Men with Debts

Men with Debts

A NOVEL BY

Anthony Giardina

Alfred A. Knopf   New York   1984

THIS IS A BORZOI BOOK
PUBLISHED BY ALFRED A. KNOPF, INC.

Copyright © 1984 by Anthony Giardina
All rights reserved under International and Pan-American
Copyright Conventions. Published in the United States by
Alfred A. Knopf, Inc., New York, and simultaneously in
Canada by Random House of Canada Limited, Toronto. Dis-
tributed by Random House, Inc., New York.

Library of Congress Cataloging in Publication Data
Giardina, Anthony. Men with debts.
I. Title.
PS3557.I135M4   1984   813'.54   83-47958
ISBN 0-394-52834-4

Manufactured in the United States of America
Published February 23, 1984
Second Printing, February 1984

To my father

"I want my place! my own place! my true place in the world! my proper sphere! my thing to do, which nature intended me to perform when she fashioned me thus awry . . ."

Nathaniel Hawthorne
"The Intelligence Office"

Men with Debts

I

VALENTI'S CHRYSLER nosed past McHale's sere yellow midsummer front lawn and Henna felt safe.

As a rule, Henna's suburb calmed him. The black shutters on the face of Mulry's house, newly painted white so that it shimmered at him like one of the silk robes Mulry's wife wore on summer mornings, soothed some errant part of him. He remembered when his suburb had been all farm. "When we first moved here," he was fond of telling his kids, "we'd wake up in the morning, you could hear the cows mooing. Right across the street!" Now the farm was covered with small, neat houses, the order of short, perpendicular streets. Stone Road. Warren Street. Elm. Beal. Forsythia. The roads were a new crop, peopled. Sometimes on his way home for dinner, in Valenti's car if they'd been out on the debit together, or in his own, Henna would see one of the neighborhood women returning from shopping at the Round-Up. The sight of a woman in a thin cloth coat, seen from behind, carrying bags of food, a child beside her or lingering behind, went to his heart with the remembered force of a story heard in childhood about a time long ago when people behaved in accordance with a code one could only dimly understand but loved nonetheless. Henna didn't understand his own time. He only sensed its gentler images—Mulry's shutters, Mrs. Mulry's silk robes, the cloth coats and the particular shade of earth brown native to the bags at the Round-Up—as outposts of a place to which he had been returned from a long primitive exile. Only McHale's long yellow grass, unwatered, untended, the jungle on the edge of Henna's lot, disturbed him. Once past it, he was safe.

Exalted by the August sun, given energy by the grays and blues and yellows of Rynn's and Slotnick's and Curry's quiet houses, Henna felt himself open to his partner. He turned and studied for a moment Valenti's ferret's profile, the pencil behind his ear, the eyes small and shot through with the insurance man's native electricity, watched him driving without caution even on these streets full of hidden ball-chasing kids, his hands on the wheel charged with the thrust of an anticipated sale. When Henna had been a new agent, just hired, Valenti had taken him out on the debit and described an insurance man's job as listening for the crack of a bat on a rolling white baseball, then running with glove uplifted to place yourself squarely under the place where the ball was going to land. "Think of yourself as an outfielder," Valenti had said, and Henna remembered the way his arms, his whole body had moved when he'd said it. Henna had tried, in his own selling, to emulate him. But for Henna, making a sale was more like putting someone to bed, tucking the covers over him and turning out the lights. In the moment of connection, he'd think of his wife and kids, and a gentleness would come over him. The policy he was selling attained the softness and healing warmth of a new flannel blanket he wanted the client to reach out and touch. In these moments, he felt himself moving beyond business. It almost scared him sometimes, you felt that anything could happen. Often, he had wanted to discuss this with Valenti, but he knew in doing so he might risk chastisement, being thought crazy. Normally they discussed only business, the common denominators of marriage, office politics, occasionally office gossip. Now he felt a desire to move beyond that, to make a gift to Valenti of his life, his thoughts. With the awareness of his suburb stretching out like a safety net beneath the wheels of the Chrysler, he thought he would risk the merely personal.

"Nancy and I went to see that picture last night, *Auntie Mame.* Did you see it, Phil?"

Valenti was distracted. Henna imagined the column of figures in his head, wondered briefly if there was something wrong with himself that he was not obsessed by money, took the time out to take his wife to the movies, spending the two dollars on a babysitter. Was he courting failure in this fashion? Was this how failure was born out of promise?

Valenti said, "Naw."

"You know that picture *Auntie Mame*. You've heard of it, right?"

Valenti nodded twice. "Rosalind Russell, right?"

"Right."

"Yeah. Sure."

"I don't know, Phil. Everybody told us what a hilarious picture this was supposed to be. Oh, Jesus, they said, you'll have a hell of a time. Laugh like hell." Henna turned to Valenti, shrugged his shoulders. "So we went, we sat there, I'm waitin', everybody around me is laughing, I'm havin' a hell of a time tryin' to figure out what everybody is laughin' at. I mean, I musta laughed two, three times, that's it."

"What kind of comedy is it?" Valenti seemed uninterested.

"Oh, I don't know—what do you mean?"

"See, there's all kinda comedy, Jack. All kinds. Pratfall, slapstick . . . humor . . ."

"Right." Henna nodded his head, worried this was being taken into depths he'd never intended for it.

"Then there's the high-class stuff, stuff I myself never found funny. Clifton Webb, that kinda thing."

"I never went for Clifton Webb."

"Then there's the Ritz Brothers, the Marx Brothers, Charlie Chaplin." Valenti's free hand swept from side to side. "That whole other side of the spectrum. Physical. Slapstick. Bing bang boom. Making . . . faces. A whole other thing. Strictly."

"Jerry Lewis," Henna helped out.

"Jerry Lewis. Exactly. My point exactly."

"The other ones. What's their names—"

"Who?" Valenti's face screwed up.

"On Saturday mornings. I watch it with the kids."

"Who? I don't follow you."

"Oh, Jesus. Moe, Larry—the Three Stooges," Henna finally blurted out.

"My kid doesn't watch."

"No? Well, they're the same thing."

"Dottie doesn't want him to watch too much."

"Very physical. Broad."

"She wants him to watch only the educational."

Henna searched for another word to describe the Three Stooges, but some impediment had obstructed the flow of his thought, something he couldn't get beyond. What did Valenti and his kid *do* on Saturday mornings? Henna was such an absolute beginner at bringing up kids that he worried about it a lot. Compared himself to other fathers. Jim Bruneau's expertise at basketball. Henna could barely dribble. It wasn't a game you played on Filicudi, the tiny island off the coast of Sicily where Henna had spent his first nine years. He sensed it was important that his children should know how to dribble a basketball, throw a baseball, pass a football in a perfect curving spiral. But these were not things he could teach them. He felt, when forced up against the evidence of life as lived by other fathers and children, as though the easy contentment, the day-off fullness of his Saturday mornings with Thomas and Leo in front of the TV watching Moe wrap the blades of a scissors around Curly's nose, was somehow threatened. Now he wondered if, on Saturday mornings, he would be exiled from their shared laughter, if now he would stand outside of it, staring at their hands and wondering what damage he might already have done them.

"So, Phil," Henna continued when, after a long pause, they were out of Waltham, on Route 2 heading into Lexington Center, "what do you do with your kid on Saturdays?"

"What do you mean, what do I do? I'm out here."

"What do you mean, 'out here'?"

"Out here! Out here! On the road. On the debit."

There was such unexpected rage in it that Henna didn't feel the sense of chastisement the words would normally have elicited in him.

"If you don't like it, why the hell do you do it?"

"What do you mean, why do I do it?"

"You don't *have* to work on Saturdays. There's no rule—"

"You take too much damn time off, you know it?"

Henna waited for it, but the embarrassment wouldn't come. Maybe things just went past him, waiting for him to catch up. Maybe tonight when he lay down next to Nancy the words might hit him with the force they lacked now. But Valenti's rage had somehow protected Henna from the assault, cushioned the blow from inside the fighter's own glove. Maybe he did take too many days off, but Henna felt centered in his work. It was for specific things. He needed time with Nancy, with the kids, to work around the house. As long as he centered his labors in the concrete, he was without reasons to kill himself working. Who knew, anyway? Maybe Valenti didn't love his wife, maybe his kid was a brat or a sissy. Maybe Valenti needed to escape them in the same way Henna needed to return to his family, or at least to keep the sense of return active, the anticipation of his slow descent from one end of Warren Street to the other, the reassuring grays and blues and yellows of Rynn's and Slotnick's and Curry's houses, and the first sighting of his own red and white Colonial. He would have kept pieces of his own earth in his pockets if he hadn't, as an insurance man, needed to appear at all times neat, businesslike, to embody what Lavolli, the district manager, called "the executive look."

Henna lit up a Pall Mall as they passed through Lexington Center.

"Lemme have one of those, will ya, Jack?"

The request came as a surprise. Valenti had been trying to quit. Dottie Valenti detested smoke. Valenti had once confided to Henna that he was giving it up to save his sex life. "She says I come to her with smoke on my breath, she doesn't want it all of a sudden. Can be hot as a bitch, Jack, she smells that smoke, boom, that's it."

"Sure, Phil."

Henna held the pack out to him. Valenti took a cigarette and accepted Henna's light. He proceeded to smoke without using his hands. Smoking never calmed Valenti. It seemed to Henna rather that the cigarette connected to an open socket, drew juice out of it, became enlivened. When one of the men in the office referred to Valenti as a "live wire," Henna always took the image literally.

Newly cigaretted, an internal change seemed to come over Valenti. When he began speaking, his tone was no different, but the energy between his words was softened, more of an approach than an attack. Henna listened through a carful of smoke.

"It's the debts, I guess, Jack. I can't seem to find my way clear through to the end of them."

Valenti's right hand went into the air, as if to pluck something from it.

"I can't say, well, if I put this much away each week, at the end of so many weeks I am free and clear. That's it, I guess. I can't find the free and clear." Valenti spoke the words as though he were pouncing on an object. "You know what I'm sayin' here, Jack?"

"Oh, sure, Phil, I know what you mean."

"I think about the kid. What the kid's gonna need. He's got me thinkin' about college. Hell, it won't be long now."

"No. They're growing up, that's for sure."

"So damn fast."

Henna looked ahead in silence, nodding. Valenti turned to him for the affirmation.

"Christ, ya blink, it's another year. You've made nine thousand dollars, but you're not a cent in any better shape than you were a year ago. But there's more to have to deal with. It's like you stay the same size, but all the buildings, all the grass, everything gets bigger."

Valenti looked at Henna again. Henna knew he was waiting for something, but that part of him that might have responded refused to come out of the silence. He was comfortable within it. He didn't want to betray to his friend the truth that he felt as distant from his problems as if the two of them existed on different planets.

Then, suddenly, the air was charged, his comfort broken.

"I had an affair, Jack."

Henna nearly snapped his neck, his motion was so quick. He fell immediately to searching Valenti, up and down. The revelation had stripped him down, in Henna's eyes. It was like seeing a friend in his underwear, bearing witness to an unexpected bestial fleshiness.

"When?"

"When? You mean when did it start?"

An edge of irritation had slipped into Valenti's voice. Henna had the sense that he was expected to understand without being told, that this was the part of the conversation where his above-the-battle stance might have been appreciated.

"Isn't it over?"

"Over? Christ, I don't know. Over. What's over? How do you know—these things, you understand, I'm not used to this."

Valenti's whole body shrugged, and the car started to veer.

"I say it's over, then I get an itch, you understand this, Jack? She's on the other end of a telephone, that's how far she is, at all times."

Henna held his breath until Valenti had straightened the car out, then asked, "Who is she?"

"Who is she? You ask stupid questions, you know that?"

"I only meant, is it somebody I know?"

"You don't know her, of course. What do you think, I'm foolin' around with Lavolli's wife or somethin'? You think I'm crazy, Jack?"

"Where'd you meet this woman?"

"Oh, it's a long story, Jack, a long story. The point is, it makes me feel, I don't know, like all of a sudden the world's crazy. I'm lookin' at women, I don't know what I'm thinkin'— crazy things, nothin' fits. I can pick up a phone now and get laid, she doesn't even care if I smoke. I could smoke while we're *doin'* it, for Chrissake, this broad wouldn't mind."

The word "broad" allowed Henna to see this woman, not as a shy blonde housewife in a prim cotton dress, but as a large, blowsy bleached blonde who perhaps referred to herself as a "singer," whom Valenti had probably encountered in one of the bars on Washington Street in downtown Boston. The transgression ceased to be a blow against the chastity of all the wives and mothers Henna knew; it became a finger pointed directly back at Valenti for his willful entrance into the dark foreignness of that other world.

"Oh," Henna said, letting out his breath at last, "she was a broad, huh?"

"What do you think, I'd have an affair with a guy?"

"No, what I mean is, she was a *broad.*"

He knew the word sounded unnatural coming from him. The easy familiarity with which certain men used the common language of sex was foreign to him. He barely understood the sexual hierarchy such language served. Other men, he assumed, had a wider experience of varieties of women, perhaps even of varieties of sex. Henna knew only one kind of each. He thought, with some small note of regret, that he would probably never be a man who could say the word "broad" as though he had a deep and personal knowledge of why, in its particulars, the word existed.

"What do you mean, as opposed to what?"

"You know . . ."

"No, I don't know, Jack. What are you gettin' at?"

"There's broads and there's . . ."

"Oh, I see. Nice women. Ladies. That what you mean?"

"Exactly."

"I got news for you. This broad was a nice lady."

Again, Henna's neck felt the pull of a quick snap, again he searched Valenti's face for the physical manifestation of an evil he felt in the car. They had both put out their cigarettes. Only a thin film of smoke remained between them.

"That surprise you? That shock you, Jack?"

"No."

"It shocked me."

"It shocks me, too."

"Course it does. I'll tell you, I was pretty damn shocked."

"Who was she?"

"That's not the point, is it?"

"It sounds to me like that's the point."

"All right, I'll tell you, Jack, but you gotta promise me this is between you and me and the lamppost. I swear to God, no one else must ever hear of this."

"I swear, Phil."

"Hand on your heart, Jack. No foolin'."

Henna readily put his hand over his heart.

"Now swear."

"I swear, Phil."

Valenti let the solemnity of the moment sink in. He seemed to be waiting for Henna's promise to seep right through his skin before saying another word.

"You swear?"

"Tell me."

"All right, Jack. You asked for it. She was a policyholder."

"No."

"I kid you not, Jack." Valenti's face went solemn for a moment; his chin receded so far into his neck he seemed to have lost it.

"A policyholder? You mean somebody on the debit?"

"That's the truth of it."

"Somebody you'd sold . . ." Henna was twisted uncomfortably toward Valenti. He wished that this could be explained more quickly; he could feel the pain in his lower back.

"No, *I* hadn't sold. She'd held the policy for years. This was a simple request for a change of beneficiary. She's a divorcée, Jack. Naturally, she didn't want to leave the money to her husband."

"Naturally."

Henna settled back. The fact of her change of beneficiary returned a sense of order to things. It had begun, at least, as business.

"What kind of policy was it?"

"Ten-thousand-dollar life."

"I'm surprised she didn't just cash it in."

"Naw. She wanted to leave the money to the kids."

"She's got *kids?*"

"Two. Boy and a girl. School age."

"She's a mother?"

"Of course she's a mother. I said she had kids, didn't I?"

"Did you ever see them?"

"The kids? Sure. But they're usually asleep."

"You see her at night?"

"It's nice. I can smoke, relax."

"What do you tell Dottie?"

"I tell her I'm on the debit. Which, strictly speaking, I am. So it's not even a lie."

Valenti stretched his neck uneasily, allowing the ambiguity to settle.

"You think just because they got kids they're not still hot?"

"Tell you the truth, I never thought much about it, Phil."

"Well, lemme tell you somethin', Jack. I never knew a broad—woman—so hot. Must have been starved for it before I came along. Hell, it didn't have to be me. Could have been any-one. You, for instance. Anyone who happened to walk through that door. Boom. That's the impression I get."

It could have been him. Henna swallowed. His crotch felt damp and vulnerable. He imagined it for a moment, then shut his eyes, pushed it out of his consciousness.

"And I'll tell you another thing. She wants it ways Dottie never even dreamed of."

Valenti was smiling now. Henna, puzzled, tried to imagine Valenti attacking the divorcée from behind, the ways dogs did it. Of *course* Dottie never wanted it that way.

"Ya know what I'm sayin', Jack?"

Valenti paused, looked at him once.

"It's *good.*"

The words seemed to create a space immediately behind them, a pause as eloquent and frightening as if Valenti were suddenly to open the glove compartment and remove a spate of photos of himself and the broad in congress. Henna clutched himself in fear. He held on to his genitals, gently massaging them, as they passed through the farmland on the outskirts of Lexington.

"What's the matter, that make you hot?"

"No, Phil."

"Scared, crazy, what?"

"Yeah, Phil. Crazy."

Henna looked away from Valenti, directly out the window. The countryside was altered somehow; it was more open now, lower, patched with color the way his own neighborhood had been, before the changes.

"What I tell you?" Valenti said.

Henna watched a boy in an adjacent field stroking the back of a cow. Henna turned to see as much as he could, but the boy and cow were quickly obscured by a long cornfield.

"I'll tell you one thing, though, Jack, and you gotta listen to this. I look at her, I don't see mortgage payments, I don't see my kid's college education. I look at her, she's all I can see. This is pure, Jack."

They were just past the cornfield when the car pulled abruptly to a halt. Valenti dealt with brakes as afterthoughts to his own body's realization that a destination had been reached. Henna wondered if perhaps Valenti didn't see the car itself as having no more autonomy than his own limbs.

"This is the place."

Valenti thwacked the gearshift into "park," wrenched the door open and stepped immediately, violently into the heat. In Henna's view Valenti was partitioned: his belly, large, raw, knowledgeable, clothed in a white shirt, a red and blue striped tie resting on the left side of his paunch and his belt buckle knotted over the unevenly hanging blue pants. Henna fought an urge to straighten his pants for him, to tell him to pull in his gut so the tie would hang right. He turned instead toward the house, focusing in on the single-car garage.

He had expected chipped paint, some sign of decay, but found none visible. Inside the garage, in the early hours of a Thursday morning two weeks before, a man named Sam Adams, the owner of the house, had affixed a fourteen-foot garden hose to the exhaust pipe of his '53 Buick, run the hose along the ground and up through a thin crack left at the top of the driver's side window and, stepping inside the car and closing the door tightly after him, turned on the ignition. Sam Adams had been the holder of a twenty-thousand-dollar life insurance policy. They had come to see his beneficiary, his widow.

Valenti sauntered up the front walk head first, shoulders heavy in relaxation, as if the impossibility of making a sale in these circumstances irritated him. It was the other side of selling insurance: the follow-up. It was very much like answering to the consequences of passion, and Henna knew this whole side of the business confused Valenti. In the larger man's confusion, he found a way out of the car and up the walk until he stood beside the slouching Valenti, square shoulders, suddenly taller, looking down on the fleck of dandruff on Valenti's slick black hair, just behind the right ear. He smiled at it, couldn't help it. Valenti looked up and caught it.

"What the hell are you so happy about?"

Then Valenti leaned into the doorbell, pressing hard.

2

"YOU UNDERSTAND your husband didn't leave you unprotected, Mrs. Adams. The man was well insured. You understand that."

Valenti was repeating himself. The woman didn't seem to have understood. She looked vaguely in their direction as though she were fighting nausea.

"Now, a death certificate may seem like a pretty stupid thing to have to ask for. We both know your husband's dead, Mrs. Adams. But the boys in the front office, see, *they* don't know. Now, this is very distasteful to me and Jack here, but see, we have to turn in that death certificate so that you and little—"

Valenti waited. Beyond the frame of the woman's head, Henna marveled at the extraordinary amount of light the room allowed. The windows on two sides of the room blazed with it. Beside this, the room's sparse furnishings seemed insignificant.

"You have a son, don't you, Mrs. Adams?" Valenti intruded.

She cleared her throat, looking straight at them, as if she had just now discovered the two of them sitting in her living room.

"Yes."

"And what's his name?"

"Johnny."

"Johnny. So that you and little Johnny can get your twenty thousand dollars. That's a substantial amount, don't you think, Mrs. Adams?"

The woman exhaled. She had been sitting forward in her chair. Now she leaned back into the cushions. The effect this gave was to lend fullness to her features. In the light of the living room, her head framed by the beige kitchen beyond, her bones had stood out so that Henna worried that she had not been eating. Against the green-cushioned chair, her skin gained color, the flesh around her cheeks and chin came forward and filled in the vacant spaces. Her hair, brown, lusterless, pulled back into a ponytail, rested on her shoulder so that the ends of it licked at her neck.

"You don't think that's a substantial amount, Mrs. Adams?"

"I suppose it is."

The kitchen door opened and a boy entered. Henna watched him pour himself a glass of milk. Then the boy entered the room but, seeing the two strange men present, hung back in a corner.

"This is Johnny."

Valenti was smiling the broad grin he used for charming kids. Henna noticed for the first time that Valenti was chewing gum. It seemed out of place, disrespectful, and if Valenti had been looking his way, he might have motioned for him to remove it. But they were all turned now, focusing on Johnny, who seemed to be receding into the corner of the room.

"He doesn't talk or what, Mrs. Adams?"

Valenti was trying for a joke. He would do that. Try to relieve the gloom. He couldn't stand mournfulness, it offended some part of him that was always, to Henna's mind, at the center of a green field, alert to the sudden whistling potentiality of speeding balls coming at him from unlikely directions.

"He talks."

Her voice betrayed a tenderness that caught Henna off guard. Something in it suggested a world beyond this one. It occurred to him that this was an educated woman.

"Rough for him, huh?"

"Yes, I suppose. Johnny, these men are from the insurance company. You don't have to stay and be polite."

Henna studied the boy. He guessed him to be about nine, ten. His own son Thomas' age. But different from Thomas, more the type of a skinny, blond American kid you saw on TV, or sometimes, on summer evenings, wearing a baseball uniform and marching off to the park carrying a glove. He found himself thinking a little better of the dead Adams for at least producing a son who looked as though he might be comfortable in the world that his own son, thus far, had been excluded from. In regard to baseball, a sport Henna worshipped from afar, Thomas showed as yet neither the inclination nor the talent.

While Henna regarded him thus, the boy turned to go. As he turned, something in the slope of his neck arrested Henna. He remembered the boy he'd seen in the field on the way here, wondered if it had been this boy he had turned to study.

The boy's leaving threw Valenti into a nervous silence. Henna understood his confusion. Valenti's style was all a matter of situation. A nine-year-old kid entering a room was enough for him to discard whatever approach he'd been using up to that point; the new element became his all. Valenti acted with props; their sudden removal necessitated a shift of thought and action he had not been able to effect smoothly.

In the silence, Henna found time to study the room's objects: the wooden floor, a large black piano in the corner.

"You gentlemen seem to be at a loss."

"What?" Valenti perked up.

Henna continued to stare at the piano. Wooden floors indicated poverty to him. He wondered why Adams wouldn't have hocked the piano to buy a rug.

"What I mean is," the woman continued, "there's very little to say, isn't there? In the first place, I'm not at all sure what I did with the death certificate. I may have thrown it away. You see, I *do* know Sam is dead. And in the second, and final, place, it *was* suicide. After all."

They both stared at her. For a moment the only sound in the room was the leaden movement of Valenti's gum.

"Nobody's denying that, Mrs. Adams."

"Then why must this conversation go on?"

"You think just because it's suicide the company won't pay it? Is that it?"

Valenti clapped his thigh and turned to Henna.

The woman, looking vaguely surprised, stared after Valenti.

"Is that not the case?" she asked.

"Hell, no!" Valenti nearly shouted.

She turned then to Henna. He nodded solemnly, wondering if he didn't appear a little silly doing that, his big head bobbing on its heavy base.

"After a year, see, the suicide clause is null and void," Valenti continued. "It's a look-the-other-way policy, see? Oh boy, you had me scared for a minute. I thought you weren't going to take it. The money."

"I'm not sure that I will."

"Mrs. Adams, for Chrissake!"

"Phil." Henna tried to calm him.

"You've got a little boy to think about," Valenti added gently.

"I'm sure your intentions are only the best, Mr.—"

"Valenti."

"Mr. Valenti. But it seems somehow—well, excuse me, but taking *money* . . ."

The words were said with unexpected anger, surprising Valenti into silence.

Then she exhaled the anger: "For what Sam did. You see."

Valenti breathed out; his body appeared to be losing wind. "Mrs. Adams, excuse me, we're just trying to help you out."

"Yes, I know. But why, exactly."

"Why what?" Valenti looked blank, almost discourteous.

"Try and help," the woman answered. "I don't think I understand."

Valenti looked at Henna, shrugged. "Why. She wants to know why."

It was the part Valenti couldn't answer. It was Henna's time now, he knew it. He leaned forward, Mrs. Adams leaned forward. He opened his mouth to explain. Never before in his career as an insurance salesman had he, at such a tender moment, allowed his eyes to slip from direct contact with the client's to steal a look at her cleavage, but here he was noticing the smallness of her breasts, as though they too had been starved. Then he looked back up. Perhaps she hadn't noticed. She seemed in readiness to receive him, her eyes open to him. He became absorbed by the intelligence there, the fine liquid sorrowful intelligence.

"Mrs. Adams," he began, "a man works all his life to try and provide for his loved ones, to protect them. Then sometimes, something happens. We don't understand it. He lets go."

He interrupted himself to study her features for some sign of understanding or agreement. Her interest had seemed to deepen, but he had the sense that it was a fleeting, almost accidental interest, and that he'd better get things right, and quickly, if he wanted to hold it.

"All that responsibility," he went on. "He does something crazy. Who knows why? We don't know why, but we see it as our job to protect him, too, to see that all his work, all the money he's poured in for your protection doesn't go to waste. Because of a moment of . . ."

"Craziness."

"Right. Thank you, Phil. Of craziness."

She smiled at him then. He looked at her breasts again. She lifted one hand to brush back a wisp of hair.

"That's very sweet of you, I'm sure."

"Sweet, nothing," Valenti said.

"Phil, let Mrs. Adams think about that for a minute, will you? Just let her think about it."

It was his tactic. He knew that after making the gesture, the client would not be able to think. That one was expected to be thinking made true thinking impossible. He knew this. Nine times out of ten, after a minute or so they responded positively out of respect for his generosity and his air of unsalesmanlike calm. The easing of pressure made its own kind of pressure, if you knew how to use it. As Lavolli had said, there are no vacuums in sales.

Valenti fidgeted. Mrs. Adams looked out the window.

"How much is twenty thousand dollars? I'm sure I don't know."

It had worked. She created a larger opening this time. He felt himself running now, leaving Valenti in the dust.

"Your husband took care of the bills?"

"Oh, yes."

"So you've never handled money, is that true?"

"Not really, no. In college, I managed for myself. But only then, really."

"Well, twenty thousand is not a *lot* of money."

"Not a lot," Valenti interjected.

"But a substantial amount, Mrs. Adams. Substantial. Enough to keep you and Johnny fairly comfortable for a few years, until you're . . ."

"On your feet."

"Right. Thanks, Phil. On your feet again."

"On my feet."

"Yes."

"Where *are* my feet? I wonder."

She chewed on a wisp of hair. Henna watched her sitting in her chair. She looked suddenly smaller, as though she were going inside herself. Valenti and Henna looked at each other.

"Wherever," Valenti said finally.

"You see, you might eventually have to find a job, Mrs. Adams, is the truth of it. But meanwhile, you go on living here on the farm."

She smiled again.

"Something funny, Mrs. Adams?"

Valenti wouldn't let it pass. That was the difference between them. If she was laughing at him, Henna would let it pass.

"No. Only the way he said it. Fahm. And the way Sam would try and say it. Form. Like a Midwesterner. Which he was not. Only he thought that was the way it ought to be said."

"Fahm. Is that the way he said it?"

"My husband?"

"No, Jack here. Fahm. Like that?"

"Yes."

"What's wrong with that?"

"Nothing, really. It's charming. Really."

"Fahm." Valenti's eyes lit up; he rolled the gum around in his mouth and lifted his head, as though this were an idea that intrigued him. "Where you from, Mrs. Adams?"

"New York, originally."

"New York?" Valenti's shoulders lifted, then he hunched forward. "Where, the Bronx?"

"No. Manhattan, actually."

"Manhattan? No kidding. Jack and I and the wives were there last year, the company held a convention. Jeez, what was the name of that place, Jack? The Italian place?"

Valenti looked hungrily over in Henna's direction.

"O Sole Mio," Henna answered.

"O Sole Mio. Jeez, the food was great. You ever eat there, when you lived out in New York, Mrs. Adams?"

"I don't think so."

"O Sole Mio. Where was it, Jack? Fifty-third, Fifty-fourth, Forty-fifth, one of those. Near the Taft. We stayed at the Taft."

He ran out of speed, sat there waiting for the next push. Henna knew Valenti would need only the slightest prod now, he had lost focus, would rant on about anything. Henna's victory had left him confused, directionless. He would chase after any shadow now, merely to gain ground.

Mrs. Adams looked from Valenti toward Henna then. In that brief exchange, only a moment, really, it seemed that the two of them inhaled Valenti's expended energy and came to an understanding. His torpor in the face of this room, this house, her incomprehensible life, was pushed aside. She turned to look away from them, as if to indicate that this should come to a close now, but the rejection didn't bother him. He thought he knew things about this woman. He knew, for instance, that she would never eat in a place like O Sole Mio, knew it without understanding why. There was nothing wrong with the restaurant. He had loved the food. In looking around the place, he had noticed lots of customers dressed in good suits and mink stoles. It was not a dive; there was a difference between it and the dives he and Valenti had eaten at, years before, when both their wives were pregnant and not up to attending the convention with them. He only knew she was from a different world. Her New York, whatever it was, did not include the Taft either. Valenti could never have understood this.

Henna sensed, too, that she had not been making fun of him when she smiled at the way he said "farm." The smile had been about something else. He did not understand, but he felt safe. He had no need to look at her breasts now. Some agreement had been reached between them, silently, while Valenti had gone on and on. He turned to Valenti now, to indicate that they should leave.

Then, looking back at the woman, he said, "Of course, you don't have to look for the certificate now. We can come back for it."

"It'd be better if you could find it now."

"Phil. It's not a problem. Mrs. Adams is, naturally, still upset. We'll come back. Next Wednesday, how is that?"

He lifted himself up holding on to both arms of the chair, but hung suspended a moment, waiting for her reply.

"Well, it's all right, I suppose, but couldn't I mail it?"

Valenti was getting fidgety, Henna could tell. He kept reaching in his pockets for cigarettes that weren't there.

"No, it's better we should come back."

He stood then. She turned to the side, looked off to a corner of the room. Valenti shrugged questioningly at Henna, asking silently why he was being so insistent. They could as easily get hold of the certificate by other means. Henna waved him off, careful to allow the woman her moment. He was certain of how he wanted to do this.

Finally she nodded.

Beyond her, in the green yard he could see through the rear windows, the boy hefted a bat over his shoulder and, throwing a rock or an old ball into the air with his free hand, cut cleanly and sent it out over the land Henna couldn't quite make out the exact contour of. The windows were not clear enough for depth perception, but he thought he saw the ball sailing far out into an orchard that, from this distance, looked spotted with color, impossibly fertile.

"What do you make of her?"

They were back in the Chrysler now, in farmland, beyond the suburbs, in the "real country" that stretched from West Lexington God knew how far. All farms.

Valenti didn't wait for an answer, which was fine, because Henna didn't have one to give.

"Odd. A little oddball, you know what I mean? D'ja see that piano in there?"

"Yes."

"Now, to me, that bespeaks money."

Henna settled down into the soft Chrysler upholstery. When Valenti used words like "bespeak," he knew he was about to be philosophic.

"Now, I'm a sensitive enough guy not to ask her why her husband killed himself. I mean, that's not something you ask right off the bat. You wait, or later, you just slip it in. When you get to know the client. 'Oh, by the way.' Something like that. Or you pretend it's official." He turned to Henna, as if for confirmation, but didn't wait for it.

"You're curious, you find out. But not right away. But I'd bet you any money it wasn't money. Not with a piano like that."

"It could have been her family's. His family's. An heirloom."

"That's true."

Valenti batted it back and forth silently, before deciding. "Naw."

"Why not?"

"You see how shiny the thing was? Like brand-new." Valenti cupped his hand as he said it.

"I didn't notice."

"What's the matter with you, you don't notice things? You gotta keep your eyes open, Jack. The details, the details. This stuff is very important. I'll tell you, I walk into a room, strange room, the first thing I do is, I look around, I give the room a very thorough once-over, to see if I can spot something, some detail, that'll give me a clue to who it is I'm trying to sell. You know, some . . . insight. It can make the difference between making a sale and coming out empty pockets. That one thing."

Henna was thinking of the appointment he'd made to see Mrs. Adams the following Wednesday. He would try to go alone, but Wednesday was a problem. Wednesday was the day he and Valenti went out together.

"So if it's not money, I say, I ask myself, what would force a guy, a guy with a wife and a kid, to kill himself? If there's money around, what's the problem so big it can't be faced? I knock that question around all the time I'm talking to her, Jack, and I get no answer. Except craziness. Something crazy. You believe that?"

"What? In craziness?"

"That a guy can just *snap?*"

"Sure."

"Or maybe there's something else. I mean, who knows? Who knows? Blame her?"

Valenti seemed to take his thoughts and go underground

with them as they rode out farther into the country. A farmer
in West Lexington had gotten married the week before. They'd
heard about it through a policyholder in Weston, the farmer's
brother-in-law.

"Maybe she drove him to it," Valenti went on, surfacing
from his unspoken debate with himself. "You see what I mean
about women?"

"No."

"Broads."

"What? What's your point?"

"The point is, you never know. Never, Jack. Not once.
Never."

The rule about weddings was, you gave the couple a week if
you couldn't catch them before the ceremony. Catching them
before was best, but sometimes you didn't hear in time. A week
was just time enough, most of the time. You wouldn't want to
attack before, you might disturb the honeymoon.

Valenti sighed. On both sides of them, the land stretched
out, covered and strange with growth. At times you couldn't
see beyond the cornstalks. Then it flattened out for a time.
Cows, sheep, some horses. It was all going. They both knew
this. They had seen it, in their lifetime, go. Still, there was a lot
of it left. It seemed so strange to be still in Massachusetts, so
close to Boston. It was like another country. Henna watched
the stalks whiz past, and remembered waking up with Nancy
on those mornings when they could hear the cows mooing
across the street. It had happened fast. They had gone away to
Lake Winnipesaukee for a vacation and come back to find the
foundation for a house laid. He was happier waking up to the
noise of houses across the street, but when he remembered the
cows there was some fondness there, too. It was the way Nancy
had looked then, not the cows. He knew this. But things mixed
together. Sometimes you couldn't separate them. They made
love in the mornings then. They conceived Thomas one morning when they could still hear the cows.

"Fahms," Valenti sighed, squinting out the window, angry

at the way the glare of the sun coming off the corn irritated his eyes. Henna, looking after him, didn't mind at all.

A maze of moving cars stood between him and his yard.

It was the end of the day: the heat created a film through which he saw his house, his car and, beyond it, his elder son spread out on the lounge chair, wearing one of the silly hats Nancy was always buying for him. This one was white, with a wide visor in the front. Effeminate. He would have to talk to her. She didn't know how to buy for them.

Thomas' body was brown and pudgy underneath the hat. He squinted down at the book he was reading. Henna guessed it was probably one of the books they made movies out of, the kind that featured stills from the movie in the center. Those seemed to be the only books Thomas read. This spring he'd caught the boy with Nancy's copy of *Peyton Place* and, thinking Thomas had been reading one of the dirty parts, had been about to hit him when Nancy stopped him, explaining that he'd only been looking at the pictures. Sure enough, when Henna opened the book to the place Thomas had been reading, there was a picture of Lana Turner in a black dress talking to a distraught young girl. The caption underneath read: "Constance Mackenzie (Lana Turner) is concerned with daughter Allison's (Diane Varsi) reaction to the news of her affair, in this scene from the Twentieth Century-Fox release." He remembered how Lana Turner's breasts had looked, as though one rip in her tight black dress would send them gushing out like falls from a dam whose delicate structure has been undermined.

He saw an opening in the traffic and walked across the street toward his son. Thomas looked up and, seeing him, gave his father a big smile.

"Hi!"

Henna plopped himself down on the end of the chaise longue.

"What are you reading, Thomas?"

Thomas held it up. *The Big Fisherman,* by Lloyd C. Douglas.

"Good?"

"It's a movie."

"Is it?"

"It's playing at the Saxon. Can we go?"

"To Boston? You know we don't go to the movies in Boston."

"But for this, can't we? It's religious, Dad. It's about Peter. He was a saint."

"Saint Peter."

"Yeah. Can we go? You like movies about fishing, and Mom'd like the scenery."

"When it comes to the Embassy, maybe. We'll see."

"Aww. When'll *that* be?"

Henna shrugged and lit a cigarette. He wanted to ask Thomas when he was going to start playing baseball, but he knew the boy was sensitive. And part of him thought that kids had a right to be happy, regardless of whatever crazy ways they found their happiness, so long as it didn't get them into trouble. But damnit, it could, it *could* get him into trouble. You had a responsibility with a kid.

"Thomas—"

"It'll *never* play at the Embassy, probably. We'll *never* see it."

"What'd you do today?"

"Nothing."

"You want to help me mow the lawn?"

"No."

"What'd you do, read? All day?"

"No."

"Then what?"

"Leo and me played a game of ganda ball."

Henna perked up. Ganda ball sounded promising.

"What's ganda ball?"

"We made it up."

"Is it like baseball?"

"No, it's like kickball. Only you're not supposed to smash it, like a kickball. You just tap it, like it's a ganda and you don't want it to break."

"What's a ganda?"

"You know what a ganda is."

"No, I don't."

"It's what a goose lays. Goosie goosie ganda."

"Ganda. Oh, yeah. Ganda."

Thomas was looking at him, smiling. Sometimes it broke his heart, Thomas' trust. It was what had always amazed him about babies, the way they trusted you to feed them, hold them, get them up and down stairs. No question existed in their minds that if they screamed and demanded, you would not do these things. He could not even approximate the wholesale process of destruction that must go through a child's mind when it sees the trust broken, its parent coming at it with a knife, or even a huge swollen hand raised. You were responsible to be worthy of the trust. Your kid looked at you with a certain vision, and you were responsible for fulfilling it. Sometimes it felt as though parenthood was nothing more than a dismissing of all the possibilities for yourself but one, and it was that or chaos.

"Say, listen. I've got an idea. You want to play catch?"

"Catch? Naw."

"Why not? Just a little game of catch? I feel like playing."

"I'm *reading* this, Dad."

"Oh, you can read that later. Lookit, this is a beautiful afternoon, isn't it?"

"I guess."

"Where's the ball?"

"I don't know. Leo's probably got it."

"Where's Leo?"

"With Johnny Bruneau. So's Mom. She found Leo tied up to a tree, and Johnny was whipping him. They were only playing Indians, but Mom went crazy. Mrs. Bruneau said she would watch them for the day, but Mom said she wouldn't leave them alone together for anything."

"She did, huh? We've got another ball, don't we?"

"Yeah."

"Where is it? Go get it."

"It's in the cellar."

"Go ahead. Go get it."

Thomas got up and walked slowly to the house, turning around once in case his father had changed his mind.

Henna opened *The Big Fisherman* to the pages of the movie stills. He searched the stills and wondered what Thomas found in them that so sustained him through the hot days of midsummer. In one, the Big Fisherman was shown holding his arms out, one pointing off somewhere, the other on the shoulder of a young warrior type, while a dark young girl looked on fearfully. What did Thomas get from this? Did he actually believe, as Henna had seen people overfed on religion believe, that religious pictures represented real events, that Peter had spread his arms in exactly that way, that the lovers had looked at him in real life the way "John Saxon" and "Susan Kohner" were looking at "Howard Keel"? In Henna's eyes, these people touched real life no more deeply than Father McCabe's sermons on Sundays at St. Jude's touched life at its factual essence. You had to understand, he would have to explain to Thomas somehow, the difference between stories, even useful stories, and life itself.

But first, he would have to confess.

Just before, the absolute rightness of his image of himself playing catch with Thomas had lifted beyond real life. He had seen it, for a split second, as a scene in a movie, a scene about fathers and sons and what they did in the afternoons when fathers got home from work. In his mind, Henna had been Fred MacMurray, and Thomas was—well, no name, just one of those perfect athletic kids he'd seen in the movies. You see, Thomas, it even happens to me sometimes. He imagined himself saying it. And then he imagined how difficult it would be to explain to his son how Fred MacMurray was not real, he was only a way of thinking about yourself.

When Thomas returned, he carried the ball like a responsibility. He appeared to be mentally ticking off all the possible sequences of events from the moment his father had plopped down on the chaise longue that might have landed him in a different place. Finally he stopped, held the ball out to his father and stood looking at the ground.

"What's the matter, Thomas?"

"Nothing."

"Don't you like to play catch?"

"It's all right."

"Don't you think it's important?"

"What?"

"To learn."

"I *know*."

"Do you?"

"Yes."

"Show me."

Henna watched a shadow pass over his son's face, noted some darkening there, as if the boy were looking at his father and understanding something in the undefined way Henna had understood Mrs. Adams, as if the little fissures in an unguarded face created an opening to the naked man, the man dripping wet and freezing, begging you to cover him in a towel. Henna saw that Thomas was a little scared by what he saw, but not his son for nothing, the boy took the ball back into his own hand and moved a short distance away.

"Where's your glove?"

"I don't need it."

"Sure you do. I might fire one in."

It was an expression he'd heard: "Fire one in." Somebody'd used it. Valenti. Somebody.

"Go get it."

Thomas walked up to the house again, stepped inside. In a few moments he was back, carrying a glove that appeared too big for him, a thing of monstrous fingers with a huge orange thumb. He stopped in the driveway and peered over the glove at Henna. Then his right arm went back and the ball came sailing over the grass. It dropped halfway between them, rolled the rest of the way. Henna scooped it up.

"Good. But come closer."

Thomas covered half the distance between them. They stood perhaps fifteen feet from one another. Thomas raised his glove so that it covered his face.

"Why do you lift it so high?"

"What?" Thomas' face peered over the freakish orange thumb.

"The glove."

"I've gotta catch, don't I?"

"But you won't be able to see it."

Thomas obediently lowered the glove to chest height.

Henna had learned this method of throwing in his adolescent days when, living alone with his mother in two rooms and being without entertainment in the evenings, he would wander down to the school playground, where the older Italian men played softball. In those days he had not yet mastered the language. He looked to the men's physical movements and expression for some clue as to how one behaved in America. They always pitched in an elaborate windup, exaggerating the arm movements. Henna wound up by circling his arm in its socket like the wheel of a gristmill. The ball flew into the air between them like a leaping handful of water. It glanced off Thomas' glove and rolled into the thick yellow grass of McHale's backyard.

Thomas turned and began walking slowly to retrieve it, as if to prolong this time of grace when the ball lay stationary, in no danger of being placed in air, a thing demanding to be caught.

"What happened?"

"I missed it."

"I know, but why?"

"It was a lousy throw."

"Was it?"

"Yeah."

"Okay. I'll try to do better."

Thomas picked the ball up and, without waiting, heaved it back. It again fell short, but this time rolled only a few inches.

"Is there something the matter with your arm, Thomas?"

"No."

"Is there?"

"I'm fine. It's *you.*"

"No. Look. When I throw, it goes straight. Yours goes in the air, like a fly ball. Why don't you throw straight? Like this."

Henna wound up and demonstrated. The throw was fairly straight. Thomas missed it again. He could not center his glove in the place where the ball was heading. It was as though something was wrong with his vision, or with the connection between seeing and acting.

"Oh. Now look, you're not trying."

"I am. We're too far."

"Too far? Too far apart? We're only . . ."

"It's too *far.*"

"Then move closer. And wait before you throw the ball. Wind up. Like me."

Thomas peered at him, having retrieved the ball. That strange look passed over his features again. Henna fought the urge to pull Thomas to him, cover his eyes. What was he seeing, what was the kid seeing? Wasn't this simple? Wasn't this what fathers and sons did? Wasn't it a connection between them, something better, more physical than a book? Thomas' eyes seemed bruised with disappointment, but not the easily remediable disappointment of a pleasant afternoon spoiled by a father's demands. Henna got the sense that he had wounded his son somehow, by a word or a throw of a ball. He had not intended it, whatever had done the damage; neither could he now call it back. The thing was begun; he persisted.

Thomas attempted to imitate his father's windup. His arm spun crazily. It appeared to be a deliberate travesty, rather than an imitation, but Thomas' face was concentrated, utterly serious. When he let the ball loose, it fell off to the side, into the rock garden that separated the upper backyard from the lower.

"What happened?"

"I tried."

Thomas stood still, staring ahead of him, his head just slightly down.

"I know. It's okay."

Henna tiptoed into the rock garden, careful to step on the larger rocks, avoiding the phlox that grew over some of the smaller ones. The ball lay in a circle of dirt, like something planted there. He picked it up and turned toward Thomas. An instinct told him to stop now, not to prolong this into some small disaster that might cast a pall over the evening. The shadows in the backyard were so cool, he thought tonight they might have a picnic.

"Okay. We can stop now."

"No. I don't want to."

"Of course you do. You don't like this, I can see."

"I like it."

"Thomas. You don't."

"I like it fine."

"You don't have to fool me."

"I'm *not* fooling you. I can play. I want to show you. Give me the ball."

"Here."

"Just get a little bit closer."

"Where?"

"Come here."

"Here?" Henna stepped to within ten feet of his son.

"Yeah. That's good."

Thomas' tongue shot out as he threw. Henna caught the ball at shoulder height.

"That's good."

"I *told* you."

Henna threw it back lightly, without a windup. Thomas caught it high up in his glove, but squeezed the glove shut in time to trap it. The boy smiled in pleased surprise, then withdrew the smile on second thought, or on seeing it duplicated on his father's face.

"What?" Thomas asked.

"Nothing."

The boy's tongue shot out again, he gripped the ball with a small focused passion, his nails digging in. Henna caught it at his knees, threw it back easily. The ball rolled up Thomas' glove, held palm out, onto his wrist, then dropped to the ground. Thomas flashed his father a quick look of embarrassment, then threw the ball back, hard. His aim was erratic, but at least the throws had some force. They established a pattern, back and forth. Thomas throwing wild, Henna having to reach out, stretch, but catching most of them, throwing back easily, without the windup, Thomas missing most, and handling the glove with so little confidence that even when he made a catch he appeared not to believe it until the ball lay fallow in his glove for several moments.

Then Thomas' throws became so consistently wild that Henna decided it was definitely time to stop.

"Your arm's tired, sport."

"I guess."

"You've had enough?"

"Yeah. Sure."

Thomas was beaming. They sat down on the chaise longue. Small beads of sweat appeared on Thomas' brow. Henna reached out with his thumb and flicked them off.

"Worked up a sweat, huh, Dad?"

"Oh, yeah."

"Worked up a sweat." Where had he heard that?

They sat there, Thomas panting, Henna staring at his yard. He lit a cigarette and looked at his son. He removed the boy's hat, touched his shoulder. They were outside of something, the two of them, as surely as if they'd been enclosed in a bubble separating them from the world. What good was his yard? He'd worked hard on it, but he'd always envisioned it as being full of something. His sons, their life. Something he could sit and watch. From up here. And say to himself: It was all right. All that time. I was fine. I produced normal sons.

Now the emptiness frightened him. Perhaps Leo. Too soon to tell, but perhaps. If you had a son who learned the ways of the world, made manifest in a boy's easy skills, you were redeemed somehow. But with sons who were not normal, you were condemned to watch the world as a thing you could not enter. Something was wrong with you. They would not let you in.

Thomas sweated and smiled. Henna loved him, and understood that love was finally useless.

"How was the movie last night, Dad?"

"What?"

"How did you like *Auntie Mame?*"

"Oh. Not so much. I don't know. No, I didn't like it."

"That's too bad."

"Yeah."

"It's supposed to be good, though."

"I know. But it wasn't."

Thomas looked away. There was nothing for him now but to return to the book. Henna wondered what he expected. That he had "worked up a sweat" entitled him to some reward? It was not enough. Not their love, not their attempts together to do the things fathers and sons normally do. He thought of Mrs. Adams' boy, the way he had walked purposefully to the refrigerator, wrapped his hands around a bottle of milk, poured and drunk from a tall glass, the fluidity of his movements, the easy way he grasped things. Thought of how those hands in all their potential, without a father now, would grasp at the physical world for a replacement. Would touch cows as if cows could rise and become fathers. His heart felt engorged with pity for the Adams boy.

Thomas was looking at him shyly.

"Dad? What's the matter?"

"Nothing."

"You look funny."

"It's nothing."

"Are we pals?"

"Yes."

"Best pals?"

"Best pals."

The world appeared a failure to him then. To its essence, all the structures failed, like a mine collapsing, or one of the human pyramids you saw on Ed Sullivan. Why should Adams have killed himself if, having produced a perfect son, his existence was justified? Money? Money could be made. Anywhere. In a store, anywhere. It was not a problem, money. It existed.

He watched Nancy and Leo now, waiting to cross the street from the Bruneaus'. Nancy in a dress so soft she could almost have been Mary Ann Mulry. But the problem was, she was not Mary Ann Mulry, she was Nancy, his wife. He knew her, he knew exactly who she was. And Leo, beside her, clutching her hand, too young to know about yet. The two of them, watching the traffic, searching for an opening, fear evident in the way they clutched each other's hand. But why not step out into the street, why not let a car hit you? For what should they live, any of them? To eat, to sell insurance, to be imperfect? Why did their lives seem so important? The world didn't work. You could fool yourselves into thinking sometimes it did, but in the end you knew McHale was right. Mowing your lawn was just a cover, just a finger in the dike. Wild yellow grass was the absolute truth of it.

They found an opening, crossed to him.

Seeing him, they both smiled.

Henna fought tears, rooted by sweat to the seat of the chaise longue. Their expectations pulled at him the way a line pulls at a strong-running fish.

But where was he running?

In his mind he retraced the trajectory of the ball or rock the Adams boy had clouted with such perfect force into an imagined orchard. Then imagined himself there, among apples, peaches, apricots, all the fruits you could never grow on his island.

3

ON THE FOLLOWING Wednesday, Henna suggested to Valenti that instead of going to Henna's house for lunch, as was their usual custom, they eat in a diner.

Valenti, the cheapskate, gave him a hard time about it. But Henna made up an excuse about Nancy "not feeling well."

In truth, he had become wary of his neighborhood. Ever since he and Thomas had played their game of catch, he had begun noticing the flaws in things, small details in his life that were somehow off. It was inexplicable to him, this new light he was seeing things in. The shining promise of all that his life had been, had ceased, during this short week, to give him comfort. Had, instead, slowly begun to break his heart.

Seated in the diner, across the booth from Valenti, he wondered if all Valenti's energy was merely a cover for the same hard intuition.

Valenti, sniffing out Henna's mental detachment, paused over his pepper steak sub and glanced across the booth at him.

"She's not pregnant, is she?"

"Who?"

"Nancy."

"Nancy? No."

"Jeesh, I was gonna say."

"What made you think that?"

"I was just remembering what you said before. About her not feeling well."

"No. It's something else."

"Hey, good. Thank God, you know what I mean? Two is enough, God forbid."

"Well, if they come, they come."

"Aw, Jack, come on. What are you, Catholic or something?"

"Yeah. So are you."

"That's not the point. Dottie's got a diaphragm, works real good, you hardly even feel it inside there. Catholic's not the point. What the Catholic Church says you're supposed to do is bullshit."

Valenti took a huge bite of his sub without pausing. The juice and oil from the peppers oozed out of the soggy bread and down his chin. Henna had to fight the urge to defend God's name and the sanctity of the Church. It was an old urge, decades old, and easily quelled.

"For instance, Dottie's got a diaphragm, that's a mortal sin, that's a black spot on her soul. She dies, she goes to hell, you believe that?"

"I don't know."

"I think it's crap. What's the matter, you don't like your peppers and eggs? You not hungry?"

"They're fine. I'm eating. I'm just not eating like you, like there's somebody behind me, waiting to grab my food away from me."

Valenti turned around, then back, his lips pursed in a mocking exaggeration of good manners. He straightened both baby fingers away from his handful of sandwich.

"Well, excuse me, pardon me. *Pardonnez-moi.*"

Then he screwed his eyes up, as if measuring Henna anew. It chilled Henna to be looked at this way.

"I'm just a man who enjoys his food, that's all."

Valenti finished and ordered coffee.

Henna knew it was time now. He had made up his mind that somehow he would break free of Valenti this afternoon. It would have to be done before they were back in Valenti's car, though. Once there, he knew, he'd be powerless to make his move. You were a captive in someone else's car. He remembered the Sunday afternoons after his mother remarried when he would be forced to ride in the back seat of Mr. Vanaria's Packard. Those hot afternoons, he'd been what, twenty-three, twenty-four? Until marriage, always someone's captive. And now Valenti's. Sometimes you thought you'd passed some dangerous or uncomfortable area of life, only to find the old ways turning up again in unexpected places.

Here in the diner, he'd done everything possible to assert his freedom. He'd wanted to eat a pepper steak sub, but, hearing Valenti order one, quickly changed his mind. Watching Valenti pour sugar straight from the dispenser into his coffee, he decided to drink his black.

Now the chance was his. Now, or never.

"Listen, I want to ask you a favor, Phil."

"Yeah? What's that?"

"Let me go out alone this afternoon."

"What for?"

Valenti looked crushed, as though he'd been anticipating this particular afternoon all week long.

"I'd just prefer it, that's all."

"But we always go out together on Wednesday afternoons."

"I know, but this is something important."

"What?"

"Look, we can get twice as much work done if we go out alone."

"I know, but so what? This is *Wednesday*, for Chrissake."

"It doesn't take the two of us to sell a policy, Phil."

"But it's the *rule*. We always go out on Wednesdays. What are you trying to pull?"

Henna bit into the last of his peppers and eggs.

"Nothing, nothing."

"What?"

"Nothing."

"You want to go out alone, you should tell me before. Not just spring it on me. Boom. Surprise."

"Forget it."

"Who are we seeing?"

"You've got the list."

"The—what's her name—the widow out in Lexington. Who else?"

"You've got the list, Phil."

Now Valenti was caught by something outside the diner. He turned and faced Henna, his neck appearing to crane out slightly so as to get a better view.

"What is it, Phil?"

"Just a thought. Just a passing thought."

"What?"

"Nothing. I never figured you for the type, is all."

"Phil, what the—"

"You a married man."

Was he joking? You had to know Valenti to know when he was joking, and even then sometimes you couldn't tell.

"You wipe that thought right out of your mind, you understand?"

"Listen. All right. You want to see her alone, go see her alone. I don't care. I'll sit in the car, how's that?"

Henna pushed his plate away, gulped coffee.

"What's the matter with you, Jack? All week long, down in the dumps. Can't even raise a smile out of you. You used to be a happy-go-lucky guy. What happened?"

"Nothing."

"Great."

"Nothing happened."

Valenti reached across the table, and Henna was afraid he was about to be slapped. Instead, his pocket was picked. Valenti removed a cigarette, lit it with the diner matches.

"Nothing happened."

"Okay."

"I think I can do the job better alone. With Mrs. Adams. That's all. The rest . . ."

"What job?" The sides of Valenti's mouth slid up, airborne with innuendo.

"If you don't cut that stuff out . . ."

"What? If it's not true, what are you flying off the handle about?"

"I'm not flying off the handle."

"Listen. Go ahead. Do it yourself. I understand."

"You don't understand *her*, that's all."

"Me? Oh, excuse me. She's crazy, what's to understand? She drove her old man to suicide, and now she doesn't want the twenty grand she's got coming to her. Excuse me. Understand. You, Mr. Profound, *you* understand her. *Pardonnez-moi.*"

"Okay, I said forget it."

"No. Hey, listen, never step on another man's turf, I say. Whatever you want, go get it. You think you understand her, go right ahead."

Henna waited to be sure the offer was serious.

"Thanks."

"Don't mention it." Valenti seemed to be inhaling his coffee, his mind already setting up new plans.

"I appreciate it."

"Enough, enough." Valenti waved him off, and they finished their coffee in silence. Henna tried to concentrate on the noises of the diner, so he wouldn't have to listen to Valenti's loud slurps. When he finally looked up, Valenti was staring at him.

"Thing is, I can't figure it."

"What?"

"I thought it was just me."

"What?"

"You figure that picture *The Seven Year Itch*, maybe that's not just something the guy made up?"

"I've been married eighteen years, Phil."

"Me, twelve. Seven, twelve, eighteen, what's the difference?"

"I'm telling you for the last time, that's not why I'm going alone."

"It's in the air. That's the only way I can figure it, it's in the air."

Valenti smiled.

"Crazy." Shook his head. Drummed his fingers on the Formica booth, lifted a toothpick to his huge yellow front teeth.

Henna settled himself, let whatever Valenti was thinking pass. He had made it. That was all. He had broken free.

"Only me, I gotta admit, I'd never pop a beneficiary."

The smile disappeared. Valenti looked sternly at his water glass, arranged his unused knife and fork neatly against it. "There is where I draw the line."

A quarter of an hour later, Henna crept up the path of his own driveway, turned and watched Valenti's Chrysler disappear down Warren Street. His own car sat gleaming in the afternoon heat. A '58 Fairlane, two shades of blue, bought new the year before. On Sunday afternoon when they'd returned from a day at Nahant Beach, he had washed it, Leo by his side, the two of them taking turns dousing the other with the hose. They'd finished just as the sun was falling behind the trees on Beal Road, up the hill. He remembered lifting Leo, dripping wet, to stare at the reflection of the sun on the Fairlane's hood.

Beside the car now, keys in his pocket, there was no need to linger. But he stood and listened.

Where were Thomas and Leo?

The yard was silent, unmoving. He could hear sounds coming from the kitchen. He moved quietly to a place outside the door where he could see Nancy washing the lunch dishes. There were no remains on the kitchen table, she had cleared them all away.

Henna was glad she was there. Before, when he'd crept so silently to the car, it was because he'd expected to be caught. When he made it, when his hand had actually touched the knob, he'd flushed with a certain foolishness. If no one is here to stop me, why am I behaving as though I am about to be stopped? Watching her from behind, the way her hair moved as she worked, her head bobbing with the effort, he felt a tenderness toward her. Her head was fundamentally innocent. When they went into the water together and she would dunk her head under and come up with all that black hair against her scalp, she looked as helpless as Thomas and Leo when he'd first seen them in the hospital, all wrinkled faces and dark, matted hair. At those moments he felt she was not his wife but his daughter swimming toward him, that he could scoop her up and hold her in his arms, no heavier than an armful of light wood. When she looked that way, he could forgive her every difficult thing she had ever been to him. Then he would scoop her up and feel the real weight of her body, and all the disturbances of their life together rushed back into his consciousness as he strained to lift her.

So it was better to stand and watch, to consider her innocence from this distance, than to go and touch her, as he felt the desire to now. It was better to watch her and feel in his heart all that he was risking.

Quickly then, he moved to the car, stepped inside. Tried to start the ignition quietly. It turned over once, twice, started. His foot breathed on the gas. He snuck out of the driveway. Safe. She hadn't heard.

Something in him had never, in moments of urgency, been able to resist the temptation to check his footsteps, to look back. In Gomorrah, Henna thought, turning, I'd have been a goner for sure. He saw her at the door, her hand halfway lifted, a look of expectation on her face. She didn't know I was home. Of course she would think that, and smile, expecting now he would see, and come back. Henna's foot pressed down on the gas. Warren Street opened before him in an astonishing blue haze. He started, remembering the way the Tyrrhenian Sea had looked through the eyes of a nine-year-old boy leaving his island forever. In the rearview mirror he watched a light breeze lift one corner of her dress.

The boy was sitting on the front step when Henna's car pulled up.

Sensing an intruder, he looked up from what appeared to be a reverie centered on his own crotch, flushed and disappeared quickly around the side of the house. Henna's arm was out. He was waving. The smile on his face suddenly felt slick, insincere. He couldn't remember the kid's name. Mrs. Adams opened the door and stepped back instantly.

"Oh."

Was she surprised?

"Remember? We had an appointment."

"Oh, yes. Of course. Come in."

Her hand went to her throat.

"I was . . ."

She looked at him.

"It's silly to excuse myself, really. I was sleeping. The light is very strong. It wasn't you. The light."

She shut it out.

Then they stood there, consoled by the darkness in the front hall.

"Well."

Henna stared hard at her. She was the first thing he'd seen since leaving his wife. All the way over in the car he had not noticed the houses or the farms. His mind had been preoccupied with images of disaster. He kept imagining things that could happen in a car, the varieties of accidents and injuries. Sometimes these images were so real they seemed to be happening to him. A bloody child rolled up onto the front hood, smashed through the glass, lay in his lap. The child's death was his fault. He thought about Valenti's idea of hell. One black spot on your soul and you would be sent there. But what was hell? What were the physical particularities of the place?

He could close his eyes now and see it, the bloody child in his lap. Some child running out into the street, after a ball. When he opened them, she had said a few words, was offering something.

"What?"

"Coffee."

"Oh. Yeah. Sure."

Then, in the kitchen, she set it before him, a white cup cracked at the rim. A tiny faded rose on each side of the handle, at the place where the cup narrowed. It was a delicate cup. It held very little. The handle was nearly too small to fit his index finger through.

"I'm sorry. I should have given you Sam's."

"No."

"Let me pour you a new cup."

"It's all right. Look. It's fine."

"It's for a woman's fingers."

"Mine can fit."

"Are you sure you wouldn't rather . . ."

He put his hand over hers.

"It's fine."

Then each of them took his hand away slowly, so as not to credit the gesture with being anything more than contact, accidental.

He sipped coffee; she pushed her hair away from her face.

He couldn't take his eyes from her. He was forgetting business. The things he'd expected to come in prepared to say would not appear. He tried to reach into himself to find the words that might start him off. If he could summon the energy, then maybe he could take them to the proper level. He was here for a purpose. He understood this, but his mind refused to focus on it. He wondered if perhaps some change had taken place in him that had left him unequipped to be an insurance salesman any longer. Before, he had not had to think, to force himself into action. Before, something had just naturally taken over in him. Now it had to be hunted down. He felt anger at himself so strong he wanted to reach into himself with his fist, pluck out the lost instinct, hold it in front of him and force it to act. But the odd thing was that Mrs. Adams didn't appear to expect that he behave like an insurance man. She appeared content to watch him sip coffee.

Then he remembered.

"Did you . . ."

He coughed. She waited.

". . . find it? The thing we spoke of."

The question seemed to have embarrassed her. He felt shamed, as though he'd asked for a loan.

She turned away, went to a drawer, reached in and pulled out a copper-colored folder, unstrung it and fished out a small, folded slip of paper. When she handed it to him, he saw that it had been crumpled, probably thrown away. An image of her searching through trash for it prompted itself. He cleared his mind and studied the death certificate.

"Would you like to go out? Outside, I mean. In the back."

He caught a little of her shame, and pocketed the document. He had not yet had time to study it thoroughly, to seek out the forbidding detail, whatever it was that had made her crumple it and toss it among broken eggs, milk containers, coffee grounds.

He left his cup on the table and followed her out onto a small patio. A chaise longue of redwood and two redwood chairs were distributed in an unrecognizable pattern. Not a circle, not a society of chairs—three chairs facing separate areas. A charcoal grill stood off to one side, half on the grass. The grass itself was yellow but recently mowed. It stretched off a hundred feet or so behind the house, at which point a row of cornstalks began.

Mrs. Adams sat on the edge of one of the lawn chairs. Henna pulled the chaise longue up next to her. The patio, the whole yard was so bare he wondered if they really lived there. Couldn't this be some elaborate joke Valenti was planning, to trap him, this house merely a stage set in which people had been deposited and rehearsed?

"I'm glad you came. Sam had so few friends, and I had none."

"No friends?"

"Does that seem strange? No. None."

"In New York you had friends."

"Yes. In New York I did have friends. One or two. I don't make them easily. Never did. One or two at a time. Isn't it funny? How it comes back to haunt you, these little—things— oh, character traits, the things we do."

She halted suddenly, in the middle of the next thought, caught by a breeze coming up off the farm. It chilled the air slightly. Henna looked out over the field, found an urge to water it, to douse it, drench it in water.

"Does the farm work?"

"No, I'm afraid it doesn't. Things grow, of course. But *it* doesn't."

"Did it?"

"No. Never."

"Did . . ."

"Sam thought it would. Sam would sit here, or stand, and stare over it and have . . . oh, visions, I suppose. Whatever that is, a *vision*. I only see what's in front of me. Or try to. But he saw something other. Not something *more*. That's fine, I think, to see the fulfillment in the seed, or whatever. Something *other*. There's a difference. It's the difference between seeing a tomato in a seed and, oh, the notion of Christian *grace* in the seed."

Henna smiled. What was "the notion of Christian grace"?

"So he'd stand here and see God knows what. Something. Some vision of the agrarian life. Something he'd read somewhere. He was a man who read, Mr. . . ."

"Henna."

"Yes." She paused, smiling now for the first time. "That defines him as much as anything, I suppose. But not . . ."

She stopped. Her smile had disappeared. A dark vein had begun to show along the side of her forehead.

"Christ, how dare I try and define him."

For moments she seemed about to speak again.

"The question, I believe, which began my little aria was: Does the farm work? No, it does not. He wanted it to. But it did not comply."

"Is that why he killed himself?"

She turned to him, bright with anger. Then, just as suddenly, the anger seemed to pass, like a cloud over her skin.

Henna felt as though asleep. All of this, dreaming. Not life, certainly. To be asking these questions, sitting here, without his briefcase. Not dreaming, perhaps. But something other than life.

"Why do people kill themselves, Mr. Henna?"

"I don't know."

"Well, exactly."

"I make you mad?"

"For a moment, yes. To assume that I knew. Could give an answer. Could sift through Sam's life and make a judgment. It's an action, after all, suicide, not a reflection on a damaged life. It is, finally, something you do."

The boy appeared on the edge of the field behind the house. Emerging from among the cornstalks, he removed his shirt, proceeded to scratch his chest and stomach and back all over. He walked straight toward them.

When he reached them, the boy stood by his mother. He looked up at Henna, then at the ground between them.

Mrs. Adams touched the boy's shirt and said, "The insurance man," in such a way that it seemed prearranged, a shorthand Henna was not privy to. "This is about money, Johnny."

Then her hand left the boy's shirt and hovered for a moment in air, uncertain where next to land.

"It's all right," Henna said, apropos of nothing.

The boy looked at him again, then went inside.

"It's awkward," the woman said. "I've kept things from him."

Henna shook his head. "Don't worry. You'll get the money." Not the insurance man speaking now, but an advocate. He was sure he would help them. Nothing in his life seemed more evident.

"You'll get it," he repeated. He suddenly wanted to see Adams' car.

"Let's," he murmured, thinking he had said the whole thing, in his current state not the best judge of his own actions.

She looked up. He could see he had not said it.

"Let's take a look in the garage."

The garage was dark and cold. Two small rectangular-shaped windows in the door allowed the only relief from darkness. Henna shivered and asked, "Is there a light?"

"It's out."

"Light bulb?"

"Oh, I suppose I should have gone to the store for one."

Strangely, Henna thought, she moved right to the car and opened the door on the driver's side. It was he who held back, feeling suddenly touchy about Adams' car. Not spooked, exactly. He had respect for the man's belongings, that was all. The car was an old green Dodge, older than anything he would ever be seen in. You couldn't sell insurance in such a car. You would not inspire confidence, not even if you washed and waxed it to a shine. His eyes had begun to adjust to the light. He saw that rust had begun to eat away at the bottom edges. Details told.

"Here. This is where he sat."

"That's fine."

"No. Come here. I want you to see."

"Why?"

A light shone up onto her face when she opened the car door. She looked stark and polished, all bone. He wanted to go back to the patio now, but how could he tell her "You need some sun on your face"? Where was she from, England? Her people? How did they get so pale, so pure and skinned-looking, like the underside of an orange after it's been peeled with a knife? Where was the protective layer on that skin? What was to keep it from being singed, pierced, pulled clean from the bone by the merest accident?

"I thought that was what you were here for."

He remembered. He was there now, in the moment. There was something clean to do. Move to the driver's side, inspect the inside of the car. That would make it business.

He crossed in front of the car and came to her side. She was concentrating on the fabric of the driver's seat. He thought at first there might be blood, then remembered that a man who dies of carbon monoxide poisoning does not bleed. It was only the fabric that fascinated her, or something she associated with the fabric.

"What?"

He wanted to know. It was intimate and dangerous to move from business activity to the realm of the personal. All around him he heard safety hatches opening. He felt like a submarine diving into deep cold water with its fissures left unsealed.

"Hmm?"

"Nothing."

"The way you look at the seat."

"Well, what do you *think?*"

Sudden hostility. He rested his hand on her back.

"Please."

He removed it.

"No. I didn't mean that, though I might as well have. I suppose it's your business to be curious. There. Sit down there."

He did as he was told, sat on the driver's seat.

"Now tell me. How does it feel?"

She crouched down next to him, stared at him with a child's eyes, searching.

"Hmm?"

"How does what feel?"

He knew instantly he had disappointed her.

She stood up.

"How does what feel, Mrs. Adams?"

She closed the door on him, moved to a corner of the garage. He could not find her.

"Mrs. Adams?"

He heard her then.

A door opening, closing, within the garage. He opened the car door and she entered his circle of light, carrying a long, peach-colored hose.

"There."

She handed it to him.

"What happened is, he went here . . ."

She pointed to the exhaust pipe.

"And what he did is, he attached it here . . ."

She focused on the appendage.

"Here."

Then her face appeared to crumple, as if from squinting too hard; it collapsed on itself and she began kicking the pipe.

"Oh, shit, shit, you stupid pipe, you stupid thing, oh, shit, Sam, such a stupid . . ."

Her crying fused into a short scream. She sat beside the car, her head against the left rear wheel.

Henna stepped out, put his hand on her head.

He had an image then, his hand on her soft hair, an inappropriate image, he knew, when he should have been all comfort, of their love, hers and Sam's. It was carnal, the image. There was light everywhere, and she was crying in Sam's arms while he, oblivious, was violent inside her. They were all light and their bodies were hard and he understood for the first time in his life how a woman might miss that. How, when the man is no longer with her, something so fleeting as how it had been one summer afternoon might be the thing, the image, that came to be a representation of all that was lost.

He stood holding her head and soon she stopped crying and rose up next to him.

"This is so silly, really."

He faced the garage door. He wanted to open it, to allow light in, to let the place stream with light.

"What must you think of me, Mr. Henna?"

She walked back to where he had dropped the hose, folded it delicately and returned it to the shelf where she had found it.

When she returned, she stood shyly before him, looked once at the car, then at him.

He waited.

"Is that everything?" she said finally.

He shook his head.

"What is left, Mr. Henna? You have your little slip of paper, your proof."

"There are forms to fill out. Paperwork."

"Did you bring them?"

"No."

"Why not?"

Her eyes held him. So sharp, the intelligence there, nailing him.

"There were questions I had to ask first."

It was a lie. The questions were simpler than any he had asked. The answers to most of them could have been gotten off Adams' death certificate. The company was interested in numbers, dates, amounts.

"I'm sorry. I didn't bring the forms for you to sign because I wasn't sure, in your state, if you'd be ready."

"I am not some weak thing, Mr. Henna." She paused. Then: "You should have brought them."

She moved past him. He found her in the kitchen, restringing her folder.

"I thought, when I come back, if there's anything you need . . ."

"No. We're fine."

"Some food, something. Or if something needed to be repaired."

"There is nothing. Thank you."

"May I see your house?"

"What?"

"I've never had a chance to really look around a place like this."

Once more the cool intelligence enveloped him. Who was he? If she asked, he couldn't have answered.

"A quick tour," she said, looking very tired.

They passed from room to room, wood floors, dull from not having been waxed in too long a time, hooked rugs, antique lamps, all "handed down," as she explained.

"From who?" he asked, and she just looked at him, rescinding some small part of her investment in the look.

She was about to show him their bedroom when they passed the boy's room. The door had been left open. The room was filled, vibrant, with an almost eerie whiteness, difficult for the walls to contain. At the center of it, on the edge of his bed, the boy sat, naked, scratching himself.

They both stopped. The boy looked up. Henna thought it was odd that he did not flush, made no move to cover himself. He stood up. One hand reached over to its opposite, scratched the wrist there. He was perfect in the white light. His nakedness, nothing seemed strange. They stood transfixed. Everything on the child's body was compact and somehow old, "handed down" in miniature, burnished to a brilliant shine by the light. Henna was so mesmerized, they all for a moment seemed so unembarrassed, like figures caught in a painting, that the shock was very great when the boy's color suddenly rose and he reached for the door and slammed it. Mrs. Adams stared at the door for a moment, blinking. It was dark in the hall.

She pointed past the boy's room.

"That's the bedroom."

But she stepped briskly off in the opposite direction.

When Henna found her, she was standing at the front door, holding his hat.

"How's Monday?"

"What?"

"For the paperwork. Monday afternoon, say one o'clock? After lunch?"

"Can I meet you elsewhere?"

"Where?"

"Oh, I don't know. Somewhere I could walk to. I don't drive."

"Where is there?"

He could tell she was wishing this was finished; she was biting her lip.

"There's *no* place. All right, Mr. Henna, you can come here."

"One o'clock."

"Yes, fine."

She opened the door for him. When he was outside, and turned around to say goodbye once more, she had already closed it.

Driving home that evening, he was pleased that he'd remembered to make the appointment for a day when he wouldn't have to get himself free of Valenti. Monday was all his.

. . .

Leo held a wrinkled periwinkle he had lifted from his plate and threw it across the table at Thomas.

Thomas tried to catch it in his mouth, but the throw was wide and grazed his left ear.

"Jesus Christ," Henna said. Beside him, Thomas held on to his ear and looked up at his father, uncertain as to how much of an issue to make of this.

"Leo, don't throw your oufiles."

"Is that all you're gonna tell him, Nan?"

She was sitting next to Leo, across from Henna, deep into her own plate of food.

"I hate spaghetti with oufiles," Leo said.

"What do you want me to tell him?" Nancy asked. She looked briefly down at Leo. "Eat them, don't throw them, Leo. Be a good boy."

"I hate oufiles."

"Leo, eat." Henna looked over at Leo and scowled. Leo's eyelids were lowered, positioned, as though antagonism were, after all, what he desired.

"I hate them."

"We picked them for *you*, for Chrissake."

"Jack, don't."

He looked at Nancy only long enough to see that she was far more interested in her food than in any sense of order at the table.

"I'll eat them."

"No, Thomas, you won't. Leo's going to eat his own oufiles."

"I only like them in the shell."

"You can't eat them in the shell."

"Why not? I bet Curly would." Leo's eyes glimmered. Clearly, he thought this was the thing to drive his father to the breaking point. "Eat the whole shell. Crrk. Crrk. Crrk."

"That's disgusting. Leo's disgusting," Thomas joined in. "Crrk. Crrk. Crrk."

"That's how Curly would do it. Eat the whole shell."

"All right, all right, no more Three Stooges on Saturdays."

Henna speared one of the periwinkles, sent it flying over the edge of his plate.

"What?" He could tell Leo didn't believe him.

"You heard me."

"Aww, Dad." The false concern in the little boy's voice was beginning to anger him.

"Aww, Dad, I don't want to live, then."

"Don't, Thomas."

"I don't. I'd rather kill myself. I'll eat oufile shells till I die. Crrk. Crrk. Crrk."

Leo looked at his older brother and offered him squealing encouragement.

"You see, you laugh, Leo, you see if I don't mean it."

"You like the Three Stooges better than we do, and we know it."

"Thomas, don't be a wise guy. Jesus, Nan, look at you, sauce all over your face."

"Crrk. Crrk. Crrk." Leo said, popping his cheeks and already, Henna could tell, looking for a new line of attack.

"What's the matter with that?" Nancy asked him. "Why aren't you eating? All of a sudden you don't like oufiles?"

"Leo's kicking."

"Crrk. Crrk. Crrk."

"Cut it out, Leo."

"Here's another one." Leo lifted another periwinkle, sent it up into the air in the direction of Thomas' head. "Open up. Uncle Sonny coming home from Korea."

"How do you remember Uncle Sonny in Korea, Leo? You were just a baby. Jack, he remembers."

"You throw another oufile, Leo, I'll whack you, I swear to God."

The table quieted down. Henna lifted a periwinkle to his mouth and downed it in disgust.

Thomas and Leo giggled at one another.

What was going on under the table?

Why did they eat like cannibals?

On Sunday, they had picked the periwinkles off the rocks at

Nahant at low tide. Today, Nancy had cooked them in the sauce. It was an old recipe, from the island, one he had lost his taste for. But the rocks at Nahant at low tide called to some instinct in them all, she, her sisters, Henna himself. At low tide they moved to the clumps of still-wet seaweed, the tiny shells clinging to the dripping walls of rock like babies suckling. You pulled them off quickly. They put up no fight. Into buckets, your legs half submerged in water. Then, at home, pulled them out with sterilized pins. Sometimes they receded so far into the shells it was difficult to stick them. In tomato sauce they were salty, chewy as small clams. The point was not to be conscious of any of it. If you thought about it too hard, you probably wouldn't be eating them in the first place. It was all ritual, from first to last.

Nancy cleared the dishes and the boys ran into the living room to watch TV.

Again, he watched her from behind, sat in his chair as she washed dishes. Wondered: Did she understand? Was Nancy smarter than he knew?

When she was finished she dried her hands on her apron, sat at the table at an angle to him, rested her arms on the table, smiled at him.

No, she understood nothing.

"Jack."

"What?"

"Don't be sad."

"Who's . . ."

"It's not like you."

"Not like me. Who . . ."

"You're not a sad man."

He looked at her, thinking how easy it was for her to define him. She had an exact image of who he was. All he had to do was live up to that image and he'd be fine.

"What, honey?"

"Do you want . . ."

"Is it something to do with business?"

He hesitated. "Yeah."

"What?"

"Oh, nothing."

"I'm sure it's nothing. You'll clear it up. You're a good insurance man."

There. Not a sad man. A good insurance man. She knew him. These were the exact things he was, had always been. The absolutes. All you needed to do was . . .

"Do you want to go out? Into the backyard?"

"Sure."

All you had to do was let her tell you who you were, what to do. Follow her.

She led him into the backyard. It was just turning dark. They walked past the rock garden down to where the chairs were arranged.

When Nancy sat, her blouse fell against her, so that Henna could see the outline of her belly. Her hair, resting against the back of the chair, bunched, became fuller, a pool of dark hair. He wanted to put his hands into it.

He rested on the arm of another chair.

"The parsley was fresh," she said.

They kept a small vegetable garden in the back.

"I had Thomas pick it."

"Not too early?"

"No. It was good, don't you think?"

"Couldn't taste it."

"You didn't eat much."

"We should go out some night."

"Why?"

"You don't want to?"

"I'm happy here." Nancy leaned back into the chair. Beyond her, his yard, his garden in the dusky summer night seemed a splendid place, if only he could think how to make use of it.

"The boys'd like it," he said.

"Thomas would rather you took him to a movie."

"He sees too many."

"But he loves it."

"Yeah, I know, Nan, but is it good?"

"Why not?"

"The kid's a dreamer."

"I'm taking him this week."

"To what?"

"The Nun's Story is at the Embassy."

In one of the bordering backyards, Henna listened to the sound of a group of children playing. An adult male voice, hard and guttural, lifted above them. Through the dense cover of trees, he thought he could see Murphy, his back-door neighbor, taking out his garbage.

"A woman's picture," he said.

"Oh, so what?"

"Nancy, you don't know what can happen to a kid."

"Thomas? Thomas is a wonderful boy. He's my angel, Jack."

"Yeah. He's a wonderful boy. I know."

He looked at her. Her eyes were on the tops of the trees, her legs crossed, one bouncing lightly over the other. She appeared happy, a wife enjoying a cool summer evening in the company of her husband. The network of assumptions appeared perfectly in place.

"You don't see anything, Nancy."

"Oh, all I know is, you worry too much."

"No. You don't see."

"You have two wonderful children, and you only want to see the bad. Look for the good, Jack."

Sometimes he thought the only time he'd been happy was when she was pregnant. The baby was like a line between them then, a clear thing he could point to, hold on to. Marriage had a shape then. What was she to him when no baby was inside her? A woman separate from him, not understanding him or very much interested. When the babies came out of her, had they taken with them reserves of personality and intelligence, pulling out of her what they needed for themselves? The babies had been greedy. For weeks he had gone without her. Perhaps then he had learned not to need her, and something had died with the loss of blind need. Maybe that was all it was when marriages went bad. Sitting there now, he could go to her. On the chair, on the grass. It was dark now, no one would see. The boys busy watching television, the two of them shaded by the trees. It might be good. They might even get another baby out of it. She was not yet forty.

He went to her. He touched her forehead with one hand and rubbed the skin there, the line of her scalp. Her face was so pure. She was so unashamed of her face.

He kissed her and waited. She smiled. She wanted to be kissed, he could tell, but made no move to touch him or kiss him back. He kissed her with force, on the lips, on her cheek. He pulled her down onto the grass, and she laughed.

He put his hand under her skirt and felt her there, so dry he had to force his finger in, so that it hurt. She gave a little cry. Deep down she was wet. She always was.

She loved the kisses so much that she felt no need to return them, but Henna's excitement was by now dependent on her response. He unzipped himself, but when he fell out of his pants he was far from erect. He forced her hand to his penis, but her touch was lifeless. Rubbing it had no effect. He finally took her hand away and they lay there, in the dark, under the trees, breathing and confused, listening. From the house they could hear the faint hum of the TV and, just over it, their two sons giggling and going, "Crrk. Crrk. Crrk."

He wondered, had he ever been violent with Nancy, blindly, murderously violent, the way Adams had been with his wife in the vision he had had this afternoon? Or had he always been too gentle with her, treating her the way you'd treat a house you've built to protect yourself? Could love ever sustain itself that way? Didn't a woman have to be the world itself, so that your hungers never reached the point where they made distinctions? You could not spend your days lusting for money and success, then come home to satisfy your hunger on top of their opposite without expecting, in the long run, to be defeated. He wanted, in entering her, to enter the mysterious world. Under the trees, he held to his loose, floppy member and despised her.

"Jack?"

He made no answer.

"You saw me today, but drove right off. Why did you do that?"

He would go up and whack Leo. That was what he would do.

"Jack?"

"What?"

"Why did you just drive off?"

"When? I didn't see you. When?"

"Today. This afternoon. You took the car."

Oh, why was life such a small thing, a matter of afternoons of "taking" or "not taking" the car? Had he ever imagined it would be larger, a matter of casting off in boats, constantly, repeatedly, for unknown places? Her voice was so small, reduced to the tiny plain on which they acted out their lives. Their lives so small they hardly needed to raise their voices. Why did people write operas? When was there ever cause for song?

"Jack?"

"What?"

"Talk to me."

Had she asked him to set fire to the house, their children, he could more easily have complied.

"Something's happening, I know it is."

He waited. Soon she would go. She would go up to the house and weep into an apron. The children, hearing, would say nothing. During the commercials, they would hear her louder wails.

He was the children listening to her crying. She was behind him. He could never stand it, not in the beginning, not eighteen years later. Eighteen years. My God. And it is still the same thing. She will cry and I will comfort her.

More.

He felt himself stiffen. That had always happened, too, he didn't know why. He turned to her and put his huge arms around her and let her cry. All the time getting stiffer. Finally, covering her. Inside. Her tears added inches to him, and he summoned a vision of violence to correspond to. In it, Adams' wife lay under a faceless man in a room as uncontrollably bright as Johnny's had been. She was screaming, but the face-less man's prodding of her only intensified the louder she screamed. In the moment Henna climaxed, the faceless man disappeared and Mrs. Adams was alone in a room, shrouded in light, gasping for air.

When they were finished, separate, breathing, it all came to-gether again, the white picnic table, the Virgin Mary in the grotto he had built the summer before, the stone fireplace, each in its place, perfect. For a fleeting moment, he understood his life. Then she rose from the ground, breaking his thoughts. Still crying, but not crying now. Weeping.

". . . all you want" was all he heard. Then she was gone.

He lay in his backyard, clutching the grass, not wanting to move. After a while, he fell into a light sleep.

When he awoke, he felt angry, as though in sleeping, even for a few minutes, he had allowed himself to let go of something.

He looked around him, saw the trees, the white picnic table, the Virgin Mary grotto and the stone fireplace and tried to piece it together again, the understanding that he had caught sight of for a moment.

4

THE NEXT DAY, back at work, life had it's old rhythm back. At his desk, surrounded by noise, by hustle, by white shirts and baggy pants and a blur of voices like his own, only the lin-gering memory of the night before kept him from exulting fully in the energy around him. He watched Connie the secretary accept Al Cutler's flirtations by exposing the pink wad of gum between her teeth, and felt buoyed up. All this life around him made his shoulders hop, his arm want to reach out and grasp a phone, shoot sales down the wires. The air was so thick with transaction it made his armpits water. He wanted to bring Nancy here, plant her and the kids in this office—Christ, here they could have a life, no questions asked! But no, the point was that their not being here was half of what made it so good.

"Hey, Cutler!" one of them shouted. "Leave her alone, she's got a date tonight with Lavolli!"

Uproarious laughter at the mention of Lavolli, the office manager, whom Henna had once promised his kids when he left the office he would personally tell to "go climb a tree." Lavolli of the famous slow-burn and foot-long cigars, with eyebrows so thick Cutler said that when Lavolli smoked they looked "like a couple of burning bushes." Lavolli, the office tyrant, had to take his wife to the doctor this morning; till eleven they were on their own.

"You think I'm tryin' to make a date with her, is that what you think, you horny bastard, Tatunjian?"

"Don't swear in front of Connie, now come on, a little rules around here." Winchell, tall, skinny, Irish, drinker's veins in his nose, seven kids.

"Who swore? Who swore?"

"You did, Cutler." Tatunjian, not looking up, involved with paperwork, gave the impression he could handle two running thoughts at once.

"What'd I say? What'd I say, Connie? Did I swear? Did I offend you? A thousand pardons." Cutler got down on his knees, kissed her hands. The laughter rocked the office again.

Henna could swear it actually moved when they all laughed like that, the office a detached object, moving through space.

"What'd he tell you, Connie?" Gennaro, the office elder.

"Oh, I'll never tell."

Connie could make them laugh now without even trying. Like Art Carney in "The Honeymooners," she came on holding a backlog of every time she'd ever been funny before.

"Saturday, in the woods back of Camp Ted, right, Connie?"
Cutler was playing it now for all it was worth.

"Are you kidding? I'll get poison ivy for sure in those
woods."

"Cutler, you're cookin' the hot dogs Saturday, right?"

There was an office outing planned for the weekend. A
yearly event. Freddie D'Alio, big heavy-breathing Freddie
D'Alio, the King of Insurance Men and, next to Gennaro, the
eldest, was in charge. He made notes on a piece of graph paper,
plotting in a delicate hand the system of balances between hot
dogs and buns, Coke and Pepsi, Budweiser and Schlitz, Gul-
den's mustard and Emma Gennaro's special home recipe for
piccalilli. His hands were paws, but sometimes, in advising
Henna, he had created figures in air, localized visions of such
delicacy that Henna, switching his gaze from hand to mouth
and back, had experienced a little shock. He was, for Henna,
the only certifiably Great Man he had ever known. Once, in a
two-page spread in *Life*, the main office listed its hundred top
salesmen throughout the country. Freddie D'Alio's face blazed
out above the number 37. Since then, Henna had regarded the
man with awe.

"Who's pitching the softball game? I still haven't got a volun-
teer."

"I'll pitch, Freddie."

"You can't pitch, Connie. We need you in the dugout."

D'Alio rode over the laughter Cutler's crack invited.

"Thank you very much, Connie, that's very generous of you,
but no women in the softball game this year. Fathers and sons
only."

"Oh, Tony, I love to play."

"Last year, too many of these lazy bums stayed out of the
game, afraid the women would beat them. This year, no.
Everybody plays. You hear that, Cutler, Mele, Winchell,
Henna? Everybody plays. Valenti, you want to pitch?"

All eyes were on Valenti, who had been jabbering into a
phone for twenty minutes straight, talking so fast, so animated
the extremities of his face and scalp seemed always to be in

danger of flying off and landing in the wrong place. He was unaware of the rest of them.

"Valenti!"

Valenti looked up, surprised, cast glances around the room, shrugged, continued talking.

"You want to pitch Saturday?"

He gave D'Alio a questioning look: What did I do?

"Pitch! Pitch!"

Valenti mouthed: What?

"For Chrissake, make your call and get off the damn phone!"

Valenti held up one finger. They all waited, listening.

"Look, nobody likes to think about it," Valenti fairly shouted into the phone. "Nobody. We all, Jesus, but you never know, who can say, in the hands of God, you should, God forbid, meet with an accident, what are they gonna eat? You ask your-self that, *what are they gonna eat?*"

"Jeez," Tatunjian whistled. "He sells like Bishop Sheen."

A slick wave of Valenti's hair had fallen over his right eye. As he gestured with one hand, the cigarette secured in it threat-ened to ignite his hair. For Henna, the tension in watching him was all in observing this contest between sales and disasters.

"You want she shouldn't be able to lie in bed eating bonbons every morning, she should have to get up, go to work in some factory where, God forbid, she should get raped by the fore-man—you know how they work the women in those places? My God! My sister-in-law, raped twice by the same foreman. A Polack. Educator Cracker Company in Watertown. I'll give you her name, you can call her—What?"

Valenti appeared then to have been shocked by something coming from the other end of the line; his hands darted out, grabbed slips of paper.

"What? It's Mrs.—Mrs. Esther Picardo."

A piece of paper flew off Valenti's desk; he broke a pencil point trying to grab it.

"Jeez, I'd give it to you, but I don't know if she's home."

He sweated, pulled at his collar. Laughter was slowly begin-ning to rumble through the office.

"All right, all right, it's Twinbrook 3-6791. Mrs. Esther Picardo. I'll call you right back after you talk to her. All right, you call me. But remember, she may not be home!"

He hung up, picked up the phone in a flash, was dialing so fast his fingers formed a blur.

"Esther? Quick, a man is gonna call you, a man I'm tryin' to sell some insurance to. Don't ask questions now, just say you were raped by a Polish foreman at the Educator Cracker Company in Watertown! You got that, Esther? I'll explain later . . . How the hell should I know the foreman's name? Something ending in -ski. That's all. And you were raped twice, remember that. And it was awful, the worst thing that ever happened to you. You got that? I'll give you half my commission, we pull this off. Ten percent. No, ten percent."

He slammed the phone down.

An amazed silence, and then the cheers began.

Valenti looked confused.

"What'd you ask me?"

They laughed even harder at this.

"To pitch, to pitch," D'Alio choked out.

"To pitch where? When?"

"Saturday at the outing."

"Saturday I can't make it."

"What are you talkin', can't make it?"

Valenti shot a quick glance at Henna.

"My kid needs glasses, Tony. Who's got a cigarette?"

"You quit. And Dottie can take your kid for glasses weekdays."

"This guy's gonna call me back. I need to concentrate."

Henna threw him a cigarette.

"You're pitchin', Phil." D'Alio made a notation, to indicate the matter was settled.

"I told you, I can't come."

"Who wants to play first?"

Gennaro rose up. A short silence, his stare cutting D'Alio off; Mele's chair creaked noisily, and Mele himself giggled, anticipating Gennaro's joke.

"We gonna get some work done before Lavolli comes in or what, boys?" Gennaro asked soberly.

"Lemme do the lineup, Joe."

"The lineup can wait, Freddie."

"Just the infield, Joe."

"I said the lineup can wait." Said with last-stand force.

D'Alio broke the momentary hush. "What are you tryin' to pull, Joe? Lavolli's across town. What are you, buckin' for the job?"

"This is an office."

" 'This is an office.' 'This is an office.' Christ, what the hell is that supposed to mean? 'This is an office.' "

"It means . . ." Gennaro was stuck. He looked around for help, found none.

"Sit down, Joe."

Gennaro, wordless, looked once more around the room, then sat, reached out for a paper, grasped it. Henna watched it shake in his hand.

D'Alio completed the lineup. Henna, right field, felt the change of mood sharply, a depressant.

Valenti was pacing now, waiting for the return call. He stopped at Henna's desk, puffing madly, shooting expectant looks in every direction.

"All right, so what happened?"

Henna had his hands on a stack of beneficiary claim forms.

"What happened when?"

"Yesterday, yesterday. The broad out in Lexington. Your big secret mission, what happened?"

When had he ever seen Valenti's eyes so cold? The eyes wanted collusion, as if they already knew the worst but needed Henna to break through his film of sanctity and admit to it. What was it about the office that created this dog-in-heat atmosphere? Cutler had told him once that he felt sometimes like he could handle three, four women at the same time. What was the essence of the prodigious sexuality of this big, hairy man whom Henna couldn't imagine even *one* woman wanting? The image of three women climbing onto Cutler's hairy body made

Henna sweat. And yet it was the life of the place, this outsized hunger. Freddie D'Alio's reputation was one of the first things Henna heard about when he was hired. He contemplated the man now, number 37 nationwide, sitting at his desk, forming lineups, calculating sales with his great paws, which, it was said, "did wonders" for women. They all embraced the world, these men. Why shouldn't he?

"What happened? Phil, what do you think happened?"

"You son of a bitch." Valenti grinned. "All right, so how does it feel?"

"How does what feel?"

"You son of a bitch, Henna. Never thought you had it in you."

The phone rang. Valenti's face went cold and ramrod straight again.

"That for me?"

"No, for Jack. Jack!" Connie called.

Henna picked up.

"Jack."

Nancy's voice. So distant now. Another world.

"Hurry up, Jack," Valenti interrupted. "I'm expecting a call on that line."

"Honey?"

"Yes, Nan, what is it?"

"I just wanted to call you, Jack."

"Well, okay."

"Are things all right?"

Valenti paced in a tight circle at the side of Henna's desk.

"Things . . . are fine, Nan."

"Are they, honey?"

"Yes."

"Do you love me?"

Valenti stopped, leaned over.

"Jack, come on, I'm *expecting.*"

"Do you?"

"Yes, Nancy. Listen, we're all busy here. You understand. You shouldn't call unless it's important."

"We'll be out all afternoon, Jack. We're going to the movies."

"Good. Fine."

"So I thought, if you came home early, we wouldn't be here."

"No, I won't be coming home early."

Both Valenti's hands shot out at his sides.

"Henna! What gives?"

"You could come with us. It starts at two-thirty."

"No."

He listened to the silence at the other end, then quickly said, "Goodbye, Nan," and hung up.

Valenti jumped to pick up his own phone, began dialing.

Before he could feel remorse for what he'd just done, Al Cutler sidled up to him.

"I joke with Connie, Jack."

"Yeah. I know."

"That's all it is. Just a joke."

"Oh, hell, Al. We all know that."

"I love Peggy, you know that."

When Cutler looked at him, Henna saw the soft pleading around his huge, doglike pupils, was respectful of it.

"Sure."

"I've never once in my life been untrue to Peggy."

"No."

"Never once."

Was Cutler going to cry, right here in front of him?

"That's good, Al."

"Even though she poops out real quick. Even though I can go on forever, Jack. I swear to you, another woman I might have made very happy. This . . ."

Cutler paused, reached for words in the air, graceless, lacking Freddie D'Alio's facility for grasping figures from thin air.

"This is the tragedy of life."

And it seemed to Henna that suddenly the whole office was imitating Cutler, grasping, missing, holding on to papers, telephones, pencils, the summer heat having snuck in and, with it, the sense that they'd all picked up their phones a second late, the prospect having just left the house or passed the moment when he was ripe for coercion.

Cutler stared at him with those large, sad eyes, meekly smiling. He went away, went to his desk, picked up a phone and sighed deeply.

What comes over an office? In the space of seconds, the energy was gone, the room seemed to have been drained of potential.

He pulled a beneficiary claim form from the bottom of the neat stack on his desk and began writing Mrs. Adams' name, address, everything he knew. He thought of Monday. In a moment the bounce returned. Back at work. Office life. Connie laughing with her mouth open at something Freddie D'Alio said. Saturday he would play right field, eat hot dogs, laugh with Connie and Freddie and Oscar Tatunjian. It would be fine. Monday he would see Mrs. Adams again, the boy.

He looked at Valenti, shot him a quick smile. Valenti, on the phone again, barely acknowledged the smile, turned his head this way, that. Henna watched a wing of Valenti's hair fly up into the air and land, disheveled, over his ear.

He listened closely to the sounds of the office, closing his eyes and allowing himself to enter its rhythm. Fragments of his conversation with Nancy filtered through, but he ignored them, determining that all he would see for now, all he *needed* to see, was the office, the outing, the million possibilities for Monday.

"Mommy, why did she become a nun in the first place?"

They were just leaving the neighborhood on their way to the outing Saturday morning. Nancy was hardly speaking to him still. Thomas, sensing something wrong, was trying to effect a peace.

"Who, Thomas?" Nancy asked.

"Audrey Hepburn. In the movie, remember?"

"Of course I remember."

"Then why?"

"Well, she loved God."

"I hate God," Leo said.

Henna's hand swung back, catching Leo on the side of the head. Leo's screams instantly filled the car.

"Jack, don't!"

"Nobody in this car says they hate God, is that understood?"

"Leo. Baby. Why did you say that?"

Leo only continued to scream.

"I know why Leo hates God."

"Why?"

" 'Cause when we play war or anything, Johnny Bruneau always plays God. Leo's John Wayne, I'm Montgomery Clift and Johnny's God. God gets to say who dies. He always makes Leo die first."

"Leo, Johnny Bruneau isn't God."

Nancy's tone irritated Henna. The way she said it made him want to believe the opposite. But he knew his impulses now were edgy, not to be trusted. He could sense his own carping nature even in the way he regarded them all now, Nancy sitting beside him in a bright white blouse, his sons scrubbed and brushed-looking. The way she had dressed and groomed them, as if in anticipation of a pleasant, edgeless outing, depressed him. He wasn't sure he wanted to have that kind of day.

"Leo," Nancy said.

"What?"

"Did you hear me?"

"He won't believe you. You love God, don't you, Mom?"

"Yes, I do, Thomas."

"So why didn't you become a nun?"

"Well, because I met your father."

"So?"

"So you can't become a nun when you fall in love, Thomas."

"Did you fall in love with Dad?"

She was silent for a moment. They were on Beaver Road, passing houses small, neat, pastel-colored, newer than their own, houses she had dreamed of living in.

"Yes, Thomas."

"What if you had, though? Already become a nun. *Then* you met Dad. What would have happened then?"

"Well, I wouldn't have married him then, Thomas."

"So we wouldn't be around, would we?"

"No."

"Are you glad?"

"Thomas, what kind of question is that?"

"I just want to know."

"Of course I'm glad."

"Dad?"

"What?"

"How come you never became a priest?"

Henna let out a snort.

"What's so funny?"

Leo began bawling again, as if he were just now reminded of his father's violent presence.

"Well, it takes a . . . Leo, keep quiet now, that's enough. It takes a special man to be a priest."

"Bing Crosby."

"Right. Bing Crosby could have been a priest."

"You like Bing Crosby, don't you, Dad?"

"Yes, I do, Thomas, but you know he's not really a priest."

"I know." Thomas' voice became small.

"You said your favorite movie was *Going My Way*, right?"

"That's right, Thomas. That was a very funny movie," and to remember, to be a father, he chuckled, knowing Thomas would appreciate it.

Nancy looked over at him. He thought she was probably ready to forgive him now, but he couldn't allow it. He was feeling too guilty about what he'd been thinking. If she'd become a nun, they'd never have married, had children; the million possible roads that might have taken him elsewhere, to a different woman, a different set of children. He knew he needed kids, but *these* kids? With Mrs. Adams it would have been different. But where had Mrs. Adams been those nights when he and Frankie Rando had prowled outside the Sons of Italy Hall, watching the cars pull up for the Filicudi Dance, waiting for the one woman to turn up who might make them want to go inside. On one of those nights he'd first noticed Nancy among her five sisters, mother, three brothers, her father pausing behind them to look at the tires on his '37 Ford. He remembered her stepping out of the car, touching the hem of her sister Evelyn's dress, the two of them conferring seriously, their lips downturned, bright red. He remembered how her forehead shone as she moved toward him, her walk sealing everything, the hem of her dress swinging lightly against her legs.

Now he thought: If she hadn't come.

Or.

Leo stopped crying.

"I know. Daddy didn't mean it. Did you, Jack?"

Henna turned, anxious to make amends, to touch Leo. Then, without his willing it, the car turned with him. Off the road, and into the bushes, where, when he finally gained control, he managed to smash into the sign reading "Camp Ted 1 mile," which the car cracked in two and then was hoisted up onto, the sign forming a natural jack, so that the car stopped there, suspended, their screams within it sounding to Henna like the noise of a whirring top winding down.

"What happened?"

"Jesus, I don't know, Oscar. One minute I was drivin' along, I made the turn into Camp Ted, I musta, jeez, made it wide, or not been thinkin', I don't know."

Henna shook his head back and forth, his tongue clicking like a metronome to keep time with the postmortems going through his head.

Nancy was trying to calm Leo, who held his knee and cried, walking back and forth with a tight, red face, a just-born face, as Nancy tried to catch up with him.

Thomas, who appeared at first to be all right, was holding his head and saying, "Boy, now I won't be able to play baseball, huh, Dad?"

Tatunjian stood before him, hands on hips, chewing on a

short, wet cigar, studying the suspended car with his accustomed grimness. Behind him the entire Tatunjian clan, still seated in the brown Tatunjian Buick, stared out at him, a communal Tatunjian squint glaring like a searchlight on Henna's shame.

"This is the first accident I've ever had, Oscar."

"Well, I knew you'd have one eventually, the way you drive," Nancy couldn't resist saying.

"I was thinking something, the next thing I knew, boom."

"You really did it, Jack."

"That's it, I wasn't thinking."

"I thought you said you were thinking."

"But not about the road. Something else. Christ, I don't even remember. Nancy, for Chrissake, tell Leo his knee isn't broken."

"You really did it."

"I *know* that, Oscar. You *said* it, for Chrissake."

"Hey, listen, I don't have to stand here shootin' the shit with you, I can take my family and go up to the outing."

"I know, I'm sorry, Oscar, we get a couple more guys, maybe we can lift the car off."

The D'Alio Cadillac pulled up then. With a renewed sense of shame, Henna watched D'Alio's huge gray head rise above the pink roof like a whale surfacing. He waved and, almost as an extension of D'Alio and a tribute to his size, Mrs. D'Alio's mammoth right arm reached out from the opposite side of the car in greeting. It looked for a moment as though D'Alio with one arm could lift the Cadillac up and carry it with him to the accident site. In the moment, Henna was reassured.

A hot dog sizzled on the grill; the men heaved.

Henna, Tatunjian, D'Alio, Cutler, joined by D'Alio's fourteen-year-old, Joey, and Cutler's thirteen-year-old, Stanley.

They heaved and failed; Nancy turned the hot dog over and shouted, "I think the fire's hot enough now!"

"Hell of a note," D'Alio said, wiping away a fistful of sweat.

"Hopeless," Cutler added.

"Nothing's hopeless," Peggy Cutler shouted. "Always remember that!"

"Just cook hot dogs and nix on the philosophy, will ya, Peg?"

"Hell of a note, hell of a note."

"We eat, we just keep trying, all I can see for us to do." Tatunjian turned to his son. "Ronnie, why don't you run up to the camp and tell them we're here, we'll be up as soon as we can, whoever can come down to help, the sooner we get out of this mess."

Ronnie, aged ten and already "shooting up," in Rose Tatunjian's words, ran up to the paved road, past the three parked cars, and disappeared. D'Alio settled into a lounge chair he had extracted from the trunk of his Cadillac and shouted, "Ronnie, tell 'em to get down here no matter *what* they're doing!"

"All we can do is eat," Tatunjian repeated for emphasis, spearing a hot dog before Rose could slap his hand and say, "Not yet, Oscar."

The children eyed each other warily, Joey D'Alio looking with fourteen-year-old lust upon the prematurely developed breasts of Karen Tatunjian. Thomas hovered near his mother. Leo picked up a stick from the woods and whipped it across Karen Tatunjian's rear, squealing and dropping the stick on the instant of contact, running into the woods as Karen turned around and, looking disgustedly in Leo's direction, then at her mother, clicked her tongue, "Tch."

Karen's father stole away with his speared hot dog, approached Henna at the side of the beached Fairlane.

"Delicious," he said, biting into the red frank. "All beef. Nepco. You want a bite?"

Henna stared at the hot dog, not thinking. The weight on his chest rendered all other considerations trivial. Life was reduced to a non-functioning automobile. The reverberations of the event seemed to encompass even the extremities of his life. What now, what now?

He opened his mouth and bit. The hot dog was cold and wet, raw.

"Jesus, it's *raw*, Oscar."

"Delicious. All beef."

"It's *raw*, for Chrissake."

"Never hurt you."

Henna spit it up at his feet, then leaned heavily on his automobile and stared glumly at the assembly.

D'Alio was in his lounge chair, holding his small daughter in his lap. Henna listened.

"And the big bear says to the little bear . . ."

Julie D'Alio looked up hopefully at her father.

"Jesus." D'Alio looked up. "Lucy, what'd the big bear say to the little bear?"

Julie pulled at a fistful of her father's chest hair.

"Lucy, for Chrissake!"

"What, what?"

"The big bear, what'd he say?"

"When?"

"When they came home and the porridge was gone. I forget how it goes."

His plea was ignored. The hot dogs were ready. Henna watched them all congregate around the grill. Even from this, excluded. Unable to develop an appetite, he watched Joey D'Alio and Karen Tatunjian move off to the edge of the woods, then farther into the woods themselves, eating hot dogs, he talking, she quiescent, grim as her father, nobody noticing, all intent on the food. Henna watched them disappear.

Thomas brought him a hot dog. "Mom says you gotta eat anyway."

"Anyway, what?"

"Anyway. I don't know what she meant. I guess we won't be able to play baseball, huh, Dad?"

"I guess not, Thomas."

Thomas pulled on Henna's pant leg, moved back and forth.

"Will we have to walk home?"

"No. No."

"How will we get home, then?"

"In the car."

"How?"

"Don't ask. Somehow. We'll get it off. Where's Leo?"

"In the woods. How, Dad?"

"Don't ask me that. We just will."

The boy hesitated now, let go of Henna's pants.

"Can you live without a car, Dad?"

He looked down at his son. It was a serious question.

"I don't know. I guess you can. If you have to."

The fire embraced them all. The famous cookout smell. The last hot dogs were black on the flames. Al Cutler waved to him from the other side of the fire, in the midst of explaining something to Stanley with the aid of a stick. D'Alio's voice floated across the air, a detail in the sensual mosaic: "Who's been sleeping in *my* bed?" Nancy, across the smoke, looked soft, tender, gesturing lightly as she talked to Peggy Cutler, her right leg bobbing up and down on her left knee. To them, it was all right, this accident. They could walk away from it, return to their lives, his misfortune a small event in the day, covered quickly by the normalcy of returning home, familiar things.

But suddenly, Rose Tatunjian was screaming.

"Oh my God, where's Karen?"

"Rose, relax, she went for a walk with Joey." Oscar tried to calm her.

"In the woods? In the woods?"

"Of course in the woods. Where do you think, into Boston?"

"And you let her? You watched her?"

"They were eating hot dogs, for Chrissake, Rose, will you relax?"

Rose Tatunjian grabbed her dress at the chest, seemed to be trying to pull it away. Now Henna understood why people wrote operas.

Rose led, and they all, almost as a unit, stared away, into the woods, stared away from the hot dogs on the smoking grill and the truncated car on its wooden jack into the sunny woods, which seemed to stretch on in shades of green forever, and Freddie D'Alio smiled, and Henna, noting the smile, felt suddenly small, a pea in the bright green world.

It was agreed that the men would search the woods while the women stayed behind to watch the smaller children. Rose Tatunjian was calmed. Oscar could be heard telling her, "It's all right, she went with Joey, we *know* Joey." His words soothed even Henna. When Oscar stopped talking, Rose's hysteria fluttered up again. Nancy went to her, held her hand. Only Lucy D'Alio ignored the situation, concentrating instead on cooking one last hot dog to feed to her Bobby, aged three.

It was Cutler's suggestion: "We men'll go in."

Henna admired the phrasing: "We men." All of them, brothers of a sort. He had trouble understanding the connection, the common denominator of male brotherhood until he heard it stated simply. Cutler made him understand something basic: men go into the woods, women stay behind. Why? Someone decided, ages and ages ago, before them. It was beyond simple logic, an impulse you blindly obeyed.

So they set off, Henna with Thomas, Cutler with Stanley, D'Alio and Tatunjian bringing up the rear. Cutler grabbed a tall stick, gathered Stanley to his side and began pointing out the "salient features of the forest."

"Now, Stanley," Cutler intoned, after pointing out birch and maple, moss and ivy, "once upon a time—you see all this land here?—once upon a time a man named Cabot came out here to Waltham, Cabot had *nothing*, not a pot to pee in, am I right, Jack, Oscar?"

"That's right." Henna nudged Thomas, gestured that he should pay attention to this.

"Had *nothing*. Came out here to Waltham, the whole city, the whole town, there was nothing in it but woods. Where City Hall is now, Main Street, Moody Street, nothing. No Woolworth's, no Kresge's, no Brigham's, no Grover Cronin's, no banks, no Embassy, nothing. Woods."

Cutler paused. They tramped ahead through the undergrowth. Branches crackled under them. Last year's fallen leaves still covered parts of the ground.

The pause had done its work. Henna turned around, could no longer see their little campground, the outline of the suspended Fairlane. All around him, as far as the eye could see, woods. He placed his hand on the soft skin of Thomas' neck, rubbed gently as they walked.

"So this man Cabot, Stanley, this fellow with not so much as a pot to pee in . . ."

"Where did he pee?"

Cutler looked down at Stanley.

"He peed . . . Stanley, that's not the point. He peed . . . somewhere. The ground, someplace. It's just a phrase, doesn't mean anything. Means poor, that's all. Poor. Not a pot to pee in. Poor."

Stanley buried a snicker.

Cutler looked down at him, disapproving, then looked ahead and down at the dead leaves and crackling branches below them until the thread of the story returned.

"So this man Cabot, poor, very poor, he climbs a tree. He climbs a tree, Stanley, way, way up—it's the tallest tree in the forest, and the forest, remember, covers the whole city, the whole town . . ."

Stanley had caught Thomas' attention. Henna, out of the corner of his eye, watching but trying not to, saw Stanley pick up a branch and mime whacking his father's long, Bermudaed ass, stopping short about two inches from target. Stanley, doubled over with suppressed laughter, nearly fell over with glee. Henna wanted to laugh, too, Cutler looked so oblivious through it all, but he remembered the story, covered Thomas' open laughing mouth with his hand.

". . . he climbs the tree, he gets to the top, and oh my God, he can see everything." Cutler's voice gathered itself in. There was a hush, and then the words continued, full of holiness, awe: "*Everything*, all these woods, from Prospect Hill over to Belmont, he surveys the whole countryside, and he shouts, Stanley, he shouts, 'Mine, all this is mine!' "

They waited, knowing there was more to the story. They had all heard it before, told it themselves, they knew what had to happen. Cutler was playing them, the ham, just as he had played Connie.

They waited, and it came, but before it came Henna could feel his own body forcing it, his arms at his side wanting to reach out as Cabot's must have, to embrace it all, and was it a trick of imagination, or could he see Tatunjian's arms stiffening at his sides, as if being held down only by a force of will? It was as if they were summoning Cabot, the old Indian fighter, the old bedraggled explorer, so poor he could only pee by exposing himself to this wilderness, peeing on it and by that act claiming it, and only when the moment was full, when their minds had been given time to form a common image down to its very edges and green details, did Cutler complete his story for them by reaching his arms out wide and thundering, "I take it!"

They all stopped. The silence overwhelmed, but only for a split second before it was broken by the loud slap of wood on skin, and Cutler was jolted forward two steps. They all turned to see Stanley Cutler's face frozen in shock, a long branch still in his hand, but only Henna and Thomas knew what had happened, that the completion of the story, their sudden stopping, had surprised Stanley in the midst of his elaborate joke, that what was intended to have been frozen in air two inches from Stanley's father's ass had instead reached its target.

"What happened, what hap—"

Cutler turned around just as Stanley was about to ditch the evidence.

"Stan-*leee!*"

Then Stanley was running, Cutler chasing him with the stick.

The others, shocked, watched until Cutler and his son were dim figures in the midst of the surrounding forest.

"It's a true story," Tatunjian said.

They were twenty minutes into the woods, the woods bigger than any of them would have imagined, so wide, so final, they would be surprised to come out, on the other side of this forest, in a housing development they were all familiar with for having driven through. For the first time that day, Henna feared for Leo.

He had known these woods, understood their place, a large square on the map of the city, separating Forest Street from Lexington Street. This was the last of something, a blur of green you drove by, dismissed, sleeping land, land waiting for someone's approach, to be awakened with an idea, a plan, blueprints and maps and bulldozers and wood. All this leveled to make way for someone's vision. Then the land would come alive. But here, within, he felt the woods' own personal distance from the ideas you could impose on them. It was still wild in here.

Before, why had he felt so small at the idea of entering? He could remember exploring every inch of wilderness on Filicudi, remembered especially the place where, it was said, his mother's sister had plunged to her death. A flat rock, shooting straight up the side of the island from out of the sea. She had been reaching out, the story went, to pick a flower growing out of the rock. The story's force hit him hard now, the fact that it might not have been true at all, just a convenient myth to keep the children from exploring. He thought of Cabot, the strong, brown, free-pissing explorer, and how the myths were different here. Here you reached out for things and they came to you, you peed in the right place and things grew.

He rubbed the soft, downy skin on the back of Thomas' neck and feared for his younger son, his hope. He wished one of them would say something. Why did they all walk so silently? Where were the jokes of the office, the easy camaraderie? He had to piss now, but not here in front of everyone. Where did these woods end? Where in all this green chaos could the children have gone?

". . . rock in my goddamn shoe," he heard.

Freddie D'Alio leaned against a tree, removed his shoe. While they waited, Henna and Tatunjian looked at one another. In amazement, boredom, mutual disgust? Henna couldn't say which, only that he blamed Tatunjian. And

D'Alio. And himself. All their children were lost somewhere in these woods. Because D'Alio handed down a sexual energy to his son, Tatunjian at least acceded to a legacy of enormous tits. And Henna had gifted his younger son with an exploring curiosity, a remnant, he would say, of ancient days.

D'Alio put his shoe back on, and they moved on. Up above, at the top of the trees, the sun broke through in patches. Now on Thomas' neck, now on the ground, shifting to Tatunjian's bald spot, then to the wide blue shoulder of D'Alio's polo shirt. They moved heavily; the sun, when it touched them, wore them down, their feet falling like bricks against the thick-leaved earth.

At last, they sat to rest.

Each of them found a tree, sat at its foot, their backs resting straight against the trunks of elms, Thomas nestled against his father's crotch.

How long had they been in here? An hour, two? Impossible to tell now. The forest had eaten the children, had Cutler and his son for dessert. In their quest, they seemed to have missed entirely the belly of the forest.

D'Alio breathed heavily. His hands were on his genitals, thoughtful, prodding, as if his crotch were the place where memory resided.

He laughed.

"I remember these woods."

He laughed again, looked at Henna.

"Remember? When we were kids? Christ, it just occurs to me. Henna, where'd you used to live, McKenn Street?"

"Yes."

"You used to come up this way, ever?"

"No. We used to play in the woods down by the river."

"Oscar. You?"

"You're forgettin' I'm from Watertown."

"Jeez. There used to be this girl. Jenny, Jenny, Jesus, Jenny Salamanca. That's it. Jenny Salamanca. Girl from over by Piety

Corner, her father ran the fruit stand down there, remember Rookie Salamanca?"

"Sure," Henna answered.

"His daughter was the first girl I ever did it with. You know that? In these same fucking woods."

Henna patted down the sides of Thomas' head, as if to hide his movement to cover the boy's ears. But no, decided instead: Let him listen. Let him hear.

"Jenny Salamanca spread her legs for me and Eddie Zambetti in these woods."

He paused, pulling the memory in. There was laughter at the tail end of it.

"It's crazy how you forget these things. I used to go around afterwards, like in a dream world, wondering how I was ever gonna get out from between a woman's legs. I figured other guys had this tremendous self-discipline, but me, I was gonna wind up like my Uncle Frankie the Stick. So skinny he had to run around in the shower to get wet, but they say he had a pepperoni on him, when it got hard it was the widest part of him, you couldn't see nothing behind it. Women? Jeez. The guy never married, but around the neighborhood every year there's a skinny kid born lookin' just like Frankie. Frankie was who they told you you'd end up like if you're not careful. You'll get pockmarks on your face like Frankie if you hang out with the wrong type of girl."

D'Alio's hands were creating a face in air, Frankie the Stick beside him in the forest. Henna could see the slope of the unbroken eyebrow, the large haunted eyes. Haunted by what? D'Alio had mentioned nothing of the grief of Frankie the Stick. It was merely the exactness of his hand motions that allowed the mind to fill in the rest effortlessly.

"So I got worried at some point, stopped coming into these woods with Jenny. Frankie died young, y'know. They said syphilis. Never held down a job, either. Lived with his mother."

D'Alio laughed suddenly at this. Henna wanted to join him, but found it difficult.

"With his mother, for Chrissake. And all over the place, women, pregnant women. He comes home, eats his mother's pasta fazool, huh?"

He rocked with laughter, created a hole of laughter in the woods, waking the sleeping Tatunjian, who looked querulously, miserably up at Henna before nodding back to sleep.

"I stopped coming in here with Jenny. You know, I stayed off women for years. For years. Afraid I'd gotten syphilis off of Jenny, was gonna die unless I went to work. I didn't touch women for a long time. I was thirty-five when I married Lucy, did you know that?"

Henna had been listening carefully, but the voice had up to now sounded detached, a voice in the forest, not of a man, certainly not of D'Alio. Men did not talk easily about themselves. D'Alio more than any of them was a man of business. Now Henna turned, looked into D'Alio's face, at the open creases, the sweat and the sudden need to be given approval to go on. Unconsciously, Henna nodded his big head, granting it.

"Thirty-five. This is eighteen years ago. For twenty years I hadn't so much as touched a woman. When Lucy came along, I don't know, I was afraid, but look, I said, you can't go around being afraid forever. I wanted kids, I wanted a normal life."

The words had come out in a rush. Now he slowed down.

"What it was about Lucy made me change my mind, made me stop being afraid, I can't remember. There was nothing special about Lucy. She was overweight even then."

D'Alio paused, his tongue licking sweat off his bottom lip.

"*Something*, though. Musta been. Do you ever think that, ever think what makes you pick one, out of a thousand, a million? One woman. Why her?"

He shrugged.

"So I had to take a blood test, before the wedding. Jesus, I was shittin' a brick before I went to that doctor, then waitin' for the results. Christ, makes me shiver just to remember. You can imagine how I felt when I turned out not to have syphilis. Like a free man. Like a free man!"

He stopped, gathered to himself the whole past. His face lit up with it.

"And that started it. Jeez, Jack, it was like I had just come out of the woods, just left Jenny and was ready to take on the rest of the world. What came over me I don't know, still don't know. You think maybe it was just knowing I'd escaped turning into my Uncle Frankie? Hell, you know what? Frankie didn't even end up like Frankie. It was TB, not syphilis, that got him. My father told me this, years later. But in those days, hell, I believed I'd been given like grace after confession, y'know?"

He turned his palms up in wonderment.

"I could never concentrate on Lucy after that. She was always pregnant. She had two miscarriages before Joey was born, one stillborn. Joey was our fourth. They told me after Joey to keep off her for a while. I kept off her for nine years, she didn't mind. I had so many others I lost track of the time. All she wanted was the kid. Then all of a sudden, she's interested again. Bang, we had Julie. Bang, comes Bobby. She's pregnant again, you know that?"

He smiled now, and Henna returned it.

"Congratulations, Freddie."

"Jack, I tell you, I can't figure life. I'm fifty-three years old. When my father was fifty-three, he was an old man."

Henna joined him now in laughter, but careful not to wake Tatunjian. When they stopped, the silence afterward was like a deep wound opened. Henna gazed into it.

"Oh, Christ. Jenny Salamanca. Jack, she was . . ."

D'Alio crafted Jenny Salamanca in air.

"Not so beautiful, but oh, what a promise. And then twenty years before it's kept. Sometimes I say damn that son of a bitch my Uncle Frankie. For frightening me to death. Twenty years is not something you can get back, Jack."

D'Alio's eyes grew dark, turning inward.

"So what do you think, Jack?"

D'Alio smiled at him. Not looking for approval anymore, just some small truth they could share. Henna didn't know what to think. D'Alio, a great man, had revealed himself to be as much at a loss as any of them. Was it the woods that did it to you, made you admit to the imminence of death? That was what D'Alio had done, and the admission had been like a soft blow against Henna's head, forcing him to move out of the range of assault.

"Is she dead now, Freddie?"

"Who?"

"The girl. This Jenny."

"Oh yeah. Christ yeah. Years ago."

Henna gripped the base of the tree, steadying himself. Thought: Somewhere in this forest, three children are lost, and here we sit snoozing, telling stories of the dead.

"Where you goin'?" D'Alio asked.

He didn't have an answer. An impulse to move, to run, to circumvent this forest, to find the *outside* of it, had begun low in him, was rising.

"Rest awhile, Jack. The day's still young."

He looked at D'Alio. The man seemed weak, clawing at the past, as though the present needed no taking care of. Yet they were lost, in the middle of a forest in the center of a town they had come to by accident and settled in without making it their own. It was not theirs yet, there was too much of the wild left.

Above Henna, a small bird fluttered from branch to branch, erratic, spinning in its pattern, so quick he could only just catch it. He felt dizzied watching it, afraid for a moment that he'd fall. Everything around him seemed to exist in the moment merely to catch him off guard.

Then, like a gift, he heard from a point not far away the trickle of water, light and uneven, a sound he could swear he'd only heard in the woods of Filicudi, the sound a salt stream makes as it flows over the high rocks on its way back to the sea. If he followed it, he'd come to a place where the rocks turned green, slippery with growth. Often as a child he'd imagined braving those rocks, feeling the loss of support beneath him, reaching out for something to grab, connecting with nothing. There was an exhilaration even in imagining it.

He listened now to the loose spray of water, his ears cocked. Without waiting for the others, he moved toward it.

Closer.

Henna moved through the fuzzy undergrowth, Thomas by his side. The two of them, explorers on the verge of great discovery or certain death. At the point of movement, Henna thought, it hardly mattered which.

His hand on Thomas' head, he had to fight the urge to hug his son. But why fight it? Early on, he'd decided that to hug a child too much was to remove hugging from the realm of reward. But little that had happened to them had ever justified reward, and feeling often hung there, heavy with disuse, in his hands when he casually touched the boy. He'd imagined, all through Nancy's first pregnancy, that he would immediately feel a connection with his child by holding it in his arms as soon as it was born. But they had kept Thomas from him; during the baby's difficult delivery, bones had been broken in two places. He had first seen the child through a glass partition, a violent, mangled face wrapped in bandages. For two days he was not allowed any closer to his son than he could get with his nose pressed against the partition. He came to see the boy as a small monster, some fault of his own seed, who would never be quite right. He had learned to love him that way, but never to feel tender as you would feel tender toward a perfect thing.

Now Thomas' hair bristled at Henna's touch. He wanted to go forward toward this destined place with the boy in his arms.

"What do you think it is, Dad?"

"I don't know, Thomas."

"A waterfall?"

"Might be."

"A river?"

"Maybe, Thomas."

They had to climb up over a long, sloping shelf of rock, covered with lichen. At the top of it a squat, short-trunked tree stood as guardian of all that was beyond.

"We'll find it, though, won't we, Dad?"

"We're getting closer."

"Maybe . . ."

"Shh."

Thomas scrambled quickly to the top.

"Dad?" Thomas whispered.

"What?"

"I can see it now. Can you see?"

Henna, in a crouched-over position, tried to grab for one of the branches of the guardian tree, to right himself.

"No."

"It's Mr. Valenti. He's taking a leak."

Henna saw now, just over the edge of the rock, Valenti watering the side of a tree, a patch of grass, clover, a small blueberry patch, barely missing a passing bee.

Thomas' laughter caught Valenti off guard. He stepped back, not quick enough to remove his pant leg from the trail of his own water.

"Jesus Christ," he said, dancing.

"What are you doing here?" Henna called.

"Yeah, I'd like to ask you the same question. Look at what you made me do. Scared me half to death."

Valenti brushed away at the side of his clothes. It struck Henna, even at this moment of confusion, as a misplaced gesture.

"Chrissake. You're gonna pay for the cleaning bill, Jack!"

"Me? What'd I do?"

"Scared me half to death, that's what you did."

Valenti cast the comment backward, moving off.

"Where you going? Phil, hey, wait!"

They followed Valenti not forty feet before they reached the edge of the forest. On the far end of the long, sloped field directly before them, they could see men and boys standing on a baseball diamond, forming up teams.

Henna gulped hard.

So close, he thought. My God, a man can be so wrong, can get scared, too scared to move almost, when he's so close to the thing itself! How do you ever know, without blindly reaching out for it, how far you are from the dreamed-for place?

He reached down to touch Thomas, but the boy was gone. Reaching back, he managed to grab a shoulder as Thomas' body wriggled, attempting to escape. Finally, Thomas relaxed into his father's grip.

Valenti had disappeared, but Henna could devote no more than a moment to wondering where, so great was his exhilaration at seeing the field divided into diamond shapes marked out in white chalk. Under the salesmen's feet, dirt rose in clouds.

He wanted to run to it, but compromised: walked faster.

5

"J A C K, where you been?" Gennaro called from his perch in a folding chair behind home plate.

"In the woods, Joe. D'Alio's kid got lost. Tatunjian's, too. And *mine*." He had nearly forgotten Leo.

"What are you talkin'? They're all here."

And sure enough, there was Joey D'Alio, swinging a bat. Leo, wearing an oversized baseball cap someone had placed on his head, appeared to be industriously digging holes in the outfield. Karen Tatunjian was nowhere to be seen, but then neither were any of the women.

"We heard about your car, Jack." Joe Mele approached and patted him on the back. "Call a wrecker, would be the best thing."

"It's not wrecked. With enough guys, we could hoist it off ourselves." But already they had convinced him of something; he felt he had entered a perfect thing.

"Jack, listen," Mele said. "It's gonna rain later on. We want to get in nine innings before that happens."

"Sure, sure," Henna found himself assenting. Behind him, he could hear D'Alio and Tatunjian's heavy footsteps.

"I thought we were lost," D'Alio boomed. "Goners!"

"Where's Karen?" Tatunjian asked, detached.

"She's with the women," Gennaro answered.

Tatunjian nodded. D'Alio looked at his son, winked. Joey D'Alio, flushed with pride, stood a little taller, two bats in his hand, working them from shoulder to shoulder.

"So let's go," D'Alio shouted.

And the field, like the office had earlier in the week, appeared to hop.

Cutler stepped forward. "We'll take D'Alio and Henna's kid. You guys can have Tatunjian and Henna."

D'Alio, retrieving his carefully prepared lineup, motioned to object, but Cutler, without losing a beat, continued, "We decided before, Tony, amongst ourselves, fathers and sons play on opposite teams."

Cutler looked down at Thomas and patted him on the shoulder. "You'll show your old man a thing or two, won't you, Tom? Ya ha ha," he laughed like a pirate at Thomas' look of displeasure, and moved away.

Stanley Cutler, red-eyed and rubbing his backside at the first-base line, shot a look of pure hatred at his father.

Henna bent down.

Thomas was clearly wishing he were somewhere, anywhere else. His body looked as if it were trying to melt itself into the ground. Henna held the boy's head in two hands, forced him to look and face him.

"It's a good game, Thomas."

"I know."

"It's a *won*derful game. It's not something to be afraid of. You know that."

"Yes."

"You're still a young boy, Thomas. Do you know that anything can happen in this life? Do you believe that?"

"No."

"Well, it can. One day you can be afraid of something, you

can be afraid of missing the ball and being embarrassed in front of everybody, but so long as you don't hide from it, so long as you're out there *in the field*, oh, one day some ball might come sailing out to you"—he watched Thomas' eyes widen slightly, hesitation and fear visible just behind the pupils—"and you're afraid, but you say, what the heck, and you reach your glove out, you reach it way up, and the ball, almost by a miracle, lands in it. You make the catch!"

The speech had no visible result—Thomas looked as scared as before—but Henna patted him on the bottom as if the boy's face had lit up in agreement and sent him over to the opposing side, where he could see Cutler already marching back and forth, giving orders.

Gennaro approached him.

"Henna, you want to pitch?"

"I thought Valenti was pitching."

"So where's Valenti?"

"He disappeared on me."

"That's the story of the whole day. He shows up, boom, out of the blue, keeps disappearing. Too bad about your car."

"Don't worry." Henna patted the sides of his legs, anxious for some simple action that would allow him to forget the car. "Sure, I'll pitch. Underhand, right?"

"To the kids. Grownups, give 'em the old fastball, right?"

"My fastball's not much, Joe."

"Do your best." Gennaro turned away, shouted, "Who's up first?"

In the course of Henna's short conversation with Gennaro, D'Alio had clearly unseated Cutler as captain of the opposing team. He stepped forward in the pose of an overweight gladiator.

"We're home team. You're up first."

"What makes you home?" Gennaro shouted back.

D'Alio paused, smiled and, spitting into the dirt, got down onto the ground on all fours and proceeded to hump it, to the huge enjoyment of his teammates.

"This," D'Alio shouted upward, then stood, wiping the sides

of his hands on his pants, picked up a glove and moved past Gennaro and Henna to his perch at first base.

The men followed him in a phalanx. Their shoulders seemed miles wide.

Gennaro looked up at Henna, shrugged "What can you do?" and moved off the infield.

Henna, starting to follow, caught the look on Thomas' face as the boy moved onto the field.

"What movie do you want me to take you to? Name it."

Thomas brightened. His face seemed to expand.

"Oh, Dad, yeah, *Indiscreet*, Cary Grant and Ingrid Bergman."

"In the what?"

He received no answer, instead watched Thomas hop off ecstatically into left field, until, at a point just beyond shortstop, the present seemed to regain its grip on his body. By the time he reached his position, he appeared tight, head to the ground, closed in on himself.

Leo, looking up at his miserable brother, smiled, waved, threw a clump of dirt that just glanced off Thomas' leg. Thomas took Leo's hand and pulled him farther out into left field, pulled the hat down over the smaller boy's head and watched him contentedly reroot himself in the new spot. When Thomas looked up, he saw his father and, as if remembering his insight from the afternoon they'd played catch, flashed his brave smile, the smile that had made Henna so uncomfortable. What was the boy seeing?

Seated beside Gennaro on the bench, batting eighth, he watched Cutler strike Mele out. The division of fathers and sons made the field look odd, unevenly mowed. D'Alio covered first by standing directly *over* the base, not to the side. It seemed the only way to reach first would be to slide between D'Alio's legs, and even that would be risky.

Roger Leblanc, son of the office's only French Canadian, tall, soft-spoken Yvon Leblanc, batted second. Cutler's pitching was smooth, direct, no frills. He pitched with force and concentration, a serious man doing a serious job. On the third pitch, Roger Leblanc hit a long fly ball to his father in center field. With enormous strides Leblanc got under it, lifted his glove just slightly, made a neat catch and threw the ball back to Cutler on the pitcher's mound.

Leblanc and his son exchanged a quick look, each utterly serious. Leblanc lifted his hand, saluting, and his son, casting his bat aside, returned it. It had the look of a compact, a declaration of this having its own set of rules, outside of whatever rules might apply at home. Henna felt warmed by young Leblanc's gesture.

Tatunjian stepped to the plate. In his dress pants and white shirt, he looked out of place. As if to remedy this, he tapped the bat against both feet, then into the dirt, a blatant imitation of the at-bat maneuvers of professional ballplayers. Tatunjian did it with no sense of ease, as though purposely exaggerating the imitation. Then he spit, and it landed on his shoe.

The first ball whizzed past him as he attempted to rub the spit off his shoe in the dirt.

"Hey, what's goin' on here?" Tatunjian shouted to the mound.

"You're in the batter's box. That's your in-play position, Oscar."

"Yeah, so what's the point? Where's the ump? You think you're gonna call me out on strikes, Al?"

The point was well taken. They had no umpire.

Tatunjian lifted the bat high now, ready.

Cutler threw a neat hard fastball.

Tatunjian swung, with surprising force, catching the ball on the underside of his moving bat, so that it chopped the ground halfway to second base. Mele's kid stood ready, next to second, as the ball hopped in his direction, glove between his legs. Tatunjian was wheezing his way to the brick wall D'Alio had constructed over first when the ball seemed to go right through Mele's kid's glove, then roll out onto the right-field green, where Gennaro's kid and Leblanc, each playing slightly off of center, charged for it. Tatunjian laughed at D'Alio's face as he tagged the bag and headed for second, where Mele's kid waited, with upraised glove, for Leblanc's throw. The throw came in time, but something appeared to be wrong with Mele's kid's glove, because the ball went right past him, heading down the third-base line on the left-field side, where Nick Taranto, third baseman, chased it. Henna noticed Thomas start to back away as the ball neared his position. Taranto finally caught up with the ball and whipped it to third, but no one had thought to cover third, and Tatunjian had already rounded the base and was heading for home when Cutler literally threw himself on the uncapturable ball and began crawling toward home. He reached out at the last minute to tag Tatunjian's leg a split second before the leg touched home plate.

Tatunjian lifted his arms in triumph; Henna watched his face collapse as the sound of gloves being thrown to his teammates and players rushing past him reached his ears, or registered in his consciousness (the two seemed not to happen simultaneously).

"What's goin' on here? I was safe."

"You were out," Cutler rebuffed, matter-of-factly.

"Get out. What are you, blind? I was on the base before you touched me."

The kids seemed to respect Tatunjian's injured tone more than their fathers did. The two Winchell boys hung back on the infield, not sure whether to come in or return to the field.

"Come on in, boys," D'Alio called. "The man was *out.*"

"Henna, Gennaro, was I out?"

The two men shrugged.

"Hard to tell from here," Gennaro sighed, working his fist into a glove. "Good try though, Oscar. Should have stayed on third."

"Never. Never. I'm gonna get you, Cutler." Tatunjian yanked a glove off one of the Winchell kids so forcefully that the kid looked as though he'd start to cry.

"Sorry, kid," Tatunjian uttered under his breath, and walked in the salesman's tired, end-of-the-trip stride out to center field.

Leo followed Thomas to the bench and sat at his feet. From the mound, Henna attempted to imitate Leblanc's salute, but Thomas, looking confused, made no return.

The first two batters he faced were the Winchell kids. Both hit grounders to short. Joey D'Alio, swift and perfect in that position, in one motion let the scooped ball fly from his hand over to Gennaro's glove at first. Yvon Leblanc, up third, forced Henna to straighten up, in emulation of the man's height. Facing a tall batter after two short ones dislocated him somewhat. He had felt some confidence after grounding out two in a row. Now Leblanc's power glistened at him. His hands and the bat they gripped, both the same color, seemed one thing. Throwing the first pitch felt like a wasted effort; sure enough, Leblanc's bat connected, sending the ball upward like a shot fired into the clouds. The ball seemed so well hit, sailed so far above their heads, it appeared for a moment that they were about to lose it to the sky. Tatunjian chased it nonetheless, full of surprising energy for such a heavy, unexcitable man. When the ball finally came down, he was under it. Lifting the glove over his head, Tatunjian caught it on the run. Leblanc accepted the impossible verdict with such grace that Henna was touched. The two opponents met at second base on their way to a trade of position, and Leblanc slapped Tatunjian on the back. Henna went beyond being touched. The word "sportsmanship" finally had a meaning for him. Leblanc appeared now to be an Angel of Rules, imposing a divine order on the splendid afternoon. With his legs moving under him on the way back to the bench, Henna wished the run from pitcher's mound to bench were longer, that this motion might continue.

Joey D'Alio hit the game's first home run, a neat, powerful line drive that flew over Thomas' head in left field so fast the boy hadn't even time to reach for it (Henna wondered if he would, even given the time, have tried to catch a ball so powerfully hit). Henna's team was leading, then, 1–0, when Stanley Cutler walked to the plate, raised his bat high up over his shoulders, swung cleanly at the first ball his father threw and sent it back with clear-eyed precision to the batter's own source of origin, sending Cutler over like a man taking a round of shrapnel in the lower belly. Stanley then proceeded to run innocently to first, where D'Alio, openmouthed, made room for him. Cutler, doubled over but still conscious, conscious enough, anyway, to desire revenge, cast the ball over in the direction of first before collapsing entirely. At first base, Stanley took a slight lead when he noticed D'Alio's lack of vigilance. When the big first baseman moved to assist the crippled pitcher, Stanley stole second.

Henna, with several of the men, moved out to the mound.

He and D'Alio bent down to assist Cutler, who was trying to speak through his teeth.

"That son of a bitch."

"It's okay, Al. Relax."

"I'll kill that son of a bitch bastard."

"Al, come on now."

"He did it on purpose, I swear to God. He aimed that ball right for my balls, did you see that?"

"Stanley didn't mean it, Al," Henna felt prompted to say.

"It's *Freud*, that's what it is."

"Al."

"What does he want, for Chrissake?" Then, getting up: "What do you *want?*"

Stanley took a lead off second.

"You son of a bitch, I'll *kill* you."

Cutler, limping toward Stanley, had to be restrained. Taken to the bench, he was forced to lie down. When D'Alio and Henna turned back, they caught sight of Valenti moving across the right-field grass, his shirt hanging sloppily out of his pants, heading toward the mound.

"You came just in time, Phil," D'Alio called out in greeting. "Where you been?"

"I told you. I hadda take my kid for glasses. Where's a glove?"

D'Alio threw him Cutler's. Valenti caught it, squinting in the direction of his fallen predecessor.

"What happened to Cutler?"

"Paternal injuries," Mele called from the bench.

Valenti's pitching was wild, unconcentrated. Henna thought: He pitches like he sells. Still, it worked better than Cutler's serious, methodical handling of balls had in that no one seemed to be able to hit his pitches, though two men went down trying.

Watching Butch Taranto, Nick Taranto's brawny, deer-faced ten-year-old, chop away at Valenti's erratic lobs, Henna, in the on-deck circle, thought two things: First, he must find a way of hitting the ball so that it went nowhere near left field. Thomas would consider it a personal betrayal if his father clouded his game by hitting him a difficult ball. He practiced swings that might send the ball to left or center and, watching Butch Taranto swing desperately, was calmed by the thought that it might, after all, be out of his control. There might be *no* way of hitting Valenti's pitches, he might have to strike out.

The second thought arrived as Butch Taranto swung and missed a third time, turned sadly to him and dropped his bat in the dirt. When Butch Taranto looked at him, he realized something that might have been obvious to any of the others but struck him as a new insight. Butch was ten, and so was Ronnie Tatunjian. The Mele kid was nine, the Winchell boys ten and nine, Roger Leblanc, Bobby Valenti and Thomas, all were or about to turn ten. Only D'Alio, Gennaro and Cutler had older kids. The rest of them had all had sons at the same time. Walking into the batter's box, Henna was not sure why he suddenly felt so melancholy. He was remembering the days, ten, eleven years before, when they'd all been busy getting their wives pregnant. How had those days been different from these? He couldn't remember the details well. They'd tried for Thomas for nine years, he and Nancy. He hadn't allowed the difficulty to get to him until the day she told him how she'd gone to St. Jude's, knelt down in a pew and asked God if he couldn't give

her a child to please let her die. After that, something in him
went sour, blame turned inward. He began to see other men as
having magical powers, powers he would never possess. When
she finally became pregnant, he hadn't reacted as he'd expected
to. In a book he read afterward, a book about pregnancy, he
read that if sperms were retained too long without being released they began to suffer the effects of senility. That was
what he guessed had happened to his desire for fatherhood: it
had been suppressed so long it became senile. He'd had to kick
it in order to feel anything.

Henna did not want to be thinking about the past as he stood
waiting for Valenti's first pitch. He wanted to hit a baseball, to
be, in every fiber of his being, bones, skin, mind, in the present.
But he couldn't help but see them all as they'd been ten years
before, couldn't help but wonder what it must feel like to meet
a woman, date her, propose, marry her, take her once to bed
and, weeks later, find out she was pregnant. He wondered how
a woman would see you then, if you had never once made her
want to die. Were they all magical, Leblanc and Mele, Tatunjian and Winchell? D'Alio had said his wife was "always pregnant." Had he, Henna, joined their ranks without truly
belonging? Was he an impostor, no more of a father in the
true sense than his cousin Vinnie with his two adopted kids?
Vinnie had once said to him, "Jack, I love them just exactly like
they're my own." Perhaps, he thought, it's easier to love
something when it isn't yours, or when the effort needed to
make it yours doesn't take something vital out of you. That
was it. He knew that was it the moment he thought it. The
others had perfect children because they hadn't made them
with discouraged sperm. His own imperfect sperm had been
able to make nothing greater than an insecure left fielder.
And as the ball came to him he knew exactly where it would
go, where it had to go.

But he missed it, and breathed a sigh of relief.

The swing at least jolted him into the present.

Valenti's second pitch soared high over Henna's shoulders.
He did not know why he swung—he knew he would miss. It

was not even properly a swing, more an attack on the ball, and it drew laughter from scattered parts of the field and from the bench of his own team.

"What are ya, swattin' a fly, Jack?" Tatunjian called jovially.

He minded the laughter only when he looked out across the field at Thomas and, catching the boy's eye, saw the same smile of understanding that had confused him earlier in the game. Then it occurred to Henna: Men had just been laughing at him. He had swung badly, awkwardly, laughably, in an open space, *in the world*, and his son had witnessed it and felt embarrassed for him. He felt a sudden chill as he saw himself now through Thomas' eyes, and was not comforted by the sight of Leblanc and the Winchell kids moving in toward the base lines from their earlier positions deep in the field. They were reducing him in their estimations, making smaller the circle they believed him capable of penetrating. He felt himself sweating, cursed himself for thinking of anything but ball and bat. He determined not to swing at the next pitch.

Which was long, graceful, and sailed right over the plate.

He had to hold his bat back to keep from swinging. Valenti put his hands on his hips, stared down at him like a prospect he was preparing to bully.

"What the hell's the matter with you?" Valenti called. "That was *perfect*."

Henna didn't know how to say the reason why he had rejected it. Valenti turned around and shrugged at his infielders. Leblanc took two steps further in.

He was choking now. Henna could not recall feeling this frightened, not in the woods, not in Mrs. Adams' garage. He looked out at Thomas, and the boy seemed to be holding his breath, wishing it over with. He tried smiling at Thomas, but the boy would not smile back.

Valenti threw him a low-breaking curve ball.

The ball reached to about his knees. He swung at waist level.

Then, hearing the ball go *smack!* into the catcher's mitt, he dropped his bat and headed out to the pitcher's mound, where he received his glove from Valenti wordlessly.

. . .

The game dragged on for an hour.

He struck out again and popped up to Leblanc in center field. Thomas struck out three times, missed two pop flies and dropped one. Once a ground ball reached the boy. He picked it up and threw it hastily to second base. In throwing, he let go of the ball too soon and it hit the ground halfway to second. The shortstop had to run for the ball to complete the throw to second, but the runner had already reached that base.

In the top of the seventh inning, it began to rain.

They all huddled under the trees along the first-base line, waiting for it to blow over. When the rain instead picked up, they decided to make a run for cover back to the site of the outing. Henna picked Leo up, grabbed Thomas' hand, and they all ran. Leo didn't want to be held, so Henna let him down, but keeping close to Leo slowed them all down. Soon they were behind the pack of running insurance men, and the ground had turned to mud. Once Leo fell. Henna picked him up and ran with him the rest of the way, the mud Leo's clothes had accrued in the fall squishing against his clean shirt. They looked comical and desperate before him, running, all his co-workers, like men being chased from a place, hounded out.

The outing was deserted.

Hot dogs had been left to burn on wet, smoking grills. On one long table, a row of Coke bottles hunched together, a bunting of drenched napkins at their base. It was as if the women and children had not left but been *removed*, in the midst of the outing suddenly abducted, carried off on horses. They moved past the deserted outing into the parking lot, where the women and children waited in parked cars.

Henna, Thomas and Leo had to run farther than most, past the parking lot, then a half mile more, down to where, Henna now remembered, his car was suspended on a broken post. If all the others took shelter in their cars, where would the three of them go? They couldn't sit in the Fairlane. He began to worry about Nancy, had a sudden vision of her standing, drenched, waiting for them. It touched his heart, to think of her hair wet, her clothes against her skin, her alone-ness, at the edge of the forest, by the car, waiting for them.

D'Alio, Cutler and Tatunjian ran before them. Henna watched the outlines of their large rumps as they moved. Finally, the cars were in sight, Tatunjian's, then D'Alio's, Cutler's, finally Henna's, just where he had left it. How wonderful if by some miracle the women had lifted the car, if he could just now drive off! He searched for Nancy, but she was not, as he'd imagined, standing alone, waiting in the rain for him. She had taken shelter with Rose Tatunjian in the Tatunjian Buick. He stood and looked around for her until she tapped on the window of the Buick, then, catching his eye, rubbed out a circle in the misted-over window so that he could see her face within. Remarkable how perfect the circle she made, just fitting her face, which appeared to him like a face seen underwater. He thought of the car sinking, how you would reach out for the face and touch glass.

She was smiling at him.

Why would she never fulfill his expectations, act out the visions that played inside his head, visions in which he fell in love with her all over again?

She rolled down the window, and he passed Leo's small, muddy body in to her.

They tried, once more, when the rain let up, to hoist the car off the broken post. Then Henna took everyone's advice and called the Shell garage to send up a wrecker.

When the car was towed to the station, Henna followed with Nancy and the boys in Tatunjian's car. He was told the front end would need to be realigned, the bumper replaced. Otherwise, damage was minimal. But the car would not be ready until Wednesday.

Tatunjian drove them all home, left them off in front of the house, and they all ran up the driveway and into the house, where Nancy ran a hot tub and stripped the boys of their clothes almost immediately.

From downstairs, Henna could hear their screams as they descended into the scalding water.

That night, after the boys were asleep, he lay on the bed beside Nancy. With the windows open, the breeze that comes with the end of a rainstorm filled the room. He stood up and removed all his clothes, then lay down again on the bed, on top of the covers. Nancy was under the covers, nestled in, ready to sleep. Henna liked the way the breeze felt, enjoyed his own nakedness. He turned to Nancy and began stroking her hair at the side of her face, beginning just at the top of her cheek. Before, when he'd come up to the bathroom, he'd entered just in time to see her rise out of the tub, her skin glistening, her hair wet, as if she'd known how he'd wanted to see her before and run naked out into the rain to accommodate his vision. The boys had been all powdered and red, standing at the mirror, combing their hair, in clean white underpants. He'd hugged Leo to him, to feel the warm skin. Thomas, noticing, turned away. He didn't know how he felt about Nancy still getting naked in front of the boys, but he knew he liked to see them all this way, in a steamy room, his garden. He didn't like to be naked in front of the boys, though. His naked body seemed an intrusion. He waited until they all left to take his bath.

In the dark, his nakedness felt more comfortable. He stood up and moved out the door, through the hall and down the stairs to the boys' room, where he stood over their beds, looking from one to the other. Soon he wouldn't be able to do this anymore. Already things were changing in the room; it was no longer a room where babies slept, all of its objects were not familiar to him. Things were hidden now, their secrets tucked away in the backs of closets, under their beds, in the corners of drawers. It was painful to recall how, when they were babies, every object they touched had been his gift to them.

He tried to forget the ways in which he and Thomas had both failed today. Told himself it was not important, but it hurt when he said that. Still, even within this painful sense of things falling apart—the car, the ball game, his vision of the world—it was possible to feel a sweetness, a melancholy unlike the one he'd felt when he first went up to bat, a melancholy without self-accusation. He thought he would go up and make love to Nancy. He had no idea what would happen tomorrow, but tonight there was no problem in knowing what to do.

He had an embarrassing erection now. What if the boys should wake up? Would they understand, or would they laugh at him? He watched them, and tried to think of all the good things they had brought to his life. He thought: Children are there to remind you, even in the midst of things falling apart, that something real endured. He tried to wrap his mind around the thought, to squeeze from it the exact thing, and felt it slipping away as soon as he tried to name it. He had been close, it had warmed him, but now it was gone. He found he couldn't even begin the thought again, to try to retrace his steps, and the sweetness went away. This is what happens when you try to put too much on things. He thought of the car, of the pop flies Thomas had dropped, of his own humiliation in the batter's box.

His erection went down. Somehow the world had entered the house again. He sat on Leo's bed and the boy turned away from him. From above, he heard, "Jack? Jack?"

Something scared him so much he clutched his balls and it seemed there was nothing there. They retracted until what he felt was the hard shell of a small animal turning away from the world.

He reached over to Leo, but the child shook him off. He stood up and moved to the stairs. Nancy was at the top, waiting.

"Jack, where are you?"

"I went to look at the boys."

"All the lights were off. You scared me."

"I'm sorry."

"I didn't know where you were."

"I just went down to watch them awhile."

"You scared me."

"I'm sorry."

As he ascended the stairs, his mind latched on to and would not let go of an image of the Fairlane sitting injured in the Shell garage. He remembered then his appointment Monday with Mrs. Adams, and the impossibility of getting out to Lexington without a car.

They did not make love.

Nancy fell asleep first. Then, an hour later, Henna.

6

ON MONDAY morning, he awoke before seven.

The clock-radio on the end table by the bed said it was only a quarter to, but he knew he could not go back to sleep. He had been extra careful with the alarm the night before. Valenti was picking him up at eight to drive him to the office, and he did not want to oversleep. He feared that Valenti might just beep, and if Henna didn't appear right away, would drive off, thinking he had gotten a ride from someone else. You couldn't trust Valenti to be careful about such things, you had to be careful yourself.

So he had set the alarm for seven and checked it twice before turning in, though he hardly needed the alarm any longer. For years, he had been waking up at seven automatically.

He awoke depressed. The early hour felt like an accusation. There was something unsettling about waking up early on a day over which you had no control. If the car were all right, he could use the extra fifteen minutes to run an errand, or get to the office early. He would be getting up now, instead of lying there facing the clock, trying to decide what to *do* with the extra time. Nancy heaved beside him, her body heavy under the covers, her face looking pale and marked with an impression of the corner of the pillow on which she slept. Henna's heart ached at the simplicity of what was wrong: if only his car were not missing!

Downstairs the boys were still asleep. He tiptoed past their room into the kitchen, spooned coffee and filled the kettle with water, turned a gas jet on under it, sat at his kitchen table and folded his hands.

It was good sitting there, waiting for the coffee. He could almost forget what was missing, the activity nearly absorbed the loss. If his kitchen window didn't face out directly on the driveway, he might have had a cup of coffee and comforted himself. But there was a large hole in the driveway, within it a puddle of dried oil.

Henna thought: I have always been an optimistic man.

He poured coffee and tried to recover his optimism, his pep. He imagined someone saying, "That Jack Henna's got pep!"

Did anyone say that now? Had they, ever?

Things would right themselves. If you had pep, you could lick the world. All he needed to do was recover his pep.

For a while, it worked. He sipped at his coffee and thought: They'll fix the car by Wednesday. I'll call Mrs. Adams and change the appointment till later in the week.

He sat content, waiting for Valenti, sure that Valenti would come, that the day would be productive in spite of the handicaps. Thomas came in in his underwear and sat across from Henna, rubbing his eyes.

"When are we going, Dad?"

"Going where?"

"To the movie. You promised Saturday. *Indiscreet* with Cary Grant and . . ."

"I can't take you to the movies without a car, Tom."

Thomas looked out the window, remembering.

"When's it gonna be fixed?"

"Wednesday."

"What'll we do till then?"

"We'll live."

"What if we run out of money?"

"We won't, Thomas."

"You can't *work* without the car, can you?"

"Of course I can."

"How?"

"There's the telephone, isn't there?"

"Nobody pays money over the telephone."

"What do you think I do, Thomas? What do you think my job is?"

"You sell, don't you?"

"Sure, I sell. I sell insurance. You know that."

"Well then, don't people have to pay you?"

"The people pay the office. The office pays me."

The boy was silent. He yawned and played with Henna's empty cup. The matter had apparently been cleared up sufficiently for Thomas, but it still troubled Henna. He could work over the phone, contact possible prospects, set up appointments for later in the week. Of course, if the car wasn't ready by Wednesday, he would be in trouble. That was all he needed, that possibility planted in his head. It wasn't long before he started thinking about the multitude of other things that could be found wrong with the car, its stay in the Shell garage extended week after week, a network of promises broken time and again, as the mechanics pierced to the heart of the Fairlane, each bolt removed revealing a deeper layer of the cancer.

"Thomas, go back to bed."

"I'm up."

"It's summer, you can sleep late."

"No, I'm up now."

Henna fixed the boy a big breakfast, to get his mind off the car. He scrambled eggs and buttered two slices of white bread, making a thick sandwich.

He thought he would enjoy watching Thomas eat, but instead thought of the reasons why he could not enjoy it, because how long would the boy be eating like this if he, Henna, didn't have a car? The hole in his day, the postponed appointment, began to eat at him. You never knew how much you counted on something until it was pulled out from under you. He wished more than anything that he could go back in time to the moment Saturday afternoon when he had made the turn into Camp Ted. If only he had been more alert, been thinking about driving instead of whatever it was he had been thinking about, how simple, how perfect life would be now. If he could have gone back in time and concentrated and made the turn right, it might all be different. It was a real effort to live in the present. It took all Henna's strength to keep him seated in the chair, his hands folded. His arms kept wanting to rise up, grasp a steering wheel. Reverse the action.

Valenti was early. Henna had been right about another thing, too: he only beeped, did not come up to the house and knock.

Nancy was not up yet, so Henna told the boys to go up and wake her. She usually got up when he came upstairs to kiss her goodbye, but today there was no time for that. He could not be sure Valenti would wait that long.

His anxiety was justified: when he stepped out the door, Valenti had already backed ten feet down the driveway.

At Henna's cry, Valenti came to one of his violent halts. The car bounced on its axles, and Henna opened the door.

"Where the hell you goin', Phil?"

"I figured you weren't ready yet."

"What do you mean, weren't ready? A guy's gotta say good-bye to his kids, doesn't he? He's gotta have ten seconds to go down the steps, open the door. What did you expect, me to be waiting in the driveway? On the street?"

"I was just gonna go pick up some cigarettes, take a ride around the block, that's all."

"You should *wait* for a guy, Phil." Henna stepped into the car and they lurched out of the driveway.

They had driven in silence awhile when Valenti suddenly hopped forward in his seat, as if surprised by something.

" 'Good fences make good neighbors.' You know who said that? Betcha don't know, huh?"

"No. Who said it? Lavolli?"

"Robert Frost. The poet Robert Frost."

Valenti grinned in triumph. Henna looked into his open mouth.

"How do you know that? Since when do you read poems?"

"No, no, no. I stayed home last night. Dottie made me watch this program on the educational channel, this whole hour-long program about the poet Robert Frost."

Valenti ran the words "the poet Robert Frost" together in such a way that it came out sounding like a man's full name.

"Jeez, I thought it'd put me to sleep, but it turned out to be very interesting, very educational. He took us on a tour of this spread he's got, up north, New Hampshire, Vermont, I forget which, and when he got to the fence he recited a poem by heart. That's the only line I remember. 'Good fences make good neighbors.' "

When they were stopped at a red light, as if to punish Henna for his lack of enthusiasm over the Robert Frost story, Valenti lifted one of Henna's cigarettes.

"Maybe you didn't hear me good, Jack. I said I stayed home last night."

"So?"

"So I haven't been stayin' home too much lately."

"Why not?"

"What's the matter with you? I tell you something, you forget?"

"What? Your affair? I didn't forget."

"That's right. My affair. No more. Phfft."

"What happened?"

"She took off."

"Took off? Took off where?"

"How should I know? She just took off. Flew the fuckin' coop. No note, no phone call, nothin'. Saturday morning we had a date, right?"

"I thought you had to take Bobby for eyeglasses."

"Bobby? Sees like an eagle. Bobby's twenty-twenty, for Chrissake."

"So you lied."

"What do you think, I'm gonna announce to the whole office I had a date?"

"No, I guess not."

"I show up Saturday morning, rooms are empty. Empty." Valenti drummed his fingers angrily against the steering wheel, looked with unveiled disgust at the shell of a new bank going up on Main Street.

"Maybe she moved," Henna offered.

"Moved? Of course she moved. What do you think I'm telling you?"

"So you'll hear from her."

Valenti blew out a long whistle of impatience, shook his head.

"Hear what? Where? You don't think she would have told me, she wanted me to know?"

"She'll have to do a change of address anyway."

"Jack, what do you think I'm telling you here? You think somebody like this behaves according to the rules of what's on our books? She's gone. She's not gonna do any change of address, and even if she does, you think that's an invitation?"

Valenti was looking at Henna now, so he had to shrug.

"Change of address. Right. She's gonna call me for the form."

Valenti's head was nodding, as though he couldn't get over the thickness of Henna, but the words were said to himself. Henna let it alone then, offered no further assumptions. He began imagining the look of those empty rooms, just vacated, and the sense of abandonment Valenti must have felt. Even in so casual an arrangement, you came to count on things. He knew it, knew it in a tender, sore spot, and cursed again the part of himself that, in handling his car so cavalierly, had thrown into jeopardy his own casual arrangement with the widow in

Lexington. He would be there in a few short hours, if only he'd been more careful. Now it was too easy to imagine those rooms deserted, the tenuousness of his grip on their whereabouts.

"Kids, everything," Valenti said, still disgusted, as they slid into the office parking lot.

His day hung so formlessly before him Henna had no real desire to leave the safety of the car. Valenti's loss, though, seemed to give him new power. Henna had to walk double-pace just to keep up with him.

Outside the three-story brick building that housed the district office, Valenti paused to put on his sunglasses. Henna had never questioned this before, had assumed Valenti wore sunglasses in the office because he'd neglected to take them off from outside. Then Valenti looked up once at the sky—as if, like a farmer, the slightest shift in the elements would have a deciding effect on his day—and disappeared into the swinging glass doors.

Once inside, Henna felt the office air hit him with the force of a suctioning blast, pinning him to the immediate. Within minutes, he'd forgotten abandoned rooms, missing cars. He spent two good hours going over his paperwork and phoning prospects, setting up appointments for later in the week. He thought a show of confidence was all he really needed; if you behaved like things were all right, events would catch up to you. The office was full until ten, the other agents usually didn't go out on calls until at least that hour. So long as he was not alone, Henna was able to minimize his feelings of loss. He even considered asking one of the other agents to drive him out to Lexington, but he felt the compact he had reached with Mrs. Adams was a private one: he must go alone.

By ten-thirty, he was alone in the office.

Across a field of empty desks, he watched Connie type a letter. After a while, she looked over at him, waved two fingers, smiled, but never broke the stride of her typing. Listening to the metallic, empty rhythm of her typing, Henna felt the intensity of his regret like a shriveling of his insides. He felt that his body might become too small for his clothes. The moment last Saturday when he'd turned into Camp Ted kept replaying in his head, as incessant as Connie's clacking *t*'s and *s*'s. It was over, he told himself it was over, nothing to do, things being as they are, the thing to do is go on. He intended to call Mrs. Adams, to continue his paperwork. But he did neither. Instead he sat listening to Connie's typing and looked at the empty desks and reached harsh judgments about himself, all of which he felt were beside the point.

At eleven, Lavolli called him into his office.

"I understand there's been some trouble with your automobile, Jack."

Lavolli sat across from him, his head swathed in smoke. His cigar was long and elegant; the man was not. Lavolli was a small, runty man, his features so tight and tough he looked as though he'd been molded inside a barrel, indentures made in his skin by a sculptor working with a blunt hammer from without.

"Yes, sir."

You called Lavolli "sir." Always. He insisted on it.

"This precipitates your not being on the debit for how long, Jack?"

The *a* in "Jack" was prolonged, a stretch between consonants, like Lavolli was exercising his mouth.

"Wednesday, the garage said, sir."

"Wednesday."

"Yes."

"That's three days, right, Jack, on your ass, am I right?"

"Wednesday Valenti and I go out together, sir."

"That's right, that's right."

Lavolli flicked ashes onto the floor, took a long pull on the elegant cigar. Henna did not understand the peculiar relationship of a cigar smoker with his cigar. At first it looked to him like Lavolli was going to *eat* it.

"But tell me, Jack, how do you expect to do any business until Wednesday?"

"There's the telephone, sir."

"The telephone," Lavolli repeated, as if delighted by the

aptness of Henna's remark. Then his face underwent a change, as his features dropped a notch or two.

"Jack, you know, this insurance business, this is a funny business, this is not like any other business. This business is unique, Jack. You know why?"

"Why, sir?"

"So long as I live, I don't think I'll ever understand the relationships between people, Jack. This amazes me, fascinates me. Sometimes, you know, I think I could go into Boston and sit on a street corner and watch the people pass back and forth. Forever. I could do that for hours, Jack. *People.* How they get along with one another, how they think, act, speak, how they look, even. Jack, this is the great thing in life, people. I just love to watch."

Lavolli was looking beyond him. He gestured for Henna to turn. Through the glass partition Henna could see only Connie typing a letter at her desk.

"Now, let's look at Connie, for instance. *Who* is Connie? Who the hell *is* Connie?"

He waited, as if expecting a reply.

"She's the secretary, sir."

Lavolli's fist came crashing down onto his desk, sending two pencils to the floor.

"I know she's the secretary. For Chrissake, Jack! Pay attention, will ya!"

Lavolli settled back, resumed his former position, studying Connie.

"Now, there's a lotta things you could say about Connie without *looking* at Connie, Jack. Things anybody could tell you. Stuff you could pick up by looking in Connie's file, or asking her friends about her. Now, let's take Artie Winchell, for instance. Winchell's a hell of a guy, but he's a lousy salesman. Just between you and me, Jack, he works hard but he's just not a natural, no native talent. Now, you ask Artie Winchell about Connie, I know exactly what he'll tell you. I bet you twenty dollars to your one dollar I can tell you just what Artie Winchell'll tell you if you ask him about Connie."

And with that, Lavolli proceeded to remove a twenty-dollar bill from his wallet and slap it on the desk. He paused, and Henna, taking up the cue, reached into his wallet and took out a single.

"What the hell you doin', Jack?"

"Betting you, sir."

"Get that dollar bill out of my sight, Jack. I'm not a betting man. Don't you guys understand metaphor, for Chrissake? A man can say something and mean something else, did that ever occur to you? I use this purely as an example, purely as an example."

And he removed the twenty as quickly as he had placed it on display.

"Now, my point, Jack, is this: Winchell's not a connoisseur of people. He doesn't look, doesn't see, behind what every slob, every idiot can see. He doesn't see the root, the center. People are like artichokes, Jack, did you know that?"

"No."

"They are, they are. They're all leaves. You know the ape-men never ate artichokes? Adam in the Garden of Eden never ate artichokes? This is scientifically proven in the Bible! You know why? They looked, the ape-men looked, Adam looked, all they saw were these sharp, tough leaves. They said, 'How the hell can I eat this? I'll bleed to death, for Chrissake!' This is true, Jack. It took Sir Isaac Newton to discover that the artichoke was an edible plant."

Lavolli placed both hands on his desk, knocking a pen and a small pile of papers onto the floor. He acted as if he hadn't noticed the upset.

"Sir Isaac Newton, brilliant man, never content just to look and see what he saw, no, he was a stripper-away, Jack, a puller-away of leaves until he got to the heart of things. He found an artichoke one day, said to himself, 'This doesn't make sense. Things that grow grow so people can eat them, right? Tomatoes don't grow for the hell of it, they're there to eat! What is this artichoke? What is the meaning of this artichoke that no one can eat? You've *gotta* be able to eat it, you can eat *every-*

thing if it's not an animal or a mineral. The artichoke is a *vegetable*, for Chrissake!' "

Bending down to pick up the pen and papers he'd lost, Lavolli revealed only his tight gray head and wide hump of back, but continued talking.

"And he looked at it and looked at it, just sat there and studied it, Jack, until the brilliant idea occurs to him. 'Wait a minute, hold on!' says Sir Isaac Newton. 'What if I pull these hard, tough leaves away, maybe something's hiding inside!' "

Lavolli's face, rising, was bright red.

"So he pulls, and he pulls, and he strips it down to the heart, Jack, the artichoke heart, and that's how we got artichoke hearts, which today people love to eat and enjoy by the bushel load!"

He paused, ate his cigar again.

"You like that story, Jack?"

"Yes."

"It's not true, Jack. I made it up. Right here on the spot. Out of my head. Whaddaya think of that?"

"It's a good story."

"Damn right it is. Only it's not a story. It's a metaphor, Jack. Something I'm trying to explain to you. Jack, listen, I'll let you in on this. A year ago I didn't know a metaphor from a hole in the ground. Remember in February all the district managers went to a seminar in the Poconos?"

"Yes."

"Well, they had this fella from New York give a speech on how to speak more effectively. That was the subject of his talk. 'How to Speak More Effectively.' Jesus, this guy was interesting, Jack. He said the mistake most people make in public speaking is they don't use metaphors. And he proceeded to explain to us what a metaphor was. I felt like an apple was dropping on my head, Jack, honest to God, this really opened my eyes. Since then, I see them everywhere, driving to work, everywhere. Metaphors! I love using them! My wife says I'm driving her crazy with metaphors!"

Lavolli leaned back again, beaming.

"What do you think of that, Jack?"

"That's very interesting, sir."

"You can cut the 'sir,' Jack. We're talking turkey. See, that's a metaphor, too. You'd be surprised how many you use without even knowing it. You go ahead, try one."

"Try a metaphor?"

"Yeah. Go ahead."

Henna tried to think. He couldn't, at this moment, think of anything being like anything else. All the things in the office just looked like themselves. He thought of saying something about the way Lavolli appeared to eat his cigar, but worried that the boss would be offended.

"I can't think of any."

"Sure, you can."

"No. Honestly. I can't."

"Look at Connie, Jack. Now, what is she like?"

Henna felt the way he had in school when the teacher asked him a question to which he knew there was only one correct answer. There were many things Connie was like, but knowing only one of them was correct kept him from saying anything at all.

"Huh, Jack? What is she like? Isn't she like a little bird out there, pecking away? Or how about a sentry on guard duty, guarding this office? How about that? A little bird on guard duty."

Lavolli was clearly pleased with his metaphor.

"Now, Jack, you notice we have learned quite a bit in just these few minutes about who Connie is. She's not only the secretary, as you say, but a little bird on guard duty. Now, you ask Winchell what she is, and he'd answer exactly as you did. And that's why Winchell is a lousy insurance salesman. You understand that?"

Henna said he did.

"It's very *clear*, Jack. You can't sell insurance to a secretary. What the hell is a secretary? A secretary can be a million things. But a little bird on guard duty, that is only one thing, Jack. One thing. You'll never make a sale trying to sell birdseed to a fish, right? They don't eat it. But you try and sell seed to a bird, you can make a killing. And that's my point. Before you try and sell, you've got to know who you're selling to, whether it's a fish or a bird or whatever. And what's the only way of knowing whether somebody's a fish or a bird?"

"By looking at them."

"Exactly. Exactly, Jack. You hit the nail on the head. Another metaphor! You see?" Lavolli laughed with glee. He suddenly appeared round and small, a painted egg in a large chair. Henna thought it, and realized that he, too, had made another metaphor, if only another one that Lavolli would hardly appreciate.

"By *looking* at them, Jack. You've got to *see* with your own two eyes before you can make that judgment. You've got to get up face to face."

Then Lavolli thrust his elbows onto his desk and appeared to be taking his own advice. His head was suddenly a foot closer to Henna's.

"So you tell me, 'Look, Rudy, I've had a little trouble with my automobile, but I can still sell over the phone.' I say to you, 'Great, Jack, *terrific*, good spirit, but tell me, how the hell are you gonna know if it's a fish or a goddamn bird you're talkin' to?' "

Lavolli said it with such force that Henna heard Connie stop her typing in mid-clack.

The office was as still as a deserted nest for the next few seconds. Henna watched Lavolli's face, which had gotten quite red, dissolve back to flesh color, then return to its original position behind the desk.

"All right, my point is made, Jack. You're a smart young fella, I trust you understand."

No one had called Henna young in several years. He was forty-three. He considered himself young. It was just that no one had bothered to confirm that self-image. For the first time since entering Lavolli's office, he began to relax.

"I'll just tell you one more thing, Jack, one more thing and that's it. When I was a young fella, a young fella on the debit, lots of things happened, Jack, that could have stopped me from becoming the man I became, the man you see before you today. But I made up my mind, each and every time some damn thing tried to get in my way, I was gonna overcome it, no matter what. If I was to have a plaque put up over my bed so's every morning when I woke up I would read the same three words, you know what those three words would be?"

Henna waited.

"Do you, Jack?"

"No matter what?"

"*No matter what.* You guessed it. *No matter what.* On my gravestone, that's what I want it to say: RUDOLPH J. LAVOLLI. HE DID IT NO MATTER WHAT."

Lavolli drew the tombstone in air.

They both studied it.

Then Lavolli screwed his eyes up and with the next few words seemed to be gunning Henna down.

"Now get the hell out of here, Jack. My point is made."

Henna left the office, walked to his desk, gathered everything he would need into his briefcase. On his way out, he whistled at Connie. She smiled, thinking he was flirting, not surprised, not stopping.

Then he stepped outside and began the walk to Lexington.

Of course it was simple.

When he was a boy, he'd walked all the time. Once he'd even walked into Boston, to the slaughterhouse, when his mother made some extra money and wanted to cook rabbits. He walked seven miles into the North End, waited until two dark rabbits had their throats slit, paid for them and accepted them in a brown paper bag, and walked the seven miles home. Nothing to it.

The walk to Lexington would be nearly as long: probably

two hours there and two hours back. Henna didn't get a lot of exercise, but his legs felt strong. He was pleased when, after two miles or so, he stopped to take off his jacket and found that he did not feel winded.

The turnoff to Camp Ted sneaked up on him. The woods covered such a small area between the junior high and the turnoff he was amazed to think how immense they had seemed from within. When Freddie D'Alio had told the story of Jenny Salamanca, had they been only a few feet from the junior high and the sandlots? It seemed not half a mile before the woods broke and he was standing in the opening, facing down the broken sign that, until recently, had held his car in a mortal lock. He turned away. He didn't want to look at, or think about, the past. He had such a clear thing to do, he was grateful for it.

The walk became increasingly less pleasant. After a while, the heat became a problem, and for long blocks, not even a paved walkway guided his feet. He had to walk on the sides of hills, past construction sites, through the parking lots of a bowling alley and a skating rink. Then, too, the only people he met walking, the only *regular* walkers, were the inmates of a state mental institution housed on the town line. When sufficient cars had slowed down long enough for the drivers to stare at him, he began to figure that they assumed he was one of them, too, a mental patient, a nut. He tried holding his briefcase away from his body, swinging it freely, as if on display, but then he thought that probably made him look more like an inmate. He was happy when he was past Waltham, past Lexington Center, where there were fewer cars to stop and stare at him.

He was well into the farmland, with, he guessed, a mile or two to go to the Adamses', when a pickup truck pulled up ahead of him and stopped. Through the back window of the truck's cab, he could just make out the driver's neck, red and rigid. He did not turn around to offer a ride to Henna. Cautiously, Henna approached the truck and looked in.

The man looked at him as though he were sizing him up. He

nodded his head, gesturing that Henna could sit down if he wanted to. Henna obliged. In the cab of the truck, he heard first the rush of air as he sat on the padded seat, then felt the waves of his own exhaustion rise. He wondered if he carried a stench on him. The driver shifted, and they were moving again.

"Where you going?" the man said. Henna looked at him from the side. The man's hair could not have been cut any closer to his scalp; it looked more like a shadow on his head.

"The Adams place. It's just ahead." He wondered, then, why he had taken the ride, with so little left to go. He thought faces like this man's were faces you obeyed, even if the thing they offered was something you didn't strictly need.

The man didn't even nod, though. Henna was surprised when, a moment later, he said, "Fella that killed himself." It was not a question.

"Yeah. That one. I sold him some insurance. Well, not sold, but I'm taking care of it."

The man still would not nod, gave no indication that he heard, or acceded to, anything Henna said. This lack of response made Henna's words stand out as if in a vacuum, and they began to seem shady, insincere. He looked at the floor of the cab and noticed bits of husks of corn.

"You a farmer?"

The man waited, then nodded. He might have known; the overalls, the boots, what else would such a man do? He wanted to ask the next question, had he known Adams?, but held back. They were there. The man pulled up in front of the house, looked up once at it. Henna looked at the man's hands, his boots. Beside him, he felt small, his clothes seemed too shiny. If Adams had lived, would he have grown this leathery? Henna wondered if this sort of hardness wasn't what the woman was used to; if, next to it, he didn't seem a little soft, unformed. It was time to get out, though. He murmured his thanks and watched the farmer shift and take off.

He stood in front of the house a moment, watching the dust the truck raised, then headed up the walk.

She came to the door dressed in a dull brown shift, her hair wet and swept back from her face, the clean skull bold and chalk white beneath fine, thin strands of hair.

His heart made a sudden hopping movement when he saw her.

She squinted against the sun, said, "Oh." In the darkness of the foyer, the door closed behind them. He was gladdened when, in a light, self-deprecating tone, she said, "I ought to get sunglasses. Always squinting, squinting."

Then she leaned against the wall and looked up at him. She had trouble looking into his eyes, focused instead on his tie. "Mr. Henna, you are so dependable. Like a well-made watch."

"I worked in a watch factory once."

"Ah. Is that it?"

She smiled queerly. Henna thought: You are like an open book, always open to the wrong pages, revealing information no one is *prepared* for.

"I've just been in the shower."

"I see."

"Because it is so hot."

She stood against the wall, folded her arms. He wondered if she intended that they should stay here forever, conduct all their business against this wall.

"Is it easier, being Italian?"

The question startled him.

"How?"

"Aren't you people somehow protected against heat. Or is that just a myth?"

"No. We feel it."

"Do you?"

"Yes."

"Something cool to drink? I have nothing."

"Water."

"Water. Yes. I have water."

They moved into the kitchen. Glancing around the house, he

was struck by how little it had changed since last Wednesday. His own seemed to transmute daily, the objects he left in one place upon leaving turning up in completely new arrangements on his return. In this house, nothing seemed moved, even touched, since his last visit. He wanted to know what they did, how life went on here, *around* things. He had a vision of the two of them, boy and mother, waiting for him all this time, afraid to change anything, having mutually decided that change was Henna's domain. He imagined the woman's body under the dull brown shift, thought of exploding inside her, sending in an infusion to get her blood moving to the wastelands, her shoulders, fingers, long arid neck. But no, no thoughts like that today, Henna. He sat at the table, hands folded, waited as she held a glass under the tap, filled it and set it before him.

He drank the water down. They sat in silence awhile. She watched him while he drank, averted her eyes when he was finished.

"How's the boy?"

He noticed a thin purple vein begin to throb on the ridge of her forehead. To comfort her, he laid one hand on hers. He looked at his hand, thought of the hands of the farmer who'd driven him here. He allowed her to slip out.

"Are there papers to sign, Mr. Henna?"

"Wait."

"No. *Now.* Please. Are there papers?"

Her sudden anger confused him; the heat his stomach had absorbed on the long walk made him feel slightly nauseous.

"Mrs. Adams, please, I want to help. Look, the place, the kitchen is empty. What do you do for food? What do you *eat?*"

She reached up to her forehead, rubbed one raw polished temple. He loved the movement. It reminded him of the watch factory, old Nordstrom opening up a watch for him for the first time, revealing the delicate inner system of parts.

"There is the garden, you know."

"The what?"

"The *farm.*"

"Things grow there?"

"Yes."

"Enough to eat?"

"Yes. Enough. You see, he did protect me, in ways you don't know."

"May I see?"

"Why?"

"I'd just like to see the farm. To look at it."

"It is out there. You can look."

"No. To have you show me."

"You don't believe me, do you?"

"I believe you. I want to see it, that's all."

She sat facing him, her mouth stiff, closed on itself. Then, abruptly, she rose, walked straight to the door, almost at a run. He had to run to catch up with her out in the yard, just past the patio. She led him past rows of corn, past tomatoes on pipes, into a field stubbled with small heads of Bibb lettuce. In each section, moving with head thrust forward, seeming to be running ahead of her body, she would fling her hands out and utter, "Here. Here. Here."

In the middle of the lettuce patch, she stopped and picked up a small, not yet fully formed head, held it up to him and said, "Here. You see? We can eat. God, we can eat, Mr. Henna. We are rich in food."

She flung the head as far as it seemed to him a woman could throw. It landed among other heads, settled. She put her hands on her hips and stared off.

"You see, he could grow things. I will not have you thinking he couldn't do that. If life were as simple as just eating, he'd be here today."

She shook her head, in flinty disagreement with the thought, then moved to the irrigation ditch at the side of the field. He watched her moving off, her head to one side, thought of grief and regret as perhaps inhabiting the right side of the brain exclusively.

She stopped just above an incline, stuck one foot into the narrow ditch and worried the topsoil. Then she stepped into the ditch and sat on the incline, one hand cupping her chin while the other smoothed the back of her drying hair, curling the ends around two fingers. He sat next to her. On the other side of the ditch, forty or so feet away, a cow snapped at a tuft of grass. She noticed him looking at it.

"Is it yours?" he asked.

She nodded.

"Of course, now we'll have to get rid of it."

Henna thrust his hands between his legs, formed a V, feeling the pockets of sweat in his armpits. He nodded.

"Which will, of course, break Johnny's heart. Oh, I don't want to. Why do we have that cow in the first place?"

"Did he milk it?"

She smiled. "Yes."

"Is it the only one?"

"Yes, just the one. The idea was, in time, to have more. But 'in time' is a concept that fluctuates in meaning, I've found. So we have the one, and Johnny's attached."

"Why get rid of it?"

"Mr. Henna, I do not see myself as a milker of cows."

"Have the boy do it."

" 'The boy.' He has a name, Mr. Henna. Why must you see this as some classical drama? 'The boy.' 'The woman.' And you, I suppose, are 'the man.' "

"No, I don't see it that way."

" 'The boy' does it. He milks that cow, feeds it, walks it. But we are going away from here. I don't know where. Somewhere, I'm sure, where a cow will be superfluous. But I do not relish explaining to Johnny the dumb lesson . . ."

She stopped, kicked gently at the topsoil.

"When I was a little girl I had a pony, Mr. Henna. And I loved that animal. We had to sell our house upstate and I was told that the horse couldn't live in an apartment in New York. But *soon*, when we're in the pink again, my father said."

She paused.

"That should have prepared me for all this 'later on' business."

She turned from him and stared down the length of the

ditch. He followed her gaze, experienced a feeling of lightness, buoyancy, loss of control, felt that it was his merely to follow her line of thought, she would *lead* him somewhere.

"Do you know anything at all about irrigation, Mr. Henna?"

He shrugged, knowing very little.

"This stupid ditch. Look at it, will you?"

"Why did he need to irrigate? You must get plenty of rain."

"Simply because a man may be foolish in his grand designs does not mean he is careless. Not careless, no. He got the idea out of a book on Oriental despotism."

To Henna's raised eyebrows, she replied, "I told you, he was a man who read."

Then, turning away, she continued. "He dug it himself the summer Johnny turned five. I helped a little, not much. You must see what's left of the dam. He and Johnny painted it together. It has a huge dragon emblazoned on it. Give him, at least, the consistency of his Orientalism."

"Does it work?"

"Does it work? Mr. Henna, it is primitive. In Mesopotamia, I doubt it would have worked. He based it on a drawing. Then, halfway through it, some of the neighboring farmers objected to his selfish use of the river water, and it became one of the great abandoned projects. Now I'm thinking of resuming it. Making this place modern, making it work. When I'm not thinking of leaving it, that is. Either one . . ." Her hand went quickly to her forehead, as if to ward something off. Henna looked for a bee, a horsefly, the motion had been quick enough to suggest one. Then her hand dropped, went back into place. "I'm sorry. I was going to say, either would be a repudiation."

Her lips seemed dry. He thought to offer water, to suggest they go back to the house. She seemed, though, more intent on talking.

"I read about a woman out in Washington, mother of twelve, whose husband was killed in a plane crash. She decided to continue on farming, put all her kids to work, including the baby, who, she says, does his share by screaming loud enough to make his needs known, to keep the others from idleness." Her fingers reached down, drew a circle in the topsoil. "She was described, you may like this, as a 'pretty widow.' I admire her guts. But possibly Mr. Dead-of-a-plane-crash worked a promise out of her before his untimely demise. I'm still trying to work out what kind of instructions Sam left. If he'd just left a note taped to the refrigerator—buy creosote for barn, spray apples, mend the north fence—do you see how simple it would be? I'd do those three things and stay in love forever."

She seemed lost in memory. Henna waited her out. Finally, she looked up, smiling with secret pleasure.

"Would you like to see his madness, Mr. Henna? His dam?"

"Yes, I'd like to see it."

He smiled, too, but she rejected his smile, instead turned away, indicating the pleasure was all her own, not to share. They were not conspirators yet, her gesture said.

He followed her along the length of the ditch, past the squash plants, the string beans, rows of peppers.

"Who? Who exactly was it who sold him this insurance, Mr. Henna? Was it you?"

"No. An agent no longer with us. Me and my partner Valenti inherited his old clients."

"So you never met him?"

"No."

"And he paid on time?"

"Always. We never had to call to remind him."

She stopped, looked again about to cry.

Henna was used by now to the system of waiting, the rhythm of her emotional flow. He felt careful with her, as though he were handling her physically. He liked the brittle toughness of her movements, thought that she was a woman still essentially unused to herself, constantly surprised by her own delicacy.

Through the trees (he looked away, into the orchard, while waiting), he thought he caught a glimpse of the boy's head, blond hair. Looking again, he could not find it.

"Can we sit down again?"

"Yes."

"Just for a minute."

"Certainly."

"I'm sorry for resenting you."

"I understand."

"Do you? Can you? This strange man, full of papers, comes knocking, knocking." She laughed. "What kind of job is this, Mr. Henna, this insurance? Is this a good job?"

"Well, yes."

"How can you do it, honestly, get up every morning, go out into the *world?* What adjustments are necessary? I'd like to know. I certainly would never be able to do it. My God, the *world.* Hello, I'm ... *Strangers.* Utter, complete strangers. What if they don't accept you, don't like your hair, disapprove? You go home then and do what? He and I could never be hired hands. But you, Mr. Henna, seem born to be one."

"A hired hand?"

"Yes. Does that offend you?"

"No. Not really."

"Of course not. There's nothing to be offended by. It is a condition, that's all. A man, it seems to me, ought to be able to just go out. Ought to. He couldn't. Could not go out. Not Samuel Osborne Adams. Not with that large head, that Olympian head, not *sell* that head. He was an extinct bird even at birth, I think. A chronic connoisseur of the misleading detail. Reading a life, a biography, he would dive into the book for self-justification. 'You see,' he'd shout, '*Frost* never published a thing until he was nearly forty!' Not thinking—it would never have occurred—that Frost was busy being Frost up until that point, and that, of course, made all the difference."

She looked up at him, bright with a small flicker of expectation that confused him. He could only think of Valenti, the educational channel. After a moment, she turned away from him.

"Do you see that barn, Mr. Henna?"

He looked. Just at the edge of the field, Adams' barn stood, pale red, imposing.

"You wouldn't know it, but it is about to fall. A scant six

weeks ago, he first heard the word 'creosote.' Or not heard it. Read it, in a book. He looked up at me, I remember, quite innocently, and said, 'Do you know that barns can fall?' One more in a series of potential disasters our eyes and ears were constantly pricked for. I'll do nothing to save it, I won't even step inside it. Someday, if by some miracle it stands, Johnny can use it to . . ." Her face went hard for a moment. She looked down. "Well, whatever use boys find for barns."

Henna could just make out the condition of the barn from here. The red paint was chipped; the roof looked as though it had given up the fight against the elements. He thought it looked like a place more suitable to her son's designs, the thing she alluded to with difficulty, than for any other use. It was not hard to imagine the boy grown up, or nearly, tall like Henna imagined his father to have been, smooth and crisp, with eyes so cold girls would not know how to judge whether they were lying or sincere. He would use them in a rotting barn, drape their blue summer dresses on rusted plows. He realized he envied Johnny the barn more than Freddie D'Alio his nights in the woods with Jenny Salamanca. You could entice a different type of girl into a barn, even one that threatened to fall on you.

"Come. Shall we walk some more?"

He'd rather listen, rather watch the barn and imagine the future life of this farm. The idea came to him very quickly.

"I'll work for fifty cents an hour."

"What?"

"Farm labor. You'll need it. I'll do what *he* did. But I'll be just a man you've hired, nothing more."

She stood over him now, smiling and shaking her head.

"Isn't this about insurance, Mr. Henna?"

"Yes, but you'll have to hire someone, why not me?"

"I can imagine what is going on inside your head."

"What?"

"Why in the first place would you *want* to work for me for fifty cents an hour?"

"I like the work. I like the outdoors."

"You could get much more elsewhere, I'm sure."

"But I wouldn't be needed anywhere else."

She looked quickly at him, squinting as though she were looking directly into the sun, then looked down, shading her eyes.

"And you are needed here?"

"Yes. I think so."

"You think so. I have a strong son. I am a woman with time on her hands."

"This place is bigger than I expected. You need a man."

"Oh. Do I?"

"Yes."

"I wouldn't have thought so. May I insult you, Mr. Henna?"

"Yes."

"Your assumptions—these things you bring here—are repulsive to me in the extreme."

She shook as she said it, as though it had been an intensely difficult thing for her to say.

"You think," she went on, still shaking, "that I am a woman who can be picked up and carried somewhere, that we are simply waiting for someone to come along and . . . jerk us into life. I assure you, we are not waiting for that."

He grabbed for her hand, and when he'd attained it, held it tightly in his own, held it even against her resistance, not looking at her, looking instead at the ditch, until resistance had gone out of it and it was just a soft hand in his own. He had no wish to offend, or win anything by force, but less of a wish to enter into a game of insistence, to argue for himself. The gesture, this taking of her hand, was meant to do his arguing for him. He kneaded her hand, then, and knew, and was frightened by, how complicated a gesture it had been.

Finally, he let her hand go and dared to look at her. She was studying him, more curious than frightened by what he had done.

"What was that?"

He shook his head, almost ashamed now. Yet she made no motion to move, seemed less frightened by him, even, than before.

"Can we just go back to the house and sign papers or whatever? Can I rid myself of you now, Mr. Henna?"

"No," he said, and the hard look she gave him made him feel he'd better come up with a reason. "I want to see the dam."

She breathed out, her head slanted forward, then drew her mouth in a little. "Follow the ditch. You'll come to it."

"I want you to show it to me."

"No. I don't want to talk anymore. It's dangerous. You must have figured out by now, I see no one else. Imagine that. A total stranger, an insurance man, is the only member of the outside world that penetrates this—well, can you call it a life? A dry farm, a bed that creaks, long breakfasts and endless hot days. Is that a life, I wonder?"

"Listen, I don't want to upset you." He thought it would be best to pull her back, away from judgments about herself. "I just want to help."

"Quit it. Just—quit. Dumb words. 'I just want to help.' Who is screaming for help? Where are the high waves, the freezing black waters, hmm? To think we would have wasted away if Mr. Whatever-your-first-name-is Henna hadn't driven up in his shiny automobile. We will waste away very nicely even with you, Mr. Henna."

She started off.

"Hold on!"

She had managed to travel a surprising distance in a few seconds, and crookedly, as though some form of indecision had guided her steps. At his words, she stopped only for a moment—her head lifted, never turned around—then started off again.

"Nobody's going to waste away, Mrs. Adams. You're wrong about me!"

"Am I?"

"Yes." He had to shout now.

"Go look at the dam!" She called it over her shoulder, so he had to guess at the last word.

Henna watched her move until she was out of sight, then followed the ditch in the direction of the apple orchard. He considered chasing her back to the house, but decided instead to take her advice. It seemed the safest thing to do.

He had not walked twenty feet before he saw again the flash of yellow hair. Moving out of the ditch toward the orchard, he caught his foot in a clump of tangled brush and fell heavily. The noise spread through the wood like the falling of a heavy log. Henna watched birds rise, alerted. The boy's head appeared, studied him briefly, ran off. Rising, Henna tried to run after him, calling, "Listen! Listen!" He watched the long-legged galloping form far ahead of him disappear; then, panting hard, at rest against the trunk of an apple tree, he looked down and noticed a small hole, clearly dug by human hands. He peered down into it, saw dark earth, black at the bottom. Had the boy dug it? If so, what was he planning to hide there? It was not wide enough for anything of substance. Money? He shook his head. What money? The image came to him of Freddie D'Alio on the baseball diamond, getting down and humping the earth. Good God, Henna, this is a ten-year-old boy we're talking about! But didn't the hole suggest it? He reached up and plucked an apple off the tree to remove the thought from his mind. Was that why the boy was always scratching himself? No, no, he was hiding a marble, something small and boylike, that was all, surely. Henna bit into the apple and grimaced at its sourness. Premature. Flinging it deep into the woods, he set off to look for the dam.

The river lay just at the edge of the orchard.

A dull green affair, perhaps a hundred feet wide, but looking deep enough. He followed the ditch to its apparent end, where it was filled with dead leaves, branches, brown detritus. Climbing to ground level, he made out the dragon beyond the muck, just visible under a black film of moss. She had called it a "dam." It was, in fact, only a sluice gate, but who could expect her to know the niceties of irrigation when her husband had built the system out of a Chinese book?

The dragon was half Adams, half Johnny. Its dual authorship was apparent from first sight, its overall grace punctuated with bits of childish mess, like a fine old house through which a child has rummaged. The face was clearly Johnny's, a five-year-old Johnny's, the eyes not parallel to one another, one an afterthought to the other, the nose piggish and central, the mouth a long, thin horizontal drawn across a plane of monstrous jaw. Below this, a massive, delicately drawn trunk, a tail of commanding length, painted orange, each scale detailed, a mosaic of scales into which a younger brush had occasionally intruded. Henna imagined the two of them, man and boy, sitting here drawing on the cement of the sluice, decorating, in fact, before their job was properly finished. (There, a clue: Adams was not a man who *finished* things, but who rewarded himself before the finish was even in sight.) But why the need to decorate in the first place? A sluice gate has a simple enough function. Why not just build it and leave it at that? Putting the pieces together, he began to envision Adams' laziness as a thing of crushing weight. Had he never had a thought for his family's welfare? There was the insurance policy, the premiums promptly paid, to answer that. Adams, then, as Distracted Man. That seemed to fit, finally. Distractions. What led a man to paint dragons on sluice gates? It was not seeing things for their functions, their use, their beauty in themselves. Yet the man was a farmer, planter of neat, tedious rows of corn and string beans, methodical, careful as to the availability of water. Hadn't she said it had been the neighbors that had prevented his finishing the dam, objecting to his "selfish use of the river"? So he had painted over the uselessness of the unfinished sluice, given it, as he had seen it, use? Art by the river. How many came to see it? By the looks of the moss, only Henna. Himself, the lone connoisseur of the Artist Adams. Approving in part. Seeing the dragon as good work, delicate. Its use seeming now no more than as a clue to character. Adams leaving tracks all over his land, as his son would leave deposits in the earth. The farm was clearly theirs. Sell it and it would remain so. No one else could so clearly, totally lay siege to this property, so firmly stamp personality on it. Make the irrigation work, it remained

Adams' sluice. Plant something in the ground, it was likely to come up with Johnny Adams' face.

He lit a cigarette and sat on the sluice gate, feeling strange in laying his buttocks on Adams' work, watched the river flow and noticed the small wooden bridge that crossed it on the edge of Adams' property, a quarter mile or so down the river. A road ran by the side of the farm.

He felt the end of it, an ending drawing him in, the cigarette feeling like a finishing gesture. He would give her the papers to sign, accept his exclusion. There was, finally, no understanding this without a devotion of sorts. Adams was another bird. The difference was not something simple, not a matter of form or sex or heritage. The difference was in personality, and with the man gone, how could his personality ever be understood? Mrs. Adams could explain and explain, it would all be a ghost to him. Adams was dead, external. There was a world of internal things to take care of: finding out how to love Nancy again, accepting Thomas' crippled adaptation to the world, raising Leo, renewing the sense of promise and forgiveness that the world had, until recently, brimmed with. In attempting to pierce through the mystery of Adams, he had drawn blood from his benevolent vision of the world. Now Adams had to be left. The world had to work. There was too much life left to have to go on with this sense of defeat, of disinheritance. He could forget things; he knew this was possible.

Crushing the cigarette underfoot, he left the sluice gate, walked by the side of the ditch in the direction of the house and looked once back at the motley crimson dragon, the childish head seeming to float on its mature body, as if the two parts were still struggling to become used to one another.

The farm seemed smaller on the walk back.

When he reached the backyard, the sun was already beginning to dip behind the barn. He had not been thinking about much on the way back, once he'd decided to end this affair of curiosity with the signing of the papers. Mystery had begun to recede; the rows of vegetables represented nothing more than themselves. He had to try hard not to see the ditch as an unhealed wound, a large brown scar on Adams' land, but he succeeded in keeping his mind turned away from its own darker resources, his thoughts cradled, like a hand played close to the vest.

Now he looked at the sun's spillage spreading out over the black pitch roof of the barn, and thought it looked fragile, as though it would fall very soon unless someone did something to save it. He remembered his vision of Johnny's future, and was saddened to think that it was all wrong, there would be no barn to take girls to. Perhaps he should offer to coat it with creosote, as a last gesture before leaving. To insure at least something.

He moved toward the barn to examine it up close. The large gray wooden shingles looked rotted, as though you could touch them and they would fall apart. He peered through a dusty window, trying to see inside, couldn't. Opening the large side door, he was struck by the initial darkness and had to open his eyes wide to make out objects in the dark. When finally his eyes had adjusted to the balance of light, he could pick out the pattern of objects, then the objects themselves, mostly old farm tools and primitive machinery. He touched an ancient yellow plow, listened to the mewlish crying sound it made as he rocked it. In one corner, he found the place where the cow slept. Its odors were faint throughout, this clearly the cow's nursery. In a separate corner, a large bench attracted him. Up close he saw it was not a bench but a desk. A small lamp was focused on its center. Henna switched it on, surprised at the sudden pitch of light.

He traced a line of dust with one finger, touched clean wood. Then he gazed out the small window just to the side of the desk and saw flat land, trees and hills in the far distance. What did Adams *do* here?

He wanted everything now to point to endings, resolution; yet here he was, sitting at Adams' desk, like a man entering the mystery business again. Outside the window, he could see a huge bluish cloud covering the low sun. The trees had already begun to darken. He knew it was time to leave, but it was difficult to do so.

He found her in the kitchen, sitting at a table, her hands flat against the wood.

Gently, he knocked on the kitchen door to warn her, then let himself in. He sat across from her, removed a handkerchief from his pocket and wiped sweat from his brow. She moved a glass of water across the table. Henna drank greedily.

"Mr. Henna, where is your car?"

"Oh, I had an accident Saturday. It's in the garage."

"Then how did you get here?"

"I walked."

She looked into his eyes.

After what seemed to him a long time had passed, she said, "I am sorry."

"For what?"

"I'm a rude woman."

"No, you're not."

"I had no idea you walked."

"I wanted to."

"That it was so important."

"Well."

She looked down into her lap then, appeared to be blushing. Henna waited. Finally she looked up. Her look implied a kind of simplicity, as if she had swept away any dark imaginings she might once have had about him, decided to accept him simply as he was, or as he appeared to be.

"Well, all there is, then, is to thank you."

"You don't need to thank me."

"I should think another man would have run away."

"No."

"No? Why not?" She pitched slightly forward in her chair. The light, quickly escaping from the kitchen, caught the loose strands of her hair, the edge of her forehead. "Stay and be in-sulted? The things I said."

"You're upset. I understand."

She was near enough to touch. He wanted to put his hand against her, into the light. She moved slightly back then, settled back in her chair.

"Oh, yes. Widow's excuse. God, that word, 'widow.' I still can't say it. It conjures up spiders to me. The seat on Johnny's bicycle has a big black-widow design on it. When Sam bought it—well, see, here I go again."

"I don't mind."

"No, I will not go on. You've been too patient, and I've been awful. Now I have prepared to apologize, to thank you, to sign papers, to be done with this, to have you finally rid of me."

"I haven't minded."

"You have a family, don't you?"

"Yes. Two boys."

"Two boys. That sounds lovely. They eat, I presume."

"Oh, yes."

"Then you need to make a living, Mr. Henna. Which you are certainly not doing here."

"This is part of my job."

"A while ago you offered to work for fifty cents an hour. That is certainly not part of your job."

"No. I'd do that extra. On the side. Your barn needs work done on it."

He folded his hands and rocked back and forth, trying to gauge the effect of this last. She sat staring at the surface of the table, her chin resting in one hand, a thin strand of hair hanging down over her fingers. In the light she looked like a young girl, thinking about a prom or a boy or a bathing suit she might want to buy.

"I had expected, Mr. Henna, please forgive this, that you were of the race of men who, presuming to help a woman, proceed to help themselves. I'm not excusing this, but we lived in Italy once."

Henna said he didn't understand.

"You have never been a woman in Italy, Mr. Henna."

"No."

"Well, to be fair, it's not the whole country, but Rome, at any rate. My mind is full of clichés, one of these days I must clean it out."

"What happened in Rome?"

"Oh, nothing happened in Rome. I was with Sam and carrying Johnny, visibly, which you would think would keep men away. But when I was alone, or Sam left for a moment, it was as though they were all maggots jumping on a piece of meat left in the sun. It formed a . . . well, a presumption. That all Italians, or Romans, at least . . ."

"I'm not from Rome."

"No? Where are you from?"

"A small island off the coast of Sicily. One you've never heard of."

"Tell me."

"Filicudi, it's called."

"Filicudi." She smiled, saying it. "Not Rome."

"No."

"Another presumption out the window."

They were smiling easily at one another now, though Henna was unsure where she might be leading him.

"It was after the war. Perhaps they'd all been starved too long. I ought to be fair to them, give them *that*."

"I haven't been back since we came over here."

"When was that?"

"Nineteen twenty-five."

"It's a beautiful country." She paused, remembering. "Will you ever go back, Mr. Henna?"

"To Italy? Oh. Sometimes I think about it."

He did not want to talk about himself, but her eyes were eager, full of lights, wanting to know.

"Well, sometimes I think I would like to, just to see how it's changed. It was very primitive, you know."

"Your island?"

"Oh, yes. No plumbing or anything. None of your modern features."

"No?"

"Oh, no, strictly primitive. Instead of a bathroom, for instance, you had what is called a backhouse."

He recognized the impropriety at once; attempting to cover it, stammered.

"That is . . ."

"Yes. I'm familiar with the term. I know what a backhouse is, Mr. Henna."

"Well, then you know . . ."

"Yes. Go on."

"Well, I'd like to see how it's changed, but I could never live there again. No, I like it better here."

"Why?"

"Why? Here you've got choices, opportunities. Over there, all you could do was farm."

"Do you never think, Mr. Henna, that *not* to have a choice would be a blessing?"

"No."

"No, of course not. You've never really had one, have you? There's a myth in this country, I hear it all the time, that one can become anything here."

"It's true."

"Oh, is it?"

He wasn't sure how, but he had brought her anger back to the surface. Her face was red and as sharp as an unhappy infant's.

"Of course it's true. That doesn't mean it's always going to happen. But the potential is there. In Italy—"

"In Italy you are born one thing, and remain one thing. Here you are born nothing, potential, as you say, and remain nothing, potential in action, chasing its tail, assuming identities, farmer, insurance man, whatever. A surfeit of choices, Mr. Henna, none of which adds up to substance. We try and claim things in this country, and end by dying on rented land. This house is a mortgaged house, it does not even properly belong to me. In Italy, at least your island was yours."

She paused, sucking in and rejecting a host of things, all of them invisible to Henna. Then she moved to the kitchen sink. He watched her pry the lid off a bottle of grape juice. She poured some into a glass and mixed it with water. The gesture disconcerted him: who was going to drink it?

"But I have a son. And that, for now, is it. Reason enough."

She slammed the glass down so hard it toppled over. Grape juice spilled onto the counter and onto the floor. Henna got up to help her. On his knees beside her, he felt the waves of her anger, decided it would be best to leave. He had unsettled even her ability to make a simple glass of grape juice; who knew the amount of damage he might do by sticking around? She would, besides, probably heal better on her own. Clearly, he touched too many disturbing places in her, and not deliberately, so there was no way of controlling it.

Quietly, so she wouldn't notice the effort being made, he reached for his briefcase, unclasped it, and removed the insurance papers. When she returned from wringing out the sponges in the sink, they were already laid out before her on the table.

"Ah, yes, the papers."

She swallowed, drew back a loose strand of hair, crossed her arms. He knew she was attempting to appear "ready for business," but there were deep lines in her face, and she looked about to erupt at any moment.

"Where do I sign?"

"Here." He pointed.

She took his pen and wrote her name, which he had never seen in its entirety (the insurance policy listed "Spouse" as beneficiary): Ann Alther Adams.

"Ann," he said.

"Yes."

"Here. Here, too."

He indicated the second place she should sign.

"Would you like it all in one lump sum or in payments?"

"Oh, which is better?"

He leaned forward, resting his elbows on the table, as he would if this were business.

"Well, that depends on whether you want to invest it or put it all in the bank, where you can draw interest, or if you want it to live on."

He found himself enjoying the opportunity to explain this to her.

"If you want to live on it, it's better to take payments. That way, *we* invest it for you."

"No, I'd better have it all at once."

"Are you sure?"

"Yes. I'll put it in the bank. I have no idea how much it will cost us just to live."

"We could adjust . . ."

"No. Just send it to me. You do *mail* it, don't you?"

"Yes."

"Then that would be fine."

He waited. He wanted to ask her how she would get to the bank—would she walk? did she need a ride?—but held himself in check. She was turned away from him; her forehead looked alive now, full of thoughts. He sensed those thoughts had moved away from him, too, toward the money perhaps. He put the papers away, fastened the clasp on his briefcase, held it in his lap.

Then he said, "Well. Goodbye."

She was looking down at the table when he said it. He felt suddenly superfluous. He thought, though, that she looked too pale, as if the rush of passion at the sink, followed by this talk of money, had drained something from her. He wanted now, badly, to touch her. He thought he could feel within himself the shape of the desire for her that had grown in his time here: it was to take effect in her, to change the color of her skin, the way she saw the world. Yet how could he do that? He remembered vividly the nights, years before, when he and Frankie Rando would take the trolley into Boston just to sit beside the Common and watch women in camel's-hair coats going into the Colonial Theater to see plays with names like *Leave Her to Heaven* and *The Male Animal.* They were tall women, mostly blond, and they walked in such a cool, unhurried manner that, even if one were alone, he knew he would never be able to just walk up to her and say, "Hello, I'm Jack Henna." With Nancy, he could say those words and know she saw ambition and Italy, and it would be enough. But to these women the words would not apply. Sometimes Frankie would watch one of them pass, and say, "I'd sure like to have some of that," and Henna, watching one long tanned leg following another into the bright, baroque lobby of the Colonial, would *want* to say, but instead would think, "But you never will. They don't belong to us." Now it came back to him, there were women who could never belong to you. When he'd first seen Mrs. Adams, he thought the power of his position might make up for the distance. But he had since come to feel a sense of intrusion stronger than the close of business, the house putting the squeeze on him, forcing him out. Distracted, he came to wonder again, as he had twenty years before, what *The Male Animal* might possibly have been about.

"Take my husband's car, Mr. Henna."

The suggestion jostled him back into the present. She was looking straight at him, a supplicant.

"What?"

"It's just sitting there."

"I couldn't."

"Don't be silly. It's too late to walk. Your wife will be worried."

"I'll call her."

"No. Please. I insist."

He looked at her long enough to tell she was serious, not just being polite. But he couldn't tell why she was serious.

"Does it run?"

"Of course it runs."

"Well."

"You can return it anytime. I don't need it."

She lifted her hands, to be rid of him. There seemed no logical way to refuse her. And besides, wasn't she giving him one last opportunity to finish things in a way that would not leave him feeling so unsettled, his hands unquiet at his sides, lusting for the unavailable? Wasn't she, in effect, opening the door another inch or so? He stood up.

"I'll return it tomorrow. My car'll be ready on Wednesday. I can walk home tomorrow if I get here early enough."

"Whatever you want, Mr. Henna."

She wasn't looking at him.

"Well, okay. Terrific. Where are the keys?"

"They're *in* it, I imagine. I haven't taken them."

He went to the garage, opened the door of the car and, seeing the keys hanging from the ignition, had to fight a mild repulsion at the thought that the last hand to touch those keys had been a dead man's. When he looked up, she was standing in the garage doorway, leaning against the jamb.

"I can't tell you how much I appreciate this."

"Oh. Please. It's the least . . ."

"You'll be home all day tomorrow?"

"Where would I go?"

"Listen, about what I suggested before." He stopped himself, feeling it was not good timing, but finally couldn't halt the flow of his own words. "Maybe I could do something about that barn. Pick up some creosote. It's a day's work, probably. Maybe two. But I'll be glad to . . ."

"Goodbye, Mr. Henna. Keep the car as long as you like."

She shut the door.

When Henna stepped into the car he felt a cold chill. Adams' presence? He shook his head. The possibility, all in his mind, of Adams' presence. Henna, he thought, you are a grown man, beyond this. He started the ignition.

With the first blast of exhaust, he panicked. The windows were all closed. He pushed the door open, leapt out, grabbed hold of the garage-door handle and lifted it, throwing his body against light and air. He breathed heavily, filling himself before descending once more into the garage. Once inside the car, he rolled all the windows down, made sure what he was breathing was untainted.

The tension left him when the car was out of the garage. Edging onto the road, he felt the beginnings of an ease and gratefulness, remembering what she had said about rented land. Why look for spooks when the answer is more likely simple economics? The car was probably not yet paid for; therefore the true owner was not, in fact, Adams, but a bank. The bank had loaned it to Adams, now the man's wife was loaning it to him.

He was feeling so good, the air rushing in against his face through the side windows of the car, that he almost didn't see Johnny Adams standing on the side of the road, at the edge of his father's property, playing with the barbed wire that ran the length of the fence. He *did* notice him, though, at the last moment, and waved and beeped without drawing a response. In the rearview mirror, he checked to see if the boy had lifted a hand, offered some gesture of acceptance. There was none. He didn't let it bother him, though. Staring through the clear windshield (had Adams cleaned it himself before death?), he saw only the road before him, uncluttered, his to master.

By the time he reached Warren Street, he could feel his vision returning, tickling at the edges of a long-empty space in him. Why this should be happening now, in this strange car, was a mystery to him, but there were the houses, here the street, and inside himself there was renewed energy at the sight, undeniable. He knew he had been on the verge of destroying this, his daily life, by a simple act of neglect, and for what? So what if Johnny Adams could whack a baseball with a purity that Thomas would forever be denied, did that mean his own son had to be disowned? And what if Nancy's expectations of him were limiting, a smaller self than the one he now felt himself to be, did that mean he had to *accept* them as the only expectations the world held out for Jack Henna? Look at me, driving Adams' car! You must learn to broaden your life, stretch the fabric without ripping it, that was the thing. Drive a man's car, embrace the man's wife, but come home, always. He felt hunger at the sight of his house: dinner, the boys, even a simple conversation with Nancy, suddenly these were as gifts to him. Mrs. Adams, too, was a gift. Even McHale's lawn, overly crisp as he confronted it, raucous with growth, hadn't the power to affect him adversely.

Inside the house, Nancy had dinner on.

His sons, in front of the TV, called, "Daddy, Daddy." He rolled onto his back and lifted Leo. Nancy, holding a spoon wet with tomato sauce, smiled at him.

Even with Leo suspended above him, little legs kicking, open mouth tunneling a shriek of joy, his happiness was not complete: in Thomas' smile, seen out of the corner of his eye, he saw the twin of his former panic, Thomas wishing to be young enough again to be lifted, kicking, fearing that that moment of his life was past. He eased Leo down onto his chest, pulled Thomas to him, held them both, tickling the soft places under their arms, the crooks of their knees, pudgy thighs, the places where, when they were babies, he would kiss them.

"You're playful tonight," Nancy laughed.

"Spaghetti again?"

"I didn't like the looks of any of the meat at the Round-Up. So I had Frank just grind me the stewing beef once, for meatballs. There's salad, too. I picked the tomatoes this morning."

"Are they ripe?"

"Oh, sure. You want to see?"

"How can I? These two buckaroos have got me strapped down."

"Okay, boys, that's enough."

The boys, hysterical, did not listen.

Henna looked up over his knees at the black-and-white image on the TV: Jane Wyman, behind a veil, tearfully kissed a child goodbye, sending it off to two adoptive-looking parents.

"What are you guys watching?"

Thomas, between tears of laughter, said, "It's good, Dad. *The Blue Veil.*"

"I never heard of it."

Nancy held a tomato up to him.

"See?"

"Beautiful."

"So spaghetti once a week is not so bad, is it?"

"No."

"Whose car is that, Jack?"

She was looking out the window.

"Oh. A client lent it to me."

"Who?"

"You don't know her. Her husband isn't using it. I'll return it tomorrow."

"That was certainly nice of her."

Did he detect a note of suspicion in her words? She sliced tomatoes as if, in her kitchen, there could be no possibility of deceit.

The boys, panting, lay beside him now, exhausted in their sore ticklish joints, laughter falling out of them like emissions from a disconnected hose.

"You guys had enough?"

"Yes, yes."

He grabbed them one final time, just to listen to their protests, and felt a potency he hadn't felt since they were each very small, and Nancy was too weak sometimes with feeding them to speak or do anything but rest against his shoulder and hand their small flesh to him. Then he would lift them up, smell them, sometimes even put their tiny penises to his nose, turn them over and sniff their small dimpled asses. Several times Leo had peed all over him, from the stimulation, but he had just laughed, feeling the warm watery substance run down the hairs of his chest, back to the source.

That night he waited for her in bed while she brushed her hair and washed her face in the bathroom, the light from the half-closed bathroom door falling across the hall, into the bedroom, so that he could see his body stretched out before him on the white sheets of the bed. Only sometimes now would he wait for her with an erection; usually it took the stimulus of touch, or the sight of her breasts in the half-light, rising and falling with her movement from door to bed. Tonight he seemed monstrous to himself, thick with desire. He grabbed himself and held on, worried it would collapse under the strain of his awareness. He wanted her quickly, to have her at this length, for the soft yelp it would draw out of her. When she finally came into the room and saw him holding on to it, she laughed lightly.

"I guess I won't put on my nightgown tonight, huh, Jack?"

"It's too hot anyway."

She sat down next to him and held on to it with him.

"Oooh, Madonna!"

Then he laughed, but soft, sexy, confident, the way he imagined Adams might have.

He'd heard that some women liked to kiss it, put it in their mouths. Though she'd never done this, he wished now she would, and of her own volition. He watched her pull on it, smiling, oblivious to his deeper desires, and felt an immense power, wondered if it was enough, this power, to take them beyond their accustomed rituals to a new place.

He reached up and grabbed her neck, rubbed it, then began to draw it down to where her hand was. Her neck was delicate and long; he saw the strain in it as she resisted, not sure what it was he was doing. Her smile held firmly in place, she looked at him with eyes more curious than frightened. He exerted more pressure, watched her neck tighten, her head within inches of the tip of him now. She looked at it with a flash of repulsion, then it hit her cheek and she cried out, her neck still under his control, twisting away from it. He forced her lips to meet it. They touched it and drew back, her mouth opened he thought to embrace it. Instead she cried out and then gagged on it in attempting to expunge him from her mouth. He slipped out of her as she fell to the side of the bed, pulling a sheet with her.

She spit and cleared her throat and then cried a bit, as if she had been waiting to cry.

He stayed where he was, watching his erection shrink, heavy desire gone.

"Jack," she said, between the outbursts he was afraid the children might be hearing, "what's the matter with you?"

He was silent, waiting it out, not giving up, regretting everything but not ready to admit to a final defeat.

"What were you trying to *do?*"

The room, pitch black, contained a new heaviness, palpable, pressing on him, as if the enormity of his desire had shot off into the air, filling little pockets of air with the weight of his need. It pressed on him as he listened to her cry, and as his body made its new plans, ordered the next charge, he fell into a deep sleep, the first layer of which covered her tears and her near flesh, absorbed them so that he felt her floating above him, his wife a dream, a former life, a naked crying girl in a deep forest. He dreamt she was his mother's sister, reaching for a flower at the edge of a cliff. He embraced her, and she fell. When he awoke, he was frightened for Nancy. She recoiled from his touch. Even in sleep, her face wore the hard frown of a skeptical attitude toward his advances. He couldn't help remembering her innocence in the early days of their marriage, her innocence even up to these last days, and wondered what he had done to lose her trust. He put his hand on her belly, felt the slow rise and fall of it, then went ahead and touched her down below. She was wet enough to enter. But his own genitals felt weary, straining to rise. Her resistance seemed as thick and heavy as a concrete wall inside her, something he could hammer and hammer against but which had solidified over time. He had contributed to it, he knew. Something inside him, he wasn't sure what, had been contributing all these years to the wall that could prevent his easy finding of her.

He lay beside her and remembered his dream of a daughter. Feeling her belly now hardening, confronting the new line on her forehead, he knew there would be no more children from this woman. What they had made now was complete. Her body seemed to be telling him that. It could no longer even induce lust unless that lust was accompanied by some perversion: the sight of her tears, or her long, thin neck straining against his going into her mouth. He saw the rest of his days as a straitlacing of desire: childless, without thrill. You made a thing and then you became the caretaker of it. All his life had been headed toward this: to be done with child making, done with desire. To sleep with a woman whose resistance was like a wall erected against you, to play with sons who would never make you proud. No wonder old people shriveled, became smaller. When hope caved in, so did the body.

He could see the two of them, old, on this bed. See their skin, and how they would be careful not to touch one another, and if they accidentally did, how they would recoil from the touch. But still, hope seemed present in the room, a butterfly or a moth with a tiny fluttering shadow. He could chase it around and around and never put his hands on it.

He touched the cheek of her wide and still-wonderful behind—*take me back, pull me back into our sense of early hope*—and felt the goose bumps rise there. He imagined her sitting up in bed, saying, "We're old, Jack. We're getting old. Don't be foolish." Could you sleep on those words? Would they ever be enough to bring you rest? She shifted on the bed, and her head, in sleep, turned to him—it seemed such a heavy thing, he was drawn to it and repulsed by it both. She opened her eyes and stared at him: who are you? The cold stare of a judge. He placed his hands on the sides of her face. "What?" she asked, her eyes looking scared. He remembered the dream, remembered losing her. He removed his hands from her face and it was like dropping her. He watched her plummet, her face become smaller. Then she turned away, retreated into sleep. She would have none of it, whatever he was up to in the middle of the night. He felt his hands at his sides, heavy with the need for flesh. He left the bed, left the room, went to the bathroom and turned on the light.

He looked at his face in the mirror. Need appeared to be drawing the skin back from his eyes, making them appear huge and bulging. His head looked so big. He looked at the scar on the left side of his scalp. His head looked like a battlefield, dank and soaked with new blood. It amazed him that he could go out with that head, day after day, and sell insurance.

He reached up and switched off the light, not wanting to confront his face any longer. He padded down the stairs, past his sons' room. Then he stood at the door leading to his backyard and looked out. He saw his yard, bordered by hedges on one side from the Lynches', on the other from McHale's by the simple difference in their lawns. As far as the eye could see, this was his. He wanted to laugh. To think he had wished, more than anything, to be expunged from the woods on Saturday, to be freed from their grip, and for what? To fail at a baseball game, be rejected by his wife, to live in the safety of this tiny bordered Eden he was paying for with his life's blood. Why not the woods, why not the wide expanse? What was this mad dash toward the chartered, the sequestered, the finished thing he had put his stamp and seal on?

He stepped outside.

The shock of his nakedness was thrilling, like a great risk whose consequences he couldn't name. He remembered—it seemed the last time he'd been naked in the open air—swimming in the Charles River, a boy of ten, twelve, the way it had felt then. He thought his body should feel different now, shriveled by use, hardened as Nancy's seemed to be. The miracle was, it didn't. It felt young, as though there were things still ahead of it. But what? What exactly could he do now?

He stood under the McIntosh and looked down at the ground, remembering D'Alio on Saturday, humping the ground at home plate. It was a foolish, childish thing to do, yet D'Alio had done it without shame, as if there was nothing in the act but joy, and a grip on life so strong it embraced even the inanimate. Well, why not? Henna got down on his knees, placed his palms on the ground before him and, trying hard to think like D'Alio, proceeded to straddle and hump the earth.

His mouth tasted grass, his body felt knuckled by stones, clumps of earth housing the wide-shooting roots of the McIntosh tree. There was no solace to be found this way. He felt absurdly foolish; what if someone had seen? Dirt had worked its way into his mouth, so he got up and went to the side of the house, to wash it out by means of the garden hose.

The water was jetting in—he drank greedily—when he noticed the car in his driveway. Adams' car had been there all along, he'd nearly forgotten it. With it came the sweet remembrance of Mrs. Adams, of their afternoon together. What was it about a marriage that had the power to negate all inroads, render every alternative mute? Here had been an invitation, and he had been humping the earth, as if no further possibility lay beyond the yard and his wife, as if, having exhausted the one, you were left with no alternative but to beat your head and body against the other.

She had given it to him. This extraordinary woman had given it to him. He had to repeat it to himself. She had offered him this car, and who knew what else? He was not just a man whose wife had rejected him, whose worldly goods had begun to shrink on him, who had nowhere else to go. Another woman, a woman he might actually love, had made a gesture. He held to these simple truths as he hovered over the car. He could feel how close he was now to delusion, to the place where he could invent any crazy excuse for its being here, give it an importance that her gesture had never been intended to contain. She had offered it, that was all. He could only guess that in the offering had been the request, the expressed wish, that he come back. Otherwise, he was sure, she'd never have given it to him.

He looked up over the roof of the car, and knowing he was now entirely visible to his neighbors, wondered what they would think if they were to look out their windows. The absurdity of his position flashed before him, and just as quickly he blotted it out. What good would it do to see himself as absurd now? Would it be better to be upstairs, in his bed, ignoring the car and whatever its invitation turned out to be? Was that what one was expected to do on Warren Street?

A car's headlamps had begun to swerve beyond Mulry's house. Henna scuttled quickly into the car, embarrassed briefly when the car's internal light further illuminated his nakedness. The car passed, though, and he could see the driver hadn't even glanced his way. Another man on a mission, looking neither to the right nor to the left, entirely focused ahead of himself.

The leather of the car seats felt cool inside, he rested his head against it. The seats and backrests were matted, and on the passenger's side he found he could stick his finger in and feel the straw stuffing. This was the place where she'd sat on their rides together, hers and Adams'. He wondered: Had he ever worshipped Nancy the way he was prepared to worship this woman, down to lovingly fingering a hole in a car seat she may or may not have created? It was enough that she had sat there.

He wanted to stay in the car, sleep there, be surrounded by the warmth of a place she had been. It made him think there was really no question left to be decided: he had to go to her, right now if it were possible. You did not finger the hole made in the straw stuffing of a car where a woman had merely sat, not with this devotion, not with this headiness, then go back inside to your wife and pretend you were prepared to resume normal life.

He sat up, clutched hard at the steering wheel, suddenly wanting a dose of absolute seriousness, at least not wanting to be making decisions based on how it felt to have your finger inside the straw matting of a car seat. He paid attention to the car's hardnesses, things uncongenial to delusion: its green dashboard, the radio dial resting permanently between 8 and 9. It was hopeless: he kept wondering if he breathed deeply enough, would he catch a whiff of the time they had coupled here, she and Adams, outside the house, safe from the prying ears of their infant son? In the erotic haze of his imaginings, he began to doze off. He awoke to the sound of his name being called. It took only a moment to figure out it was his wife, looking for him.

The sound of her voice was like a thin, sharp blade piercing his skin. It was coming from the general vicinity of the porch. He felt his body tense, instinctively lifting toward the sound. He remembered the rebuttal in her behind, though, the judging eyes awakened from a dream in which he played no benevolent part. There were all the signs and symbols of a marriage falling apart, love having ended. To ignore them was to put oneself in the position of a man without instincts, one who couldn't tell the difference between a fish and a bird. He steeled himself and listened to her calling him, the repetition of his name. He saw little images of himself receding with each repetition. It was the hardest thing he had ever done, not to answer.

When the screen door had slammed and the night returned to its detailed silence, he removed himself from the car and walked into the depths of his backyard, as far as he could go. Having refused to answer her, he did not want to be found in the car, so close by, his evasion as obvious as his nakedness. In the backyard he could always say he didn't hear. But that was foolishness, wasn't it? Things happened in an instant—limbs were severed, truths discovered—and everything was changed. The changes themselves had to be faced: I love another woman. He could imagine himself waking up with that knowledge every morning for the rest of his life, never being able to tell anyone. Eventually the pressure would be such that he would feel himself being drummed into the floorboards, stuck in a position where he was of no use to anyone. Things happened, Henna, it was of little use to cover tracks before you knew where they would lead.

From the depths of his yard, he looked up once more at his house. Under the branches of the McIntosh, he could see the place where his sons slept. He could see, too, in its outline and solidity, how well the house had been made, how safe a place it really was. This oughtn't to have but nonetheless did surprise him. He saw how much it was, and would remain, his. The life inside, his creation. Even if he were to leave it, he was not sure how much, if anything, would change. It would not burn down, or crumble. His sons, imperfect as they were, would never wear another man's face.

It was, finally, what allowed him the thought of leaving: how well he had done this, how solid were the contours of the life he'd created, how little was required of him now. In his sons' room, under the cool leaves of the McIntosh, he could perceive no danger. It all looked safe, as if there were nails in his life. It had the autonomy of a house: you did not have to stand inside it, holding it up. Walk away and you would be surprised how firm the whole thing was.

7

WITH THE FIRST light, he felt the wetness on his face, and thought he had been crying. Then his eyes offered up the simpler explanation: all around him, his grass was wet with morning dew. He had slept there, outside, under the trees.

An amazement came over him—the thread of actions and decisions from the night before seemed to be unraveling from the tight ball they had gathered into in his sleep. At the same time, he began to feel the grip of the cold on his body, and his bladder felt so heavy he thought that discharging it here might create a small lake in his backyard. Nearly doubled over, he headed for the house.

A logic, distant and muted in him, spoke up the instant he started forward. It was as though there was something wrong, or not thought through, in his movement back to the house, the very reason he had slept outside being to deny himself the house's comfort. The amazement—the pleasant sensation of having done something ribald and uncharacteristic—was lessened, too, by the ache in his bones as he moved forward. He remembered that he had, at some point the night before, thought of himself as young. His body mocked the sentiment now, straining against movement. At the moment, it seemed there was *nothing* his body could do.

When he was nearly up the porch, just two steps ahead to cover, he heard a sound like a gunshot very close to him, ducked and covered himself. Turning to the place it must have come from, he saw McHale opening his garage door. The sound had to have been the click the door made when McHale unlocked it. Now McHale stood shaking his head, and Henna wanted to duck from that, too. Where now was the sense—the thing he'd felt so powerfully the night before—that his neighbors didn't count, could hold no sway over him? It seemed that

McHale stared at him a long time before disappearing into his garage. Only when he was gone did Henna become fully aware of his nakedness, and a charge went through him, a chagrin so total it had the effect of a pin stuck into an open socket. Then McHale's car started up, and his heart began to thump wildly. He was certain now that McHale would not just drive calmly down the driveway and into the street, not observe the common rules of behavior. He imagined briefly, obscenely, that his behavior the night before might have unleashed a wildness in the neighborhood. He was afraid McHale would, instead, drive across his lawn onto Henna's and, accelerating, head straight for the porch. He wouldn't leave until he'd leveled the house. When McHale instead did the unexpected, the habitual thing, it had the effect of drawing him into an uncertainty mistier even than this sunless hour. What good were actions and decisions if the world didn't go along with them, if, instead, it resisted them, as McHale seemed now calmly to be doing, not even looking back? It was as though last night meant nothing, and it angered him until he realized he'd made no statement, there was, strictly speaking, no way for McHale to know his morning nakedness was anything other than an aberrant act. His hopes, his plans, had not been on display; it was a flaw to think that, in judging the outer man, McHale had been judging *him*. Quickly then, before he could make himself any more vulnerable, he ducked into the house.

In the bathroom, he relieved himself quietly, taking a long time, allowing relief to work its way through him like a masseuse hitting all the right places. When he was finished, he shivered and flushed, then realized he didn't want to leave the bathroom. It seemed the only place in the house he could use with trust now. He turned on the tap and began to fill the tub with hot water. When the heat hit his face, he knew instantly that he'd found something to absorb the next hour, and after that there wouldn't be many, and each of them filled with use—dressing, breakfast—before the time came to get in the car and go.

. . .

When he opened his eyes, Leo's face was peering at him over the edge of the tub. The water had begun sloshing over the sides, and there was a sizable puddle on the bathroom floor.

"What are you doin', Dad?"

The words had the rhythm of a repetition, and Leo's eyes were lit by mischief. For a brief moment, Henna felt the victim of one of his son's tricks.

"What happened here?" Henna asked with some anger, though by the time he got the words out he had figured it out for himself.

"What are you *doin'?*"

He was groping now blindly for the submerged taps. Leo's obvious glee at finding him in this state was irritating.

"You *know* what I'm doing. I'm taking a bath."

"And you fell asleep."

That was obviously the punch line. Leo did not have to wait for Henna's assent before letting loose a high whinnying hiccough of laughter.

"You watched me, didn't you? Why didn't you wake me up?"

He was out of the tub now, soaking up water with clean towels, a choice he knew would earn him some chastisement from Nancy later on. When he looked up at Leo, he wondered where the laughter had suddenly gone—wasn't he as ridiculous now as he'd been in the tub? He saw the boy was poised uncertainly between laughter and something else, a fear that had a kind of cruelty in it. It amazed him that his younger son had reached the age of choice—why didn't children just hang on as long as they could to their blind impulses? The choice seemed to imply some kind of judgment: Leo was deciding whether to laugh at his father or be frightened by his rage; either way, an assessment would take place, and Henna wanted none of it. He reached out blindly for the child, and hugged Leo to him, clasping him hard by the buttocks. Don't judge me! The little boy's fists dug hard into Henna's throat, and he was out of his grasp before Hanna could find a safer, tighter place to grab. Leo had decided on fear. He hid himself behind the radiator that stood next to the tub; there was just enough room behind it for his body.

"Leo," Henna said, approaching.

He could see the boy's face through the bars of the radiator, partitioned. The high red mark on the boy's forehead reminded him of Leo's birth.

"What?" the boy asked sullenly.

"What did you think I was doing? You think I meant to hurt you?"

Leo's face colored. He wouldn't meet Henna's smile. Henna was reminded of the sudden violence he'd inflicted on this child in the car on Saturday.

"Come out," he said.

Leo still wouldn't budge. Henna was beginning to ache now for some semblance of normalcy. He felt an urge to strip the boy, to pull him into the tub with him, to return to the ease with which they related to one another in the days when Leo, still an infant, would wake in the middle of the night and Nancy would bring him into their bed. Then it had only been a matter of warmth: the boy's small body would curl into the hollow Henna's arms made. They would lie there, and Henna would be overwhelmed with a sense of good fortune: he had planted a garden that would feed them all, he was sure, into the foreseeable future. What could he offer now that the boy couldn't just as easily get for himself? Worse, what would be the worth of his offering if, as he intended, the boy were to be left fatherless by evening? He shook his head; it was too harsh, he couldn't accept it—that word, "fatherless"—he could be sure of nothing. He was groping once again for the wet towels, to find an action to contain this sudden loss of direction, when, as if to aid in this blunting of thought, Leo threw a cake of soap at him, hitting him directly over the right eye.

"Leo!"

He went blind with rage for a second, and struck the radiator. Leo cowered behind it, unreachable. Henna tried to reach through the bars—in his rage, he sought skin to touch, pinch, squeeze—but Leo managed to make himself even scarcer. Henna watched the little boy's stomach go concave at the approach of his father's fingers. Finally he stood up and reached over the top. Leo's hands went up to cover his head. Though Henna had intended to lift the boy up by his underarms, he could too easily imagine scraping his son's head against the bars, drawing blood. It was too pathetic, the memory of it would make him resist any flight he dared dream of. He leaned over the edge of the radiator and patted Leo's head. His hand felt heavy and uncomfortable in the act. He commanded his voice to be gentle: "Hey."

"What?"

"I'm not going to hurt you."

Leo looked up. There was no judgment now, only a soft reproach.

"Come out," Henna said.

"You won't hit?"

"Hit? Since when do I hit?"

Leo didn't have to say anything. His expression didn't change, remained questioning. Of course Henna hit.

"No. I won't hit."

Leo came out. He stood in front of his father and touched his knee, felt the hairy knob, Henna noticed that he'd made the boy's pajamas wet. He bent down.

"Tickle me," Leo said.

"Tickle you? Is that what you want?"

Leo nodded, and Henna complied. He tickled under Leo's arms and listened to laughter that sounded strangely false to his ears. Weren't kids supposed to be a little more forgiving of chaos? It made him feel foolish, as though the tickling idea should have been his own.

When he stopped, Leo lifted his hand and put it back onto the last place he had tickled. "More."

Then, as he resumed, Leo's laughter held to the thin strip between falseness and a genuine response. He wished now that Leo's face would simply collapse, but it was as though the boy was afraid to close his eyes, so determined was he to test the waters before giving his father any real power. Even in the midst of laughter, Leo seemed to still be studying him. And why not? Here he was, still naked, formerly dangerous, a man who'd thrown so many moods at his son in the space of five minutes that it was no wonder the trust had been revoked. He felt an urge to get up, put clothes on, do something formal. But for now, the boy seemed to want to be tickled; he thought it was the least he could do.

When Nancy entered the room, they were still at it, each of them reluctant to stop. He could feel a stiffness go into his arms immediately, though, as if the tickling were now exposed to the glare of a hot light, in which he had to prove that he was doing something simple, something good. Such an innocent gesture, this tickling, and it was being made to do so much work!

"Daddy's tickling me," Leo said.

She frowned (he'd known she would), staring after them to the puddle on the floor, the sopped towel in its midst. But there was something else, too: in her cheeks was a high pink blush, not the morning paleness he was used to.

"What happened?" she asked, and he had to ford through the deep stream of events before he was sure exactly what it was she referred to.

"Daddy fell asleep."

She wouldn't look at him now. Instead, she bent down to sop up the puddle with a new towel, and he watched concern darken and then erase the colors on her face. In an instant—his fault!—she was turned into a charwoman, on her knees, cleaning up his mess. He turned away from this vision of her, picked Leo up and then stood above her, holding Leo, suddenly not sure what to do with himself. When she looked up, he could tell she was seeing his sex, hanging stupidly before him; he watched her glance at it and then return to her char work. Who had ever convinced him it was supposed to be an image of power, this instrument? From her angle, he was sure it looked no more powerful than the sopping-wet towels in her hands, another part of his mess. The shame was that he felt the tantalizing presence of physical life in the room, as though their attraction to each other were a layer of skin several layers below the outer—on her entrance he had felt it sharply and immediately—this was, after all, a woman he wanted. But she had to comply, or what was the use of it? The way she was wringing out the towels made him feel the hopelessness of her rejection—why were the towels, the neatness of the room, more important than him? She left the room before he could figure it out, and when he and Leo were alone again, facing each other, it was as though a visible confusion and expectation lingered in her wake; the two of them were unsure where next to step.

He took Leo to the sink and dried him on it. Then, after he'd crossed the room for a towel, he looked back and registered how easy it would be for Leo to fall. He did nothing, though. It was as if Nancy had already taken the boy from him; his very safety seemed a thing he'd already handed her. He was surprised when, on her return, she let out a half scream.

"It's okay, it's okay," he heard himself saying.

"He could fall."

She might as well have hit him with the idea. He had no doubt that if words could solidify and become clubs, she would have used them that way. She carried a huge white towel. She opened it to take the boy to her bosom. Then the two of them were gone from the room.

He dried himself with the paltry towel he held in his hands, then wrapped it around his middle. Confronting himself in the fogged-over mirror, he could only see an arm, a shoulder, part of his trunk. He thought: She is always *taking* things from me. Then he entered the bedroom. She was still drying Leo on the bed, as if he had made the boy so wet it would take all her attention, and the major part of her day, to get him dry again. He went to a drawer to find underwear for himself, absentmindedly opened hers instead. The hefty nylon smell of Nancy's underwear lifted toward him; he felt he'd invaded some private sanctuary. Then a more frightening thought occurred: What if, overnight, she'd emptied the house of what was his?

She looked up at him, confronting her underwear. What perversion now? In her face was the same stiff denial of him she'd worn in sleep. She'd crossed over a line, too: he'd become a foreign country to her. He could still recognize the memory of beauty in her face, but she seemed to have become suddenly not beautiful. The hard small animal inside her—the animal that loathed him—was moving outward, affecting her features, changing the whole cast of them without actually affecting a line. He looked down, tried to find his drawer again, for a moment couldn't imagine where it was. In his total sense of disorientation, he nearly fell over from dizziness. In the space of a morning, she'd done all a man on the verge of leaving could have asked for—removed from his house, and from her face, every possibility that had once existed for a life.

At seven, he remembered to call Valenti.

His family was seated around the breakfast table, turned away from him, absorbed in eating: the way they were seated made him think of them as a family composed entirely of edges, parts that butted up against one another. Only Thomas made himself available now and then, Thomas crunching on a piece of toast, looking up and eyeing his father: What's up? What's that in your eyes? He thought Thomas knew too much. The boy's availability was no more tempting than an inquisitor's.

With Valenti, he was abrupt. He referred to Mrs. Adams as "the beneficiary out in Lexington." He made quick work of the information that he wouldn't need a ride, then, just as Valenti began to pursue details, issued a quick and formal "See you at the office" and hung up.

When it was finished, though, he began to follow Valenti's line of inquiry on his own, and it left him with a sick feeling at the base of his stomach. In truth, he had no idea what the day would bring. He knew he would go to the farm, but that was all he knew. Suppose she did accept him, though, suppose he were actually to go through with the leaving of them, what would they think it had been for? It was too easy to imagine Valenti coming here, explaining it to them, telling them how it was "crazy," Nancy nodding her head, agreeing, "He always had crazy lusts." He could imagine Thomas, too, searching for some movie in which there existed a correlative for his father's action: he remembered one in particular they'd seen together, in which young executives on the train from New York to suburban Connecticut went goggle-eyed at the sight of every large-breasted thing that happened by. He wanted to cry out to them now: It was not that way! All morning he had been holding on to the idea of staying here, of denying the other, as if it were a line cast into a murky, depthless pool. Wasn't it more a passive act, this leaving, than anything else? They no longer had anything to say to him. His use had been worn out. Even the way they ate breakfast, Nancy refusing to meet his eyes, seemed an unconscious expunging of him. But would they remember, after the fact, the real way it had been? No, they would weep, they would gnash teeth. Valenti would shrug. He saw himself sticking a knife into an innocent animal, drawing blood. It was because he was seeing it from outside, he knew, but how else was he to see it from here? He had to leave, he had to go to the woman, nothing would make any sense until he did. He lifted his briefcase and made to go.

Nancy interrupted him. "What time will you be home?"

He watched her take a napkin and wipe a smear of butter off the table. The question was apparently not a loaded one. He was able to watch her, detached, thinking: This may be the last time I watch her wipe butter from a table. Then wondered if that was so, if *any* break could be made that cleanly.

"I don't know," he said finally.

"What about supper?"

She still had not looked up. Had she only confronted him with the question, he could have defied her and felt justified in doing so. Now, the habitual way she asked the question touched a part of him that itself loved the habitual, the everyday. He had to curse it, to force it down: he was seeing his empty plate, empty chair, the falling light sucking hope down with it as they all sat waiting for him.

"You just go ahead and make supper, Nancy."

He said it as though laying out a course for her: do this, stick to the norm, minimize the damage. But what else could she do? Cry into the sink? The children would still need to eat.

Any further involvement in their dailiness would keep him there, he knew. He could recall mornings when escaping from their tiny, postponable demands had been like a quick tripping over quicksand. He could imagine now lingering a second too long, allowing her to ask him to bring something home with him: ears of corn. Driving to Mrs. Adams', he would imagine them waiting, hungry; he would want to turn back. This leaving had to be a business like any other; allow emotion in, and you're sunk.

He opened the door and went outside.

The car was warming up when Thomas appeared at his window. He pushed his nose against it, as Henna started to roll the window down.

"Can I come?"

Henna shook his head quickly, then looked down at Thomas. The boy's brown head staring up at him made him wonder how much he had meant by the question. Come with me where? Into my new life? The tugging he felt was so strong he tried to envision Thomas on the farm, with the cow, playing with Johnny.

"Come where?"

"This is a new car. I never drove in it."

"It's not ours, Thomas."

The unstated pulled Thomas' lower lip down. Henna was sure he, at least, knew everything.

"Just a ride to the Round-Up then?"

"What do you need there?"

"I need to buy something."

"What?"

Thomas smiled. "It's a surprise."

"For me?"

Thomas' smile held. He gestured for the boy to get in, and they drove mostly in silence the short distance to the Round-Up, Thomas hovering close to the door, examining the upholstery, the dashboard in front of him.

Once Thomas asked, "Whose car is this?"

In his caution, Henna answered, "The office's."

"You said the beneficiary."

"When?"

"On the phone, before."

Henna panicked. Had he heard everything? But when they were stopped in front of the Round-Up, Thomas looked up at him, his face a round healthy globe, searching for nothing but the vague approval he had always asked for, the thing Henna had never quite been able to give. He looked at his son now and thought: I gave him those wide cheeks, that forehead, and now he will use them to break my heart. How had Thomas' face suddenly attained the power to fly over the place where mere approval resided, to attack him in a tenderer part? Did Thomas *know* his face's power, or was he being guileless now? Whatever, Henna suddenly wanted to hug him. He started to, and noticed a car in his rearview mirror, waiting for him to move. It was enough to halt the impulse. Thomas opened the door himself and slipped out.

A foot or two onto the curb, Thomas turned back, waved to his father, said, "Bye." Henna mouthed the word in reply, then watched the revolving door of the Round-Up embrace Thomas and carry him inside. Such powers the boy had, his baby was now able to go into a store, to buy something without him. Through the window, he could see the checkout girl (girl? she must have been fifty) bagging groceries. He pressed his foot down on the pedal and bore down, considering as he did the tenuousness of a store's, of *any* store's, construction. What if a beam should go, or a pipe leaking gas remain unsealed? He was leaving his son to such uncertainties; more, he was doing it willingly, as though you could trust the world to do your husbandry for you. It felt mad, a foolishness he had spent his life defending himself from. What, even, was the boy going to buy? That he might never know was instantly more than he could bear. He braked—not knowing why—heard a honking behind him, then the screech of brakes. The car behind him had missed him by inches. In the rearview mirror, he saw the man's—a stranger's—face, red, scrunched like balled paper, waving him angrily forward. He obeyed.

At his desk in the office, he lit a cigarette, exhaled smoke and thought of the day stretching ahead of him as though it were a long groping toward the nebulous, a promise for which there existed no hard contract. The vagueness of his future was making him soft—his arms and legs felt as heavy and useless as they did in dreams. He watched the smoke rise above his head and wondered if he weren't actually leaking substance, deflating like a huge rubber blowup of himself.

The heat in the office felt incendiary. As he looked across the room, it was as though a haze were hanging over it. But even in such torporous circumstances, he noticed Yvon Leblanc managed to look crisp and white, in a bright starched shirt. Leblanc was hard at work already, while Henna sat slothful, indigent, planning to leave his family, allowing himself the pleasure of smoking. He stubbed the butt out and tried to imagine what Leblanc would think if he could see into Henna's mind now, Leblanc who had always seemed such a positive draftsman of his own life, planning everything out squarely, cleanly, lines on ruled paper, Henna's own image, once, of the way to live. He tried to focus on his own desk, to put things there in order, when out of the corner of his eye he noticed Valenti's thigh jiggling against his desk. Henna bristled, preparing for an onslaught of questions. Instead, a photograph was thrust before his eyes.

In it, a young bride and groom stood leaning into one another against at thick arrangement of drapery. Their heads and faces appeared thin and as yet unformed, and their bodies looked uncomfortable, as though they'd been thrust into poses that didn't suit them.

"So?" He looked up. Valenti's hair, haloed by the fluorescent light above him, looked singed.

"My cousin sent it to me in the mail."

"Just married?"

"A week ago Satidy."

"So?"

"We're still workin' together Wednesdays, right?"

Henna wanted to say no, but couldn't. His head suddenly felt overheated, as though too much pressure were being exerted there. One change in a life, and what else was affected? Would the Wednesdays still exist, he and Valenti still covering the farmland, approaching the newlyweds, offering succor to the newly widowed? Could all that still go on if he changed his address to Adams'? It had to, but he had no idea how it could. What would he do, come into the office and make an announcement? "I left my wife. I'm now living with the beneficiary of one of our policies out in . . ." Crazy. He could not conceive of that moment in his life. But here was Valenti, proposing the customary. Henna was grateful when the sound of Connie's voice calling to him saved him from having to answer.

Connie gestured to the phone. He picked it up and heard Nancy's voice.

"Jack. Hi."

The word sounded strangely formal coming from her. He felt blank, immune to whatever message she carried. Then it occurred to him: one of the boys was dead. Thomas had been crushed by the falling roof of the Round-Up. Leo had fallen from the sink. He hated the length of her pause. He wanted the message immediately.

"What is it, Nancy?"

"It worried me, you saying you'd be late tonight."

So that was all. "Nan."

"Where were you last night?"

He felt again the retreat into blankness, decided to give her an honest answer. "I was outside. I heard you."

She was silent.

"Why?"

"Look, I'll explain."

"When, tonight?"

Now it was his turn to be silent, but he could imagine her

suspecting, tracing him down, showing up at the Adams' before he could get there.

"Listen, Nancy, I told you, I don't know when I'll be home. I have to be late."

He let her cry awhile. When she was finished, he felt cold, not certain why. He was beyond helping her. Any gesture would be a sop. Where they would end up would be with her, on her knees, cleaning up his mess.

Still, when she finally said, "Okay," there was something in it that nearly pulled him out of himself. In that moment, he didn't want to be the sort of man who made women say "okay" in just that manner, sounding hollow and distant and lost. She hung up, though, and he was left with a feeling for which there was no use, an energy that had no direction to go in. He could actually feel it die then, the pull back toward her, and was glad he hadn't acted on it.

Valenti patted the picture and gave Henna's shoulders a squeeze.

"Workin' late, huh, Jack?"

Henna nodded, distant and unfocused. Before him, the photograph blurred, became two distinct images. He studied it: nothing else to do. What drew them together, these two? What made them think they could have a life? Their pairing seemed as arbitrary as any, even animals seemed to have more of a plan, more of a chance at long-standing fidelity. Who was it, which bird, who, it was said, upon losing its mate, pined always at the site of the nest, remained forever faithful? He tried to imagine that bird's flight, its trajectory through the sky, the awful loneliness. It amazed him, and left him with a small, nameless ache.

The morning began to seem endless.

He became conscious, *too* conscious, of the image he'd had the other day—what was it, just a week before?—when Cutler had come to his desk and started telling him about the trouble he'd had with his wife, his failure to awaken her to all his erotic potential, when Cutler's hand had tried to describe the arc of his potential in air, and failed, and Henna had seen, beyond him, all the other insurance men suddenly missing their connections, going a beat off, lumbering doggedly where swiftness was all. It had come to him in waking dreams, on rare occasions over the years—usually after a disturbing encounter on the debit—the lack of a guarantee that one would ever again make a sale. Who said that it must necessarily happen? Because it had happened before was not, on these occasions, comfort enough. Because it had seemed, when he was conscious of it, as he was this morning, a high-wire act, he also knew how easy it would be to fail. At heart, it really *was* all rhythm, all pep. He had neither this morning, only the sense of a load: words to be communicated, expelled. He wanted to go directly to Mrs. Adams, dispense with the work of the day. He studied the papers on his desk, searched for a word or a clue that would let him back in.

He remembered once watching a ball game on television, when an old-timer had been called in to relief-pitch—in baseball, "old-timers" were often younger than he was now—and hadn't been able to deliver, his arm seeming to have gone permanently out. After a few pitches, it had been sadly obvious he would have to be removed. So the manager had gone out, chatted with him a few minutes, squeezed his shoulder, and the pitcher had walked off the mound. Then the crowd had, astonishingly, gone wild, applauding him, cheering him for his very failure, it had sent his triumphs into such relief, made them glow with a brilliance only something finished can have. Now Henna wondered at the unfairness: he had been selling insurance as long as that pitcher had been throwing curves, and yet if he were to be removed, he wouldn't go out to any applause, but in disgrace. How long was a man's selling arm supposed to last anyway? The perceived cruelty was made even more bitter by the fact that he knew it would not be shared by anyone in the room now. If he were to go in and present it to Lavolli as a "metaphor," Lavolli would probably put his cigar out in Henna's face.

Outside, Adams' car seemed to absorb heat unnaturally. It

felt like a special punishment, to be confined to that room, to be sitting there waiting for someone to come and get you. When he parked at the first house, it came almost as a surprise to him that he could get out, relieve himself of the car's heat. Perhaps inside the house they would offer him water, he could mop his brow. He could—a new thought—reveal his humanity to them. And in his obvious humanity, wasn't it just possible he might even find a new way of selling insurance?

He was greeted at the door by a young man, clean-cut, wearing chinos, and the man's pretty, blonde-haired wife. They seemed happy enough to see him, and on his way into their living room, he wondered if he hadn't always exaggerated the demands of selling.

When he began to pitch, he thought it might actually work, this new detachment. He heard the words arriving like a train he had to run a little to catch, but as long as he kept pace he felt he would be fine, they would always be there ahead of him. It was Valenti's "look once around the room" that undid him, a remembered bit of advice he thought might come in handy now that he was trying things a little different. When he looked around, he started to find things that unsettled him: artificial flowers that looked so real you had to study them to ascertain the difference, a stack of magazines whose titles—Car & Driver, Argosy—were at once familiar and completely strange. He found himself in the midst of a silence he wasn't sure how to cover. He lunged toward the end of his pitch a little desperately, and when he arrived at the word "death," found himself going too fast, brutalizing the word like an old death-hardened fish he was pounding against their immaculate coffee table. Something had gone awry, but now that he was at the end, there was no way to go back and smooth over the speech. It felt bottom-heavy in his mouth, all death, no comfort, the exact antithesis of his former approach. He wanted to run out of the house, or shout, "This is a different man, the one who said these words, this is not me!" Instead, watching the man look away from him, look down and scratch his ankle, he heard himself say, "Of course, nobody here's saying you're going to die, ha-ha!" His laughter sounded idiotic even to himself, and they looked at him strangely, embarrassed for him. Of course they were polite, said they'd think about it. But Henna, on his way out, felt a shame like he hadn't felt since school, when each failure, at arithmetic, at spelling, had made him want to banish himself. He remembered, starting the car, that the woman had gone into the kitchen at the beginning of his visit to prepare a pot of coffee. It had never come, never been offered. He stepped on the gas, couldn't get away fast enough.

At an ice-cream stand that stood just off the highway, as solitary as anything commercial could look (and thus, he reasoned, not a place where he was likely to be found), Henna ate vanilla ice cream and tried to form a plan. To go through the rest of the day having experiences like the one he'd just had would be killing; he was sure he'd never be able to do it again, never be able to get up in the morning and, as Mrs. Adams had said, "sell that head." His head was looking elsewhere, obsessed: how could he expect it to do any worldly good in this condition? Better to give it a rest, write the day off.

The density of his thinking made him distracted. He accidentally knocked the scoop of vanilla onto his lap, then realized he hadn't brought napkins into the car with him. He had to stand up, shake the vanilla off, walk to the stand with a huge stain on his thigh. In a neighboring car an old woman and her husband stared out noncommittally at him. Their stares implied no judgment: this is what happens in the world, you eat ice cream, it spills, you clean it up. That he had spilled it because he'd been thinking of a woman not his wife held no weight here. That the force of confusion engendered by his plan to leave his family had acted to make a stain on his pants was dismissible. The couple stared at him as if they wouldn't know where to begin to make a judgment, yet he ached for one. He wished the woman would shout out, "Go to work, you lazy bastard!" Then at least he would know he was someplace.

In her place, he did it to himself, made a judgment, demanded the exquisite torture of work. To go to Mrs. Adams now, on a matter not related to business, would be like placing his cool, fragile desire in the center of her yard, under the broiling sun, for the duration of the afternoon. How could it possibly survive the heat, the length of time until coolness came, light fell? He could only protect it by buffering it with actions that turned away from it. Even if he were to fail at selling insurance, he had to keep trying.

Then, late in the afternoon, after the day's failures had multiplied—not all his fault, some not at home, some only vaguely promising, others downright hostile—he retrieved from his wallet the address of a couple he had put off seeing for a week, so unpromising had they seemed: an academic couple, teachers at Brandeis, childless. He had expected posters of Karl Marx, strange smells erupting from the kitchen. Instead he found a neat house, gray clapboard. A dark-haired woman answered the door, let him in.

Her husband was in his study. She was polite, offered Henna tea. Asked what kind he preferred, he said, "Whatever."

The husband, interrupted at his work, did not look up. He motioned for Henna to take an empty seat. Henna looked at a poster on the wall, charting the various strata of the earth's crust. While he patiently studied it, the man looked up once, distracted.

"Insurance, is it?"

Henna nodded, and the man went back to his work. Finally, he turned around and asked to see it.

"See what?"

"The insurance policy," he said brusquely.

Henna took out a sample ten-thousand-dollar life, handed it to him. The man, without another word, proceeded to read it.

He waited quietly for his tea. He watched the man's salt-and-pepper crewcut bristle as he ran his hand through it, told himself to stop, not to notice anything, to concentrate instead on the matter at hand. Apparently, nothing more was required of him. Eventually, he assumed, a question would be asked and he would answer.

The man, lighting his pipe, not looking up, said with some annoyance, "I don't know why I never bought this stuff."

He flipped a page quickly. The man's wife came into the room, handed Henna tea. "Camomile," she said. He sipped it, dutifully.

Finally the man looked up. "What's the loan value on one of these?"

Henna referred him to the proper page, pointed out the chart of value over time. He watched the light over the man's head move as he shifted the lamp's position to shed more of it onto the paper. Outside, Henna knew, the light was blazing, but here, they seemed able to control it, to use it only for focus. The tea, as it went down his throat, was immensely soothing.

The man, puffing, repeated, "I don't know why we don't have this."

His wife, sipping tea, said, "We all have our contradictions, don't we?"

The man looked at her like he wanted to slug her.

"Well, nobody's asked me before, have they?"

When the man scowled, his face looked as though you could hang things on it. He stared at Henna a long moment, then, as if he were about to throw him out, said, "All right, I recognize this company's name and I suppose I ought to have it. What is this, ten thousand?"

Henna told him there were other policies, explained the difference in premiums. He opted for a thirty-thousand-dollar life. It was the biggest policy Henna had sold in weeks.

When he realized what had happened, he wanted to cry. He became ebullient, began cracking jokes, the way he'd done in the old days, when selling insurance had been as natural to him as whistling a popular tune. Back in the car, he actually did let go a few waiting tears, stopped himself lest they were watching through the window, then took off.

So that was that. All he'd done was sit and wait, as though he were selling a thing that couldn't be sold, a thing of such obvious value all you had to do was hold it up and let it be seen. You did not, finally, have to be a messiah of your wares. You could be what Lavolli derisively called "an order taker." The difference chafed, but maybe he could slip by in the latter category, maybe they'd never find out. He could hear his history being told, years from now: "Used to be a crack salesman, then something strange happened. Met this broad out in Lexington" (he could hear the voice, hear the language; it didn't matter, he could accept its variation on the truth). "Left his family. Oh, he never quite lost it, but he was never that good anymore. They kept him on, he made his money. But you know, the funny thing" (they would say this, he was sure of it), "he was a lot happier from that point on."

He felt a lightness, a skipping motion, as a clear path opened, light negotiating it. He had been set free; did it matter what they said of him? By any of the world's weighing measures, what he had just effected, in a house he'd been previously afraid to enter, would count as serious business, enough to get a man by. There was a middle ground, after all, between his old life and chaos. He had needed that certainty; now, he was sure, nothing would stand in his way.

Adams' farm had come to exist for him more as memory than as physical reality. When he finally arrived there, late in the afternoon, and was parked in front of the house, studying it, he found himself surprised by small details, an old weather vane he hadn't noticed before: What's that doing there? In his mind, he tore it down, replaced it. He wanted the farm to exist only as he remembered it.

In the car, he searched blindly for the words with which to begin. What would he even call her? Ann? Mrs. Adams? He remembered Valenti's advice to him as a young salesman: Go up to the door, knock, then step back a foot or two. That way they don't think you're pushy, they're more likely to let you in. He considered it, then wondered why, at this point in his life, he was putting himself in the position of a schoolboy. Valenti's advice hadn't done him any good anyway. He would be his own coach, keep his own counsel; his legs shook and his stomach pumped sweat, but he held to himself as to a last friend.

He was on his way up the walk, moving more swiftly than he would have told himself to, and having lurched out of the car not out of anything so calm as a decision, when he heard himself say it, and saw the words as clearly as the title on a deed, the definition of all that would follow: my God, I am actually doing this. He felt himself let go of some last hope that his passions could be tamed or subverted by the external: a car accident, a sudden phone call telling him that one of his sons was in the hospital, a clipping of the car's wings from on high. Under his own power, he was walking into a house where the body of his desire waited, and suddenly the need for form, for words with which to be ready to declare himself, receded. He knew he had the words, would find them in time. If you believed in something, they just naturally followed. It was only when you stopped believing, as he thought he'd done with insurance, that they disappeared, and you were forced to grope. The important thing was that the last turning away had not happened. He was here.

The garage door had been left open, exactly as he'd left it yesterday. Was it no more than that small detail that incited this newfound sense of arrival? He knew he would have to be careful, that what he was seeing as a sign of his necessity could, in fact, be no more than an enormous lethargy on the woman's part. He decided to enter that way, just to close the garage door, but when he'd done that, found he was actually inside the house, the darkness was so frightening he had little time either to consider the import or decide whether this was the correct, the proper way to enter. Fright opened the door for him, and he found himself in the hall of her house, the stray burglar she'd invited. Invited. She'd left it open because she knew he'd be back. It had to be that. No one would risk his life so cavalierly unless he expected, at any moment, to be saved.

The house inside was almost eerie, so vibrant with late-afternoon light that the rooms seemed like reeds being played on by it. He loved the light, was amazed by it, but wondered how people could live in such light without seeing each other differently, as ghosts. This was a house where a child lived. He always had to remind himself of that, so ineffective had the boy been here. He found holes outside instead. He left his deposits in the earth.

He called out once, "Hello!" surprised at the sound of his voice, aware of its habitual salesman's boom, incongruous here. He said to himself, "Shh," and moved into the kitchen.

There, he was startled by a shaft of light that seemed almost negative: walk into it and you will disappear.

Where was his cup from yesterday, her copies of the forms they had filled out together, their last bit of business? He'd expected to find traces of himself in this room, was looking forward to finding them as a hook to his presence here. But the room was empty of him, and he worried. Suppose, overnight, she had gotten hold of herself? Suppose the need for him had been gotten rid of, too? Suppose the open garage door had been just that: a lapse? He wished there were business at hand, a clean purpose for his presence, a paper he could take out of his briefcase and have her sign. No such thing presented itself. He was here, alone, to tell her about a desire so thick, and so immediately irrelevant, it was as if he'd gone miles out of his way to describe a dream he'd had the night before to a person he hardly knew. He cursed the light, it had effected all this: he'd expected to feel at home.

He had to leave the kitchen. Suppose she found him here: what would he say? The light, its exclusiveness, felt as though it were draining things from him. He wanted to greet her from a position of strength, not this terrible weakness even something so simple as the light could induce in him. But she was not in the living room either. The idea that the house had been deserted, that the garage door had been left open because they were no longer there, arrived like a strange letter, one he was afraid to open, certain that the news inside was bad. But where would they have gone? She was from New York, they could have gone there. She'd said nothing about family, but he assumed there must be one. It was certain, then: he was standing in a deserted house. He'd acted too late. Even the furniture looked uncongenial: a wicker chair he'd never noticed before stared out at him from its corner, daring him to sit in it. He knew he would not be comfortable sitting in it. He thought of a tall skinny man with long legs draped across that chair. How he would laugh at Henna and his dreams. "My wife could never love you," the man would say. Henna could almost hear him saying it, the high educated timbre of his voice. He was certain the man was right.

But he heard a noise just then, the scraping of a chair against wood on the floor above him, in the place where he knew her bedroom to be, and against the tall skinny man's no doubt sage advice, he raced to it.

The strip of carpeting on the stairs absorbed his footsteps, and he crept down the hallway to her room. He thought of calling, but he remembered how his voice had sounded downstairs, the inappropriateness of tone. He didn't trust his voice today. He thought he would wait until he was closer, then announce himself gently.

A few feet from her doorway, through an opening of several inches left between the bedroom door and its jamb, he saw her. He stopped, uncertain now whether to retreat, to blurt out an excuse or even to announce himself. She was sitting on her bed, pulling on a robe, her left side naked and visible to him. Her shoulders and the tops of her breasts looked fresh and pink, as if she'd just come from a bath. Even as he noted this, he thought he should be forgetting it, making it not seen. Her arms, as they reached into the arms of the robe, seemed too thin; the skin barely wriggled with the movement, and her rib cage threatened to penetrate the thin layer of whiteness covering it. Once the robe was on, her fingers began eagerly clutching at her right ear, the one invisible to him, and her head tilted that way. He moved his foot unconsciously against the floor, sending a creak the length of the hallway. She turned, something dropped. He heard a soft lopping sound on the floor as she called out questioningly, "Johnny?" But he knew she had seen him.

He moved backward, held up a hand as she came toward the door and slammed it. The hallway darkened. He looked down at the green strip of carpeting, the wood extending on either side of it. On the wall, a small painting of a girl sitting in a garden was framed in plain brown wood. He looked at these things as if the world were somehow descending away from him, and he would live now in a corridor with only these things to look at. He had failed. He had come here and, within minutes, had effortlessly achieved the thing he had spent the day warning himself and planning against. Beyond admitting that, he could do nothing but look at things and wonder what would happen next. He had no idea what to say, or how to excuse himself. Any control he might once have had over how the events in this house today would go had slipped away from him. He had allowed it to.

Finally, when it seemed she had no intention of opening the door to him, he walked the half dozen steps down the hallway and knocked on it. There was no immediate answer. He knocked again.

"Go away," he heard from inside.

"I want to explain," he mumbled, not sure even if she could hear him. Explain what? Everything she could guess at, he was guilty of. Spying on her. Invading her privacy. That none of it was intentional, or that his intention might be a different one than she could guess at, seemed, at the moment, a weak excuse.

He waited a few seconds, then tried the knob and found that the door opened. Light inched across his feet, up his legs. He saw her on the bed, her head downcast, as if she were waiting to deliver him bad news. He stood there awhile, allowing her time to begin. He found that he was strangely grateful to be standing there, to be inside the room, or nearly. To know that she would have to say something to him now, that it was not yet over.

"I didn't see anything," he said, not sure why he wasn't waiting, as he'd intended, for her to begin. He watched her eyes close. One of her temples was throbbing now.

She stood up and started for the door, as if she would go

right past him. He grabbed her wrist, to stop her, but the contact seemed to set something off in her; her hands started lunging out at him, wet, hot towels slapping against his skin. He tensed against the blows, but allowed her to continue. It didn't hurt badly. At least she was not out the door, at least she had not left him alone in the room.

"Go ahead," he said.

It made her stop, his permission. She stood and tried to catch her breath, as if it were running away from her.

"Are we never going to be free of you?"

She couldn't look at him as she said it. She looked downward. He wanted to chastise himself for her, not make her go through this agony.

"Or do we always have to be on the lookout for you? Tell me. What right do you have to do this?"

When she finally looked up at him, her face was so fierce, so changed by her anger, his panic returned. Since he'd entered the room, he'd thought there'd still been a chance. Now he could not believe anything could happen between himself and a face so belligerent.

"I didn't . . . I meant to call your name, warn you, something. I wasn't sneaking. I didn't see. Anything. Honest."

The sound that came out of her then seemed so uncontrolled, undirected, he wondered what she had intended it to be: laughter? a shriek? It was somewhere between the two. He wondered if he weren't robbing this woman of her most singular gift, that of language, and if he wouldn't, if given time, turn her, too, into a charwoman. The thought was horrible, he tried to blot it out. He lifted his hand, then, to put it onto her shoulder. She pulled away. He started, surprised to find himself returned to something, some piece of comfort given back. It was, for a moment, as if he hadn't seen any part of her.

She stood then with her face up to him, her chin jutting forward, as if expecting something. Below her chin, he could see the design on her robe, a Chinese emblem. He took a moment to look, to notice, to still time. He realized that he could make out the shape of her breasts against the fabric. The sensual—his memory of all that he wanted from this woman, all he'd imagined from the first—seemed to have entered the room and deposited itself in the place where the Chinese robe met her breasts. He could feel the beginnings of arousal, thought that was perhaps the worst thing that could happen now.

"Look," he said, losing sense of what train of logic he should be following now. The word was more a signpost to his confusion than proper communication. He moved to the bed, to hide himself and what he feared might happen. Above him, she remained standing as still as a bird, poised and ready for flight. He had to look down, because to look at her now, as the color drained from her face and it slowly returned to its natural shade, was too painful for him. He was realizing now what he should have known from the beginning: she was the most beautiful woman he had ever seen.

"Look," he said again.

"Yes. You said that."

He lit a cigarette.

Dumbly, he gestured the pack toward her. She shook her head.

"Look," he said for the third time, and his voice sounded like a small boy's, impossible to the task. What was supposed to come after? Why had he never been taught, in all these years, words adequate to passion?

A sudden pity for him must have taken hold of her. When he looked up, she looked not so stern. Her head was bobbing wonderfully on its axis. He would hold it. He would protect it. Why couldn't he say that?

"Don't you *see?*" she began, and the stress, coming after he'd expected to be forgiven, put a knot in his stomach. "Johnny and I live here, Mr. Henna. This is our house. We can't have someone always barging in."

"I wasn't barging. You don't see . . ." He thought now he could begin to explain.

"You have attached yourself to us, Mr. Henna. I would like to know why. It's not for *us* anymore."

She was still angry; the calm had been deceptive.

"It was an accident you were naked. I didn't mean for that to happen."

"Mr. Henna, you are not answering me."

He puffed twice on the tiny stub of his cigarette. He felt he'd drained her of patience; at any moment, she would jab a finger at him. It was like being scolded, that humiliating. He felt the words coming then, the only available ones, and his hand half lifted, as if to pull them down.

"I love you," he said.

The words erupted harshly, too quickly; he was not sure if they sounded even as sincere as he wished. He looked up, cautiously to see how they had registered.

Her face offered little. It looked as though she might be disappointed by the news: *that's* what you've come here to say? He heard the floor creak under her. It hurt him to know that at a moment like this you could hear a floor creak, your words had to coexist with the sounds of the natural world ignoring you.

He turned away. His cigarette was beginning to bore a hole in her white bedspread. He squeezed the fire out.

"Yes," she said, her voice lying down at last.

He looked up, hopeful. Her eyes were on the small hole in the spread. The word, the hopeful word, had had nothing to do with what he'd just said.

"Did you hear me?"

She looked at him quizzically, pained.

"Yes."

He nodded, his head tilted.

"Now will you go?"

"Go?"

"Out the door. Away. To your home. Away. Message delivered. Accepted. Thank you. No, thank you."

She moved back to the door, stood beside it, to guide his exit.

Was this to be it, then, his "message," as she'd called it, delivered, rejected, then to be ushered out the door? No, it was because he'd chosen the wrong words. They'd told her nothing. It had been like handing her an emotion: what could she do with it? He had to dig deeper, find words that encompassed a plan, something she could enter, too.

It occurred to him, then, the extent to which he'd been living internally. All she knew of his day was that he'd come in, surprised her, mumbled a few words, told her he loved her. But where, to trace the rest, could he begin?

When he looked up, exhaustion had replaced every other emotion on her face. She had that facility, to change emotions without his help.

"Please, Mr. Henna. I am so tired."

He watched her as she stood leaning against the door, looking out into the hall. For a moment, before she closed her robe, he noticed one breast was mostly visible. It was small, perfectly molded in the shape of an upended Bosc pear, and it fell into her robe with the swoop and delicacy of a swan's wing. He thought it would be such pleasure to touch it. Then, seeing her pull the robe tighter, he knew it wouldn't do any good to talk to her in the language of his flesh; this wasn't what he was here for, not first, not until much later. For her to think so would be to defeat his plans. She could then peg him: you are exactly what I imagined at first, and was repulsed by.

He cleared his throat.

"Last night," he began.

"No, don't tell me. I don't want to know what happened last night."

She looked at him once, with hardness, as punctuation. Then she looked out into the hall, seemingly arrested by something there.

"But you gave me the car." He had not intended it to come out as a whine.

She turned to him then, and a gentle smile passed over her lips.

"Is that what this is about? The car? I gave you the car because I felt sorry for you, Mr. Henna. It was hot."

He cleared his throat again. He thought he'd been about to make progress, now she was diminishing him, making him a creature deserving of pity, subject to the sun's excesses.

"I would have walked," he said, as if that changed the meaning of her gift.

"Yes, I know. And I should have let you. But an act of charity—it seemed to me, in my delusion yesterday, that you had done something rather selfless for me, and I ought to be charitable in return."

Her hair was so alive, her nose pointed so solemnly forward! It was impossible that the act could have been charity alone, why couldn't she admit it? This was not a charitable face, but a face that knew its intent. She would not have made this mistake, not purposely. Overnight she must have changed her mind. He thought his work was cut out for him now, and had to fight the urge to go to her and hold her.

"Mr. Henna, this may be difficult to believe, but all I meant by that gesture was 'take the car,' " she said to the floor between them. "I meant nothing more, nothing beyond it. Is that much clear?"

He nodded, certain of nothing.

"Now will you go? Can I make this simple statement and have myself, for once, understood. Go."

She was leaning toward him, her face once again full of color.

"No," he said, still nodding, searching for the beginning of an explanation.

"Then I will call the police."

She reached for the phone. He had to allow it. He couldn't keep her from calling the police without presenting himself as a criminal. If that was how it was to end, so be it. To be escorted out, in disgrace. His heart thumped heavily. He could imagine Lavolli finding out. "Jack," he would say, the way he said it, in preface to firing him. No, he could not believe that would actually happen. She dialed two numbers and hung up.

"I will not call the police."

She brushed the hair away from her forehead. The wisps of it moved like dust particles in a shaft of light. She kept her eyes on the phone, uncertain of what she had done.

"You would lose your job, wouldn't you?"

He nodded. "But I don't care about my job."

"You have a family, Mr. Henna."

He remembered Thomas going into the Round-Up, thought of him choosing, from among the stacks there, the one thing he wanted to surprise his father with. Then he thought of Thomas finding his father naked, prostrate, on the ground in his backyard, and withholding the gift.

"Yes, but I was about to tell you."

"Please, can we talk *facts*, Mr. Henna. I don't want to hear about your love for me. Forgive me, but it seems entirely beside the point. Can we look in front of us for a moment?"

He looked up at her. The suggestion, her clearheadedness, made him gulp, as though a new idea had been presented to him, one requiring a response.

"Facts. You want to talk facts." He fixed his gaze on the bottom of her robe. "I told you one. I love you. Fact."

He was surprised at the sound of his own voice. He hadn't known it could be so easy to say such things. When he looked up at her, he saw she was staring into the wood on the floor, her mouth tensed. He only half expected a response, waited only a moment for it.

"You're still beautiful," he said. "You're still . . . young. You've got a boy."

She moved her foot along the floor.

"Do I want another husband, Mr. Henna? Am I aching for a lover? Is that your assumption today?"

"No." The hollowness of his response made him turn away.

"I tried something, failed at it, am not looking to try again."

"You didn't fail. It's not your fault he killed himself."

"How do you know?"

"I know. A man wouldn't kill himself if he had a woman like you to go to, unless he was blind, or crazy . . ."

"Yes." Her face had closed in on itself, become sharp and red. "One always sees one's . . . love as the solution to the problem. It's beyond your comprehension that someone might see the person he loves as part of the problem itself. Isn't it? Mr. Henna, have you ever known a suicide?"

"No."

"Then please don't presume to talk about them."

The way she was looking at him made him feel suddenly small and worthless, as though everything she'd always said about him and his presumptions was, after all, true.

"Now I have listened to you, Mr. Henna. And I believe you are sincere when you say you love me. But in a larger sense, I can't accept that."

"Why?"

What she did then astonished him. It seemed, at first, a slight movement, the opening outward of her palms on either side of her body, but the effect it gave was like an ascension of all of her parts into a higher, sweeter plane, lifting above all the bitterness and anger he'd had to contend with since finding her on the bed. She seemed, in the moment, a younger, less certain woman, one whose uncertainties made her tremulous.

"Because I've no idea what you see," she said, "or who this person is you say you love. It's not me, not the self I know. I am unworthy of love, Mr. Henna. Yours or anyone's."

Her hand then, as if it were a separate, judging part of her, began to slice the air. She looked as though she wanted to revise the room, change the places of all its objects.

"Oh, God, here I go being melodramatic."

She moved away, her hands wrapped around her body suddenly, as if she had gone too far, and the robe had opened.

"You don't believe me. I know. You think I think less of myself than I am. I assure you, to go on living requires me to invent, each day, a self worthy of getting up in the morning."

She breathed hard, tightened her grip on herself, then let her hands fall.

"All right, have I said enough?"

He stood and kissed her. That is, for a second, before she turned away, his lips brushed against her dry lips. It stunned him. She was the first woman, besides Nancy, that he had ever gotten this close to. Now the fold of her robe against her shoulder as he touched it seemed immensely larger to him than his own wife, a thing that could contain a thousand Nancys.

"I am a widow less than a month," she said, still turned.

"I know."

"Don't you have a religion, or something, that prevents this?"

"Yes," he said, and tried again.

Her hand forced him back. He stayed far enough away so that she would not feel him. He put both hands on her shoulder, and drew her closer, still not touching. Her eyes were so frightened, he couldn't kiss her. His lips touched her forehead, cheeks. He wanted to worship her, to communicate worship. What part of a woman did you kiss when you wanted to do that? The eyes? Too much like a father. His lips went to the ear offered him as she turned to the side. He absorbed the lobe and tasted blood.

Pulling back, he saw the pinpoint of red, wondered, had he bitten her?

He licked it again, to hide the wound from her. When he pulled back, it was gone.

"I'm sorry. I made you bleed."

"Oh. Not you. I was doing something foolish before. But please, no."

She looked straight up at him, as if the kissing had had no effect. He pulled her to him, knew now that she could feel him, was ashamed and humiliated by the fact, but had, somehow, to let her know.

"I love you so much," he said, meaning it now.

She looked at him without reproach, without particular fear. She was mulling something, quietly, keeping her own counsel, before letting him know.

"And where is this to end, Mr. Henna? On the bed here, or somewhere out on the farm? Is that what you propose?"

He shook his head no, then moved back so no part of him was touching her.

"No. I want to help out here. I want to help Johnny."

He said it slowly, each word measured. It was an effort to return to the sense of help.

"And do you suppose that's what he wants?"

"Who?"

"My son."

She looked at him clearly, a measuring as succinct as any he'd ever received. It took only a minute. Then she allowed her eyes to slip. The quickness, the finality of what she had just done made him furious. He wanted her to measure him again.

"Look at me," he said. His bravery thrilled him, the simplicity of the demand.

At last she did.

"I'm not making myself clear. I want to stay here, but I won't demand anything. I'll live in the barn, I'll make a bunk for myself there."

She laughed.

"And shall I clang the triangle to call you in for breakfast? Shall we call you the hired hand?"

"Don't laugh at me. It's not a joke."

"No. Forgive me."

She stared at him another minute, then went and sat by the window. He was standing above her. She motioned for him to sit on the bed. He knew what he must have looked like, standing above her, hulking over her, but he did not want to sit. As soon as she moved away, he wanted to be embracing her again. But he sat down, wanting to be compliant, not wanting to represent a threat. He bunched a fistful of the bedclothes in his hand and squeezed, trying to make his need go down. When he looked up, she was staring at him from the window seat. Again, the intent, serious, entirely private mulling washed over her features.

"That first day you came here, and we sat across the room downstairs, and that ridiculous man, his name—"

"Valenti."

"Yes. Mr. Valenti."

He became angry at this. Valenti should not be mentioned here. Valenti had no place.

"Listening to him as he went on and on, I wanted to just rid myself of the two of you, just say, 'Oh, go, go and take your money. I will not have this.' But there was a way you looked at me. I thought to myself: It's time you dealt with the real world.

You seemed entirely serious, Mr. Henna, as though you'd accommodated yourself to something Sam and I had spent our lives ignoring."

She paused, she collected.

"And then you began to pry, and I wondered if I hadn't become the victim of a ruse. Still, it is my fault as much as yours that I allowed . . . the attraction."

She looked at him now, entirely serious.

Henna thought this was amazing, this was wonderful. It was as though there were suddenly pulsebeats in his arms so strong they would lift him.

"Appointments with you were the only fixed things in my days." Her hands came to rest, open, on her lap. Her head dipped forward, just slightly. She smiled the vaguest smile.

Henna hung back, in wonder. Was she inferring that romance had once entered her head as a possibility? As much as he wanted it, he couldn't get over the fact that in some small part of her, she might actually have considered it. Now she was looking at the door. Her eyes had become tired.

"Will you take my husband's car, and will you go now? I've said everything. I want you to have the car, as a gesture."

She was making an end of it. But no, she had said before there was an attraction, he couldn't let it end there. He felt intensely the sense of a loose string, an idea somewhere—probably right in front of him—that, if he could only find it, could keep him here.

"And how will you survive?" he asked, hoping that almost any idea, if followed to its conclusion, might yield an opening.

"We will survive."

"You're not being pragmatic. What will you eat?"

"There is food. I have explained that to you." Her head went forward, as if she were unsure of the fact now, and wanted the former argument to suffice.

From his position on the bed, he leaned forward, rested his elbows on his knees, clasped his hands together. They had moved, somehow, closer to one another. Only a few feet remained between his clasped hands and her knees.

"You think it's enough to live off this farm? You think you won't need things. What are you eating tonight?"

"I haven't thought."

"I could run into town, pick up some things for you. Meat." He thought this might be the thing he was looking for: he would cook for them.

"That's not necessary."

"What's in the refrigerator?"

"Mr. Henna, there is no need . . ."

"What's there?"

"Broccoli." She stopped a moment, her mouth still circling the word, as if she'd been caught at something. "I picked it myself yesterday."

"You're going to eat broccoli? By itself?"

"Yes. What is wrong with that?"

She looked angrily at him then, but not the way she had before. This argument was occurring on another level; some of her anger, he could tell, was directed at herself.

"Just broccoli. For a growing boy. You've gotta make more of an effort."

"I do *fine.*"

"For now."

He stopped, pointed his finger at her, but gently, chastising, wondering how far he could go with this.

"Look, it's been less than a month. You are, you're doing all right, but a kid has got to get more than vegetables. Without a car, it's like you're cutting off his life support."

She looked at him with an intense hardness in her features, set against him. Quickly, though, it seemed to cave in, as though she were looking for a new line of defense.

"Broccoli, by itself," he clucked. "Did you know I can cook?"

She looked down, away.

"I might have known," she said, under her breath.

"What?"

"I said I might have known."

"Well, would you like me to?"

"No."

"I will. I'll cook for you tonight."

"Mr. Henna."

"He's gotta eat." He reached out, and could just take her chin in his hands. He was surprised she allowed it. "You hear me? You can't starve him, and you can't just feed him broccoli. You say you want the real, you want me to be real. I'll teach you how to cook things. That's all. Then I'll go. If you want to go on dreaming, fine."

As he said the words about cooking, he was remembering Nancy, her skills. He felt oddly grateful for them. He stood up.

"Listen to me. I'm not going to hurt you. I won't kiss you again if that's not what you want. I'm not here for that anyway. The one thing I want to do is help you."

He rocked back on his heels, looking at her face, the odd mixture of moods there, like the surface of water when your line is tight and you have no idea what you might bring up.

"Now don't fool yourself. You need help. One meal, one bit of health, so I know things are all right here. I can't leave until I know that."

He took her chin in his hand again. This time, though, it made her look uncomfortable, so he took his hand away.

"I'm sorry. I won't even do that much if it's not what you want."

But he hugged her, quickly and tightly, as if it was the last time he would do so.

"I'm sorry for that, too. But that's all. A promise."

He moved to the door. To wait for her to say yes would be a mistake. Only his energy was unstoppable, his desire for permission the one thing she could still affect. If he moved, he could deny her that. He felt close enough, too, to the point where she would allow it, where a simple action might get him over the edge. He could see now there were tiny ripples on the surface of her skin, the way she had looked when she'd decided not to call the cops on him after all.

"Look, I want to make things up to you, that's all. I came in and embarrassed you, and I want to apologize. I'm across the room now, see? I'm not even close. I'm not going to hurt you. I just want you to know I'm a guy you can rely on. Anything you need, I can do it for you. I want to."

It ached him to have to phrase his desire in these terms, to geld and nullify it. He wondered if it counted as deceit. He wanted to make a joke, to break through this crust.

"A guy you can rely on," she repeated, weighing it like an oversweet morsel in her mouth.

He ran his foot along the floorboards. "I don't know how to talk. I don't know how to say anything." He wanted to joke. He didn't know where this would lead. "So, I'll go downstairs, I'll see what you've got, then I'll shoot down to the store, come back with the goods."

"This is absurd," she said.

"But that's not no." He said it before thinking, worried that in reintroducing the issue of permission, he might have undone himself. There must have been something jaunty, just slightly ridiculous and unthreatening in the way he said it, though. She was looking at him the way you would look at someone you could afford to be amused by.

He gestured, with one of his hands, for her to sit tight. But when he followed his hand's gesture to the floor, he noticed a small, shiny object there. He went and picked it up, regretting now that something was keeping him in the room, keeping him from acting.

She coughed, then admitted: "My foolishness."

She was sitting straight up in her chair, as though he had caught her at something she was ashamed of. He was holding a tiny gold earring in his hand. The source of the blood on her ear was made clear.

She bit her lip.

"I wanted, before, to see if they would still go in. I wondered what a touch of glamour would feel like, these days."

She was trying to appear proud as she said it. It touched him immensely.

He held the small gold stud in his hands. He knew he should leave it and go out the door. She was too vulnerable now. She would not stop him from cooking. But something about the earring, and the small drop of blood he remembered, kept him there.

"Let me try," he said.

She looked up. "No."

He moved toward her.

"Mr. Henna."

"You wanted to look pretty."

They looked at each other. In her eyes was some frightened sense of how quickly and thoroughly he understood her. Her head bobbed slightly, as though she were gesturing with the ear and then holding back at the same time. He touched her ear. The way she shuddered now made him drop the earring. He searched on the floor for it.

When he rose, she let him take her ear. Resistance had gone out of her. She started to cry, silently, as he gently touched the place in her ear where it had been pierced, years ago. A spot of red appeared. He'd missed. It grew. He ran to the bathroom, saying, "Jesus. Jesus." When he came back, she was still crying. He had cotton and witch hazel in his hand. He drenched the cotton and applied it to her ear. He thought he'd ruined everything, and now would have to go. For the chance to put an earring in her ear! His foolishness, inability to stop himself, seemed a flaw so enormous he wondered how he ever thought he'd get around it.

But when he'd finished, when the blood had stopped and he'd moved away from her, he saw she'd been affected in a way he couldn't have guessed.

She was not looking at him. There was nothing to indicate she cared for him any more than she'd done when he'd first come into the room and she'd lashed out at him with her hands. But in the moment before she spoke, he knew he'd somehow been given permission to stay.

"Mr. Henna, you seem to have a talent"—she stopped, had to clear away some obstruction to the words—"for finding places in me that no one has touched in a very long time. Forgive me," she said coldly, gathering herself.

She was staring into the center of the room, into the space between them, as though alluding to a third force, something they might as well both admit existed. It was, for him, a strange, curiously freeing moment. Perhaps she had never before resented him so much. But he had his permission now. He lifted his hand halfway up—the gesture seemed from another time, he was not even sure what he meant by it—then headed for the kitchen to begin his work.

8

HE SEARCHED through the refrigerator, hauled out broccoli, parsley, a clove of garlic. Otherwise, there was nothing usable: a tall juice container full of water, a bottle of ketchup, a glass dish holding half a slab of butter. He searched for a pencil to make a list of the things they would need. Now that he'd been given her silent permission, he would have to decide what, from his limited repertoire, he could make them.

He looked out the window and realized, with gratefulness, that the light was leaving him alone now. The sun had gone behind the barn. In the coolness and hesitancy of this light, he could almost see himself on this farm, a part of it. Out the back window, he could see his image, returning in the evening from the fields. It was a comfortable image, he seemed secure in it, and wondered if he should allow himself that comfort. He'd been intensely aware, since leaving her bedroom, of the tenuousness of his being here now, her hesitant allowance of it, that it had been achieved by nothing he'd said, but by the incident with the earring. He had not understood what had happened—he cursed himself now for the limitations of his experience with women, his former mad dash toward the university of his wife, leaving him a faulty interpreter of the behavior of all other woman—but he knew that somehow, in his medicinal handling of her ear, even in the clumsiness of it, he had done himself more good than all his words about starving the boy had. But, because he didn't understand just what he had done, he thought that at any minute she could come down and change her mind and he would have no defense against it, no way of saying why he must stay.

When he sat down and began to write at the top of the list the word "milk," he noticed his hand had begun to shake. They had a cow. That they might have milk stored elsewhere seemed but the latest in a wealth of secrets the farm was holding back from him. He would have to go and ask. But to keep asking seemed to be placing him further and further back from the place where his will could have any effect. He could just go and buy it, but then imagined himself returning, them going through his purchases: "We don't need this. Or this. This we already have." Eventually their inferences would come down to him, the man himself, as a thing they didn't need. His hand was still shaking as he crossed the word out.

What *did* they need? As he had in the room before, he felt the presence of a single path that, if followed, might gain him admittance here. He remembered the woods the other day, the search for his son, his near-despair just before the point where he'd found the way out. The important thing would be not to give up, not to be frightened. He decided against going to the store, it would be too risky to bring home unnecessary items. He would have to apprentice himself a little first, watch how they operated, use what was here. He searched one cupboard, found a box of crackers, spaghetti, cupcake holders, an old box of Bisquick, toothpicks. In another, oil, vinegar, salt, pepper, a box of Bay's seasoning. Sparse, but it would have to do. Nancy would know how to do something with this. He should have paid more attention. If there were tomatoes outside, he could make a sauce, but that would take hours. It was nearly six. They would be hungry.

Then, considering the broccoli, he remembered a dish from the old country, a simple spaghetti and broccoli concoction of

his mother's. He'd had it only a few times since marriage, but
he remembered he'd loved it. He set about cutting into the
broccoli, making two deep incisions in the base. It made him
happy, to have arrived at so simple a solution. He reached
down—the rise and fall of his passion in the room before had
left his crotch feeling damp and moldly—and scratched there.
When his hand came back up, it had the testicly smell of unal-
layed lust on it; he could imagine it infecting the food, their
knowing him at his basest. He washed his hands quickly. Outside the kitchen window, he saw now that Johnny Adams had
been watching him.

"Johnny!" he called through the window when the boy
turned and started to run. His characteristic gesture, Henna
thought, though this time it was his own, not Johnny's, sexual
secret on display. He ran out the door after him.

The boy stopped halfway to the barn. He looked back at
Henna, solemnly, as though his running away had had to do
with something prior, not with Henna's appearance at all.

"What?" he said.

Henna held the broccoli before him. He'd taken it with him.
He wanted to say, "I'm going to save that barn for you." Instead he said, "I'm cooking."

The boy looked up, locked eyes with him for only a second,
just time enough to show Henna a contempt so deep he wanted
to flinch from it but, strangely, didn't. He couldn't help it, he
still found the boy beautiful. His skin had been burnished so
brown it was as if the sun were molding him, making him over.
He thought of his own sons, how they would get tans and lose
them. This boy, his mother: their combined beauty was so astonishing he thought he would cry. Then he thought of Adams
climbing into his car, breathing the deadly exhaust, tried to
imagine a despair so deep it could make even the sight of such
beauty intolerable. This was inconceivable to him. No matter
what had gone wrong, just the possibility of looking at this boy
and saying, "I made this," should have been enough to pull him
through.

"You're going to love it," he said.

"Love what?"

"Dinner."

The boy's words were aggressive and frightened at once: "I'm not hungry."

"No. But you will be. It's almost suppertime."

The boy gulped hard. He was ashamed to show what he was feeling. He looked down. It seemed to be just now adding up for him: his own powerlessness to keep Henna from taking over. He moved into the barn, out of Henna's sight.

Henna stood awhile against the door, listening. He heard a rapping against glass. Mrs. Adams was at the kitchen window, motioning for him to come. The broccoli was still in his hand. He held it up foolishly: See! I'm cooking.

In the kitchen, she leaned against the sink, not looking at him. She was wearing the brown shift she'd worn yesterday. Behind her he could see the dark barn. It was as if they were each enclosed in darkness and he was standing at the doors of their closed rooms, listening.

"Mr. Henna, perhaps this isn't a good idea."

"No. I'm cooking. It's already started."

"Well, then perhaps you should show me how to finish."

"It's a recipe from my island. You could watch me, but you couldn't do it yourself."

She looked at him, appraising what he'd said, but somehow softer, less brittle than she'd been before.

"Are you going to insist on eating with us?"

It was a clear, simple, bluntly phrased question. It was like the tightening of a fist around the base of his stomach.

"I hadn't . . ." He couldn't finish. Of course he'd intended to eat with them, but now it occurred to him, the act of help ended with the cooking. His staying would have to be a gesture on their part. He couldn't invite himself.

"You'll cook and then you'll leave, is that the understanding?"

"Yes." He nodded. There was no other answer. He wanted to put the earring in her ear again, to return them to that place. She was negating it with logic, with simple requests. He would not think beyond the cooking. He would simply do it, and pray for a reprieve.

She waited until he was finished nodding, stared at him a second longer, then closed her eyes.

"It would hurt him very much," she said.

She smoothed the skirt of her shift. He wondered why she chose such a dress, the way it hid the wonders underneath in such a dull, shapeless boxing. Her cheekbones quivered. She was thinking something. He wished to God to know what. Her hand went up to brush away a wisp of hair. The fading light caught it in flight. When she left the room a second later, he found himself still staring at the window, where her head had been framed.

He stood the broccoli up in boiling water and arranged the lid on the pot so that the broccoli would remain standing as long as he needed it to. Then he chopped garlic, poured a small amount of oil in a frying pan and let the garlic cook slowly. He absorbed himself in cooking. He would do it all slowly. The longer he was here, the greater were his chances of being allowed to stay.

When the spaghetti was cooked (he'd put it in the same boiling water that the broccoli had cooked in), he drained it and the broccoli in a strainer he'd found under the stove. It was wonderful the way the broccoli fell apart when he mixed it with the spaghetti. Then he poured the oil and garlic over the mixture and tossed it together some more. His mind had gone blank in all this cooking; he'd nearly forgotten that his work had a purpose, and that the purpose excluded him. He'd become a man doing a job, with no idea what would come next. Their own actions, the woman's and the boy's, were apparently stilled; no sound came from above him in the house, and he had not seen the boy come out of the barn. He would have to call them soon. He set the table, then when that was finished (set for only two, he wouldn't force himself, though he kept one dish ready on the sink), garnished the bowl of spaghetti with a few of the parsley leaves. He'd never done this before. Usually when he cooked, he did it in such a utilitarian manner it seemed needlessly refined not to eat out of the pot itself. Now he placed the dish on the table, went to the stairs and called up to her.

It was a few minutes before she appeared. He was annoyed that the food might be getting cold. When she came she looked at the food, not at him, said, "Oh," and brushed back her hair, as if it were bothering her. She looked like she couldn't quite figure out what he had made. Then her face changed. Apparently she had determined to eat it, whatever it was. He felt so foolish now, standing there, exhausted by his effort. They would not appreciate it. It was the wrong direction to go in, he knew now.

"I'll call Johnny," she said.

He watched her, through the kitchen window, as she walked to the barn. Again he watched her body underneath the dull shift. It was as though he had made love to her, knew secrets that allowed him to look at her in a special way. But he had not made love to her; indeed, what he had seen was a thing he thought he had best forget. She would not like to know he was looking at her now with a proprietary interest, a sense of having been places other men were not allowed. He thought of walking with her in a city, in a crowd; clutching her arm a little tighter when he saw another man looking at her. But he knew how inappropriate that would be. He had no more rights than any other man. He wished that they were still upstairs, he were still watching her in the Chinese robe. With an exquisite pang he thought of what another man might have done in that situation, what Valenti might have done. But that was foolish: she would have called the police on Valenti, she had called him "stupid."

Johnny was not coming out. She knocked twice on the door and received no answer. He heard the words "All right, then!" and saw her come marching back to the house. When she was inside, she said, "Sit down, Mr. Henna. You and I are going to eat."

He was not surprised. He took his dish from the sink and

filled it with spaghetti, then filled hers. He poured them both glasses of water.

She said, "Am I *wrong?*" and turned over her water glass. She only sat and stared at it, though. He cleaned it up. When he was finished, she looked over at him, not demanding anything, but rather sweetly, he thought. Her face seemed, for the first time, round. He wanted this to be an intimate conversation they had every night when they sat down to dinner. He wanted that to be the familiar shape of her face when she recounted something rather touching that had happened to her that day, how a fat woman had knocked her into the cat-food counter at the supermarket. He wanted her to touch his forearm lightly as she told it, to say, "Isn't that funny, dear?" He thirsted for intimacy from this woman in a way that was deeper than lust.

"Perhaps you'd better go."

He stopped eating. It surprised him. He was imagining the fat woman in the supermarket. Now she was putting in motion again the apparatus that would remove him from her life.

But Johnny appeared at the door, and saved him.

They both looked up. The boy looked beseechingly at his mother, the mixture of moods that children are capable of working away at the bones beneath his skin. Henna thought: These people's bodies are like tents under which such a variety of life happens; yet the bodies themselves go nowhere, move through only these familiar rooms. He'd never known such a wealth of internal life before. It seemed a thing with powers of its own, moving toward him, then away, invisible to him yet constantly affecting his position, like a tide.

"I had just asked Mr. Henna to leave," she said.

The boy would not look at him.

"I think that's cruel, don't you? He's made this meal for us, after all. He has stayed here, and cooked for us, when he has other things to do."

There was a cold, forceful anger underneath words which seemed to trip along the surface of meaning like flat stones.

"I hate you," the boy said, still looking at his mother, though Henna was sure the words were directed at him.

The woman got up and slapped him. Then she sat down again. Henna stood up, determined to leave.

He watched the boy's face redden deeply before he started to cry. In his youth, when American boys had cried like that, he'd been shocked. He had not thought of the boys who could speak well, whose parents had been here for years and years and who seemed quiet and dry, as possessing such reserves of passion or being acquainted with a *heat* like the one he and his mother lived in, where tears were as much a part of the day as the noon meal. That he had caused this pain was excruciating. He would go, he had to go.

"Sit down, Mr. Henna. This is quite delicious."

She didn't mean it. The falsity was almost cruel. Johnny sat down, too, then, his head in his hands. Through the covering hands, Henna saw his red face.

"Look," he started to say, and thought that nothing whatsoever could make sense now, no logic could intrude with any force on a scene so primal. He would have to sit and wait. That she seemed to require him now was enough.

She spooned spaghetti onto Johnny's dish. He looked at it and moved it away.

"I want you to eat that."

Her voice had lost anger, become so loving, in so short a space of time, he looked at her and expected to see a different woman. Somehow, though, he had become, in the space of a minute, excluded. She and her child had locked into one another in such a way that he felt, once again, as though he were listening, behind a door, to an event going on in a room closed to him. Light was falling more quickly now. He wondered if he weren't, in fact, sitting in darkness while the two of them snatched at the available light.

"Are you going to eat?" she asked.

The boy looked again at the food, one hand at his forehead, sobs still issuing from him in short, raspy groans. He picked up a fistful of the spaghetti and broccoli and squeezed it in disgust.

She took his wrist and shook it until he dropped the food.

"This is not what we eat!" the boy said.

"We're eating it now, Johnny."

"No. When we eat spaghetti, we have it with sauce. When we have broccoli, we have it plain, on the side."

He removed the broccoli, separated it on his plate, to show her. His words, punctuated by gasping, painful efforts to catch his breath, were an effort to reveal to her a truth so formidable he could not believe she would have transgressed it knowingly. Henna was an interloper who had undone the very nature of their most private act, the silent breaking of bread in the evening, a ritual whose rules were sacred.

"Mr. Henna makes it this way. It's from your island, didn't you say? Perhaps you could tell Johnny about your island."

She placed a forkful of the spaghetti in her mouth as if it were an unpleasant duty. Henna panicked at the suggestion: what could he possibly say now that would convince the boy of anything? But again Johnny saved him.

"I don't want to hear about any island."

"No," Henna affirmed, nodding.

"Perhaps you should, Johnny. Perhaps you should know something other than what goes on on this farm."

The boy looked up at her. He looked as though he'd been betrayed, and had no inkling as to the source.

"Tell him, Mr. Henna. Tell him how you lived."

Henna cleared his throat, fumbling for an answer. The question was simple enough, but, because of who it came from, and who he would have to answer to, made him feel his own history as a long bankruptcy, something he might as well make up on the spot.

"Well, it was a lot like this, but not, not really," he started.

The boy dropped his fork loudly, deliberately.

"Johnny."

The woman continued to fork the food in. Did she like it?

"We would only farm in the morning, you see, until it got too hot. Then, in the afternoons, the men would go out and fish."

Johnny was not looking at him. He played with his food, digging the fork deeply into the spaghetti, then turning it over, drawing up bits of oil and broccoli that had settled on the bottom. Henna looked at the woman: what more do you want me to tell him?

"And that was all you needed."

"Oh, yes. There was a miller, for bread. You'd thrash your own wheat, then bring it to him. And you made your own wine."

He stopped. He could go on now, get lost in the telling, but he wasn't sure what point she would have him make, and was afraid of missing it. He tried to gesture with his face, for her to guide him.

"And tell me. Tell Johnny. Do people there still live that way, now?"

"No." He shook his head.

"Why?" She was too eager, stepping on him. She bit down hard on a forkful of broccoli. He could hear the grating of her teeth on the tines of the fork.

"Well, most people went away, for one thing. And the island, see, was cultivated by terracing. All the way up the hills, the land was dug out to make, like, terraces. Once you let that go, it's hard to restore it. The overgrowth is tremendous, it eats up all the work that went to make it."

"But if you wanted to, you could."

"Could what?"

"Restore it."

"Oh, sure. It'd be a lot of work, but I suppose you could."

"And live exactly the way you once lived. Idyllically. Could you return to that, Mr. Henna?"

"Could I?"

"Could one?"

It was odd. She seemed to be ignoring the boy, but everything she said was directed as much to the boy as to him.

"Well, that'd be hard," Henna said. "There's no more miller, for one. And everybody now makes their money off of tourism. The Germans like to come in the summer, and the people on the island rent out rooms to them. You could do it, I suppose, but you might be laughed at. All the food is shipped in now, the connections to the mainland are better. You could do it, though. You might not be too successful . . ."

He let his voice trail off. Her head, poised above the plate of food he had fixed for her, seemed to stop in motion.

"That was not quite the point I was hoping you would make, Mr. Henna." She dug once more into her food.

"Why?"

She coughed, freeing a bit of broccoli. "I was hoping you would say it would be sheer folly, even trying to do so."

"Well . . ."

"Isn't that what you believe?"

"No, I could, I could see a man trying to live again that way. I could see it if he didn't care about the modern things. It wasn't a bad way to live, really. It's like what you said the other day, about owning what's yours."

"What did I say?"

"How it's better to own what's yours. Not to rent. Not to have too much of a choice, either. Though, well, we've got a choice now, don't we?"

"Your father's idea," she began brusquely, ignoring his question, speaking directly to her son now, "was to *try* to live that way."

She looked at the boy a long moment. Henna was unsure whether the expression of intense concern on her face meant she would cry or merely wipe the boy's face with a napkin. She did neither.

"But there is no more miller, is there, Mr. Henna?"

He was startled to be included again.

"No, the miller sends bills instead," she said.

She forced another forkful of food into her mouth, but seemed to decide immediately against it. She held a napkin to her mouth and coughed the food out. The sight of it saddened Henna.

"See?" Johnny said. "I told you this food's no good." In his voice was the sense of how desperately he wanted her for his ally now.

"The food is fine," she said, getting up, removing her napkin and depositing it in the wastebasket. "I've just had enough of it, that's all."

She sat down as though they were waiting for her to resume.

"I had Mr. Henna tell you that story, Johnny, because I wanted you to understand that what we have been through these past years, the way we've lived, is not the common way to live, not the usual. And if we are to crawl back, somehow, to a more usual mode, you have to expect the uncommon. Mr. Henna here, making us dinner. We can't see it as an affront to your father's memory. We have to see it, rather, as the thing we most need now, which is help."

Henna felt graced by her words. He beamed, and looked toward Johnny, not feeling he quite deserved this.

"I don't need any help," the boy said.

"No, I don't imagine you think you do. You'll do just fine, won't you, with no one to drive you to school, and with twenty thousand dollars to get you and your mother through the rest of their lives together."

"You could learn to drive," the boy said.

"Fine. And who will teach me?"

The boy's inability to answer that question was apparently too much for him. He grasped the edges of his plate and spun it so that it landed perilously close to the edge of the table.

"Does that mean he's got to teach you?"

"No!" She was furious. "I was using him as an example."

Johnny knocked his plate onto the floor, looked up once, briefly, and ashamed, at his mother.

When Henna looked at her, her face was round again. The world was momentarily overwhelming her. She would never beseech him, though. He would just have to stay attuned to her moods, hear the unspoken. He bent down to pick up the fallen meal.

"Help him," he heard her whisper to her son. He was not sure why, but he was thinking of the boy inside her, the things that sort of relationship implied. When she said, "Help him," or anything, in fact, at all, could she ever feel she was talking to a being strictly outside herself?

"It's all right," Henna heard himself saying. "I made the wrong thing, I guess."

"It was fine," he heard her say above him, again. How many times had she said that? Yet through the entire meal he had remained unconvinced.

He heard Johnny's chair shuffle above him, too, knocking into the table in what must have been an effort to get as far from Henna as possible.

He finished his cleaning job, then stood above his chair, suddenly not sure he had the right to sit down again.

"Well, we're doing just fine, aren't we?"

She was looking at her son. Why didn't the boy just go? He and the woman had things to talk about now. But Johnny sat there, standing his ground, evidently determined to make a shambles of whatever either of them proposed.

"Mr. Henna, there are some things I'd like you to look at."

When he looked up at her, he thought he had never seen that expression on her face before. From what he had witnessed of her behavior thus far, he'd come to think of her as a woman who thought exhaustively, came to a decision and then acted passionately on it, even if her face left some indication that she was not entirely sure it had been the *right* decision. But here the idea had just seemed to *land* on her. He could not afford to be scrupulous, though.

"Sure, whatever," was what he said.

The blankness in her features gave way to a hard setting of her jaw, as if *against* the idea and his easy assent to it. But when she looked at her son, these negative signs fell away. She got up and went to look for whatever it was she would show him, leaving Henna alone with the boy.

Henna sat down. The boy shifted in his chair, then, turning subtly away, looked up to where his mother had gone. Henna tried to think of what to say.

Behind the boy, he could see the barn now, losing the last light, a deeper crimson climbing slowly—upward or downward?—with the sun's descent. There had been no clouds, so there was no vibrant sunset to deck it out gorgeously, just a slow unfolding of new colors, forcing him to look at it differently. A barn unused seemed such a huge, delicate construction, such an enormous waste. As it had when he'd come back from the walk to Adams' dam, it had the power to stir his soul, to make him want to put it to use. He wanted to tell Johnny, "I will save it for you." It felt so oddly poignant to be sitting across from this boy, with the power to effect changes that would deal him a life a little better, perhaps a great deal better, than the one he would otherwise have. He could see the boy and his mother trekking about, living here and there as refugees, in rooms, having little to say to one another, until the day came when the first girl to act kindly toward him became the girl he would marry, most likely a dull girl, one who would never know him in his entirety. And in the sad nights of his marriage, he would lie down beside her and think: At least I am not alone with my mother, in rooms.

Henna knew, too, what it was to be fatherless. All he could remember of his own father was in a picture, kept by his mother, of a timid man in a dark gray suit whose huge, watery eyes had already begun to suffer the effects of the illness that had finally killed him. His father's death had happened early, and Henna thought his own life had been in large part altered, made more cautious by it.

"I'd like to, with your permission, do some work on that barn."

The boy looked at him.

"Why?"

"It's falling."

"It's not. That's just something my mom thought. My dad knew."

"Knew what?"

"She made him worried, so he went in and looked. It was fine, he said."

How quickly this boy could make him feel superfluous! The barn was fine. So would the boy's life be, probably. In New York, she would fall back on family money, send this boy to a good school. He would not marry the first nice girl that came along, he would not even *meet* a girl like Nancy. Or if he did, he would desert her. He was that supercilious, that superior. It was a mistake to assume that everyone was exactly like Jack Henna.

"Well, I could look at it again" was all he could muster after that. And it seemed instantly unnecessary, another looking at the barn, a following in Adams' footsteps. He would have to come up with something different, an alternative to Adams, if he were to make any headway. He had to remind himself, this was a guy who killed himself, removed himself forcibly from these people's lives! Here they were treating him like some kind of god, a man in whose footsteps you'd better fear to tread.

"You loved your dad, didn't you, Johnny?"

The boy looked down at the floor, then quickly up again, as if in looking down he might have missed his mother's return. "Yeah," he said finally, but phrased it as a question.

"I don't want to take his place. I don't want you to think that's what"—he paused—"what I'm up to here."

The boy was silent, poised like a runner on the hood of a Mercury.

"Not at all what I'm up to. Your mother needs help, and she's a proud woman, she won't ask for it. I happened to notice, just in coming, that there are a few things that might be done here. Things she wouldn't ask for."

The Mercury runner would not budge.

"Look," he said, "the last thing I want to do is make you unhappy. The last thing."

"Then get out," the boy said, and finally looked straight at him, aping maturity, issuing a challenge Henna would have thought beyond him.

He found himself talking to the boy's feigned maturity, as if he were discussing his problem with an adult.

"And go where?" he asked.

The boy's mask crumbled; he'd become a child again. Your one defense against children was your capacity to ask them questions beyond their ability to respond. He remembered that.

"Do you understand, Johnny? I have no place to go."

He could feel his own forehead crinkle. He wanted to show the boy his weakness without exploiting it. He must not look helpless. Children stepped on weakness with the deliberation with which they attacked cracks on the sidewalk. He would talk to the boy like a man and see what happened.

The boy had no response, however. The complexity of the idea Henna had presented to him was peeling back years, turning him into a younger boy. He remembered his inability to explain to his children why his mother cooked rabbits. Yes, they are the same cute things we see hopping about, but now they are dead and we eat them. Logic had always been a thin weapon against repulsion. But it was not quite repulsion he was faced with here, rather an inability to understand how a man could have no place to go. It amazed Henna, too. Home was still there, it could be gotten to—he'd told Nancy he'd be late, there would be little explaining, even, to do. But the actual transmission of himself from this place to that was hampered by considerations stronger than geography. He would still be at this table, regardless of where he was physically. He would still be trying to answer this boy's questions. He would still be waiting for the woman. He would still be wishing, with a desire that seemed to coalesce with an awareness of his own vital functions, for a return to the intimacy they'd known in her room before, when he'd touched her ear.

When she finally appeared he could sense the automatic easing of tensions in both his body and the boy's, and the lifting upward in them, too. Her appearance was like a call to attention. She carried papers. That he'd known this was a source of amazement to him. Thus far, nothing that had happened in this house had been what he'd expected. Now he was being asked to do exactly what he'd been prepared for, and the inconsistency of this was slightly jarring. He wished that he had glasses to put on, so he could look different, more businesslike, less like the man who had begged Johnny for understanding.

When she handed him the papers, though, he was disappointed by their individual lack of heft. He had wanted contracts, deeds. He had wanted to sift through the language of officialdom, to make clear to them where they stood in the world, what they owned, how much they had coming to them. Instead, what he found were envelopes with windows in them, Adams' name printed out again and again in the dull black script of cost accountants. Bills. Oil bills. Medical insurance bills. Bills for electricity. Bills from companies whose names he couldn't connect with a product or a service. Sorting through them, he glanced once over at Johnny—he had hardly looked at the woman, he realized now, so eager had he been for the papers—and felt a strange sensation, something not far from guilt. The boy paid no attention to him, staring directly into his mother's waist, but Henna was acutely aware of the potential embarrassment of what he was doing, going through a man's bills, things previously intimate only to Adams, like searching with your fingers over the scars in a dead man's skin.

The boy reached out, as if to embrace his mother's waist. The gesture was too subtle, Henna thought. It did not insist on itself enough. It demanded that she pay closer and stricter attention to him than she was. Henna noticed because his eyes were still half on the boy. But the woman's attention was on the bills she'd handed to Henna. He saw the boy's hands recede. He knew that she hadn't even noticed. He thought of saying something: *he tried to hug you*, but knew that gestures like that couldn't be saved by explanations, had to be acted on in the heat of the moment. Once the gesture failed, intent usually died with it. The boy probably wouldn't want to hug her now. He could only make matters worse. He went back to the bills.

Nothing had been said, though, as to what he was expected to do with them. He looked up at her. Her head was oddly held, slightly tilted; her face seemed to have been arranged in a pose of seriousness. She looked uncomfortable in the pose.

"These are bills," he said. Did she know, or had she just grabbed all Adams' mail and deposited it here as if to say: Make sense of it for me.

She cleared her throat. "I know." Then she sat down. "You

remember Mr. Valenti asking me if I'd ever paid bills, taken
care of finances ..."

"That was me. Who asked you."

"You remember."

"Yes."

"And I said no."

"So you want me to look at these for you?"

"I would like you to tell me." She cleared her throat again.
She had not looked at him since beginning the discussion.
There was some difficulty he wasn't clued in to. It had to do
with Johnny. She hadn't looked at him either. "To tell me
which have to be paid now and which can be put off. I have no
idea."

She looked at Johnny then, though the words seemed to be
directed, he thought, toward Henna. The boy played deliberately, Henna thought annoyingly, with his fork. His face had
begun to redden.

"I am thirty-seven years old," she began quietly, "and I have
no idea how these things work."

She touched the wood of the table, her fingers putting stress
on it. Her words, though, seemed enormously careful.

"And you expect me to somehow learn things without being
taught."

Johnny glanced up at her then, his eyes dark against darkened skin.

When she turned back to Henna, her face still carried the
weight of difficulty she was having communicating with the
boy: it looked as though there were an invisible hand pulling at
her skin.

"Now would you look at them and tell me."

He fingered them.

"It would take a while."

"Take as much time as you need."

She began to collect the plates. The boy still said nothing,
but clutched his fork when she tried to take it from him.

"Johnny."

He clutched it harder. It seemed sad to Henna that the fork was the only object available to him with which to make a last stand.

"Are you going to let me have it?"

"He can't stay."

"He is going to look at the bills."

She took the fork from him. He let it go. When she had deposited it in the sink, she ran quickly to the kitchen doorway and switched on the light. The way she did it reminded Henna of the way he'd seen her running out in the field the day she'd shown him the farm—the way intent pulled her head forward.

"Do you see that?" she asked. "Do you think it's magic, or divine right that light comes on? It is a thing we have to *pay* for. Do you understand that?"

To Henna, it seemed that the boy was getting a complete education in the ways of wandering insurance men and electric light bulbs, all in the space of a few minutes. No wonder he looked as though it was all too much for him.

"Now, we have a certain amount of money, and a great many bills, and the ways of such as the electric company are entirely foreign to me. Perhaps you can tell me, Johnny, about how great their quota of patience is, how long they will let us go without paying before the day comes when I turn this on and nothing happens?"

"I don't care about light."

"No, of course not."

The boy rose and switched off the light, to prove his point. The natural light, by contrast, had become cavelike.

"I'll need that on, if I'm going to look at these," Henna said quietly.

The boy stood his ground by the light switch. It seemed a stronger stance than the fork had allowed him. Henna pitied him, and moved to the living room.

From the living room, the sound of their quarrel was muffled. It soothed him, after being so long in their presence and feeling he was behind a closed door, that here he was in fact in that position. Their argument, and his place in it, could not cut him so quickly now. He had removed himself, and been given a job to do. This seemed, for now, to give him a firmer place in this household than any he'd previously enjoyed. He sat down in the wicker chair that had, not two hours before, looked so forbidding, the very chair from which the imagined Adams had chided him for his misguided attempt to win his wife, and felt enormously pleased with himself. He wanted to hold the bills up in his hand, display them. *Look: I am here.* The outside world, the world in which cars passed in the newly enveloping darkness, seemed a thing of diminished importance, like the currency of another era. He listened to the few cars that passed and felt warmed by the insideness of his position here. It felt as though everything of importance to him was contained under this roof. He riffled through the bills eagerly.

He tried to make two piles: one for those to which she should pay first attention—the oil, electric, medical insurance; another for those that could wait awhile—a book club, a local lumber supplier and a farm machinery dealer who had apparently been repairing Adams' tractor. The bill informed him that it had been ready to be picked up for two weeks.

At the bottom of the pile he found an envelope he'd over-looked at first glance. His own company's trademark stood boldly out in the upper left-hand corner. He opened it and read the cover letter and circular advertising new riders to existing policies. The letter began: "As you are the only insured member of your family . . ." An old urge rose in him. He was amused to discover it. She was uninsured. The boy was unprotected. He would make mention of this, nothing more. He folded the cover letter and put it inside.

He heard the screen door slam in the kitchen. Then, after several moments of silence, the water began to run. She was washing dishes. It was as if they'd been here forever, these were habits. Once the boy was gone, what was left to disrupt? Perhaps she would make coffee, bring it to him. He remembered she had none, nor liquor. She'd allowed the house to empty of habit. He would have to bring about its return. Perhaps even washing the dishes was an aberration, something normally put off till morning. It felt strange now, to be sitting in this house. He thought comfort here was as evanescent and quick-dipping a thing as light. The house could catch it for a moment, but always seemed on the point of losing it.

He was sitting in the dark when she appeared. She was drying her hands on a towel.

"I thought you needed light."

He'd been studying the bills under what natural light was available. He had to fumble for an excuse. "I didn't want to run up the bills anymore."

He switched on the light beside him. He gathered the bills quickly, so that she could see he hadn't been ignoring them.

"I regret putting you through that scene," she said.

"It's all right. I've been going through them." He coughed and held up the first bill: the Book-of-the-Month Club.

She shook her head, and sat down. She paid no attention to what he was holding in front of her.

"Now these here"—he pointed to the neat pile he had made—"are the ones you should pay first attention to."

She still would not look at him. On reflection, he thought he might have said "we" instead of "you."

"And these others, these I think we can wait on."

She lifted her head and stared at the two piles of bills. In the glare of the light bulb—he realized now how rarely he had seen her in unnatural light—the wisps of hair she seemed never to be able to control cast shadows on her face. She was tired. Exhaustion drew her features in, like an artist crimping on line, drawing in short, stubby, staccato movements. There was absolutely no expression on her face.

She got up and left him alone for a moment. When she returned, she carried Adams' bankbook and an envelope from the bank.

"Here," she said. "This is what he left."

Henna opened the savings passbook. The figure was $396.21.

His bank statement indicated that he had written checks for
$721.47, leaving a balance of $221.30. He added it up.

"You've got six hundred and seventeen dollars."

"And the bills?"

"Does the bank know he's dead?"

"I don't know."

"Was there a will?"

"Nothing."

He fingered the passbook.

"I can put the savings money into the checking account, can't
I?" she asked.

"We'll see."

He looked at the book. Only Adams' name appeared there.

"What do you mean, 'we'll see'?"

"Your check from the insurance should be here in a week.
You'll start your own account."

"So this money . . ."

"There may be trouble. I don't know. When a man dies
without any will, and leaves money in the bank, sometimes
there's trouble. We'll see, that's all. Meanwhile, I'll give you
some money to live on."

"No."

She sat down. He totaled up the bills. Heat, electricity and
insurance came to $314.00. The due date on each of them had
passed.

"Meanwhile, I'll take care of these bills."

The blood seemed to have drained from her face. She stared
blankly at the two piles of bills. Then, so quickly he was not
prepared for it, a sob shook her body, then another. He
watched the spaces underneath her eyes turn red, color charg-
ing in as if from some underground river beneath the skin. She
put her hand to one eye to stop herself.

"I hate this."

"I know."

"You do not know. Please. You do not know."

She tilted her head and let the sobbing overtake her again.

"What have I been doing? What have I been doing these years? Waiting for Sam. I loved him, Mr. Henna. It was not a good marriage, but I loved him. Oh, *shit.*"

The last word was so harsh he would have blotted it out, had he that power.

"They're only bills," he said, he thought, weakly.

"And what else do I have? What is this life anymore? It was his dream, not mine. I resent being left with it."

She rubbed hard at the tops of her eyes with the back of her hands. The gesture was meant to stop the sobbing, but it failed.

"I hate this," she said.

This time he was silent. He waited. Finally, she stopped. In the silence after her sobbing, he felt the loss of all physical desire for her. In its place came an overwhelming pity that was like physical repulsion. He recognized how outside himself she was, how separate a thing, how even more incomplete than he. His gestures, at least, had had some significance.

He recognized, too, how fine a thing it had been to come here, how brave to stay even in recognition of the loss of the original dream: to make her his. She would not be his, not in any of the conventional ways. He would not make love to her: he *could* not. She had loved Adams, and he would leave that memory intact.

He took the bills up and pocketed them.

"What are you doing?"

"Nothing," he said.

"I can't let you."

"No, it's no problem." He laughed, quietly, for her. "Other guys, they worry about money. Me, I guess I've always been smart, never overstepped myself."

She swallowed. Her eyes looked to be filled with liquid. A thin smile played on her lips. It appeared not to be an easy thing to do.

The house was so quiet it seemed you could hear things from far away. When he shifted his foot, the sound arrived as a loud intrusion. He laughed at it, and that, too, sounded loud. The way she was looking at him now was indecipherable. He remembered his admonition to himself to pay close attention. She had lost him, though. She had gone too fast.

"Will you . . ." She stopped herself and looked at him as if to get a new angle. "Will you be going now?"

He could feel the bills in his pockets, and the silence in the house seemed to hold no invitation. He thought he should do exactly what she said.

"I guess."

"May I walk you out?"

"Oh." He laughed.

"It's like courtship, isn't it? In reverse. The fact is, it was I seduced Sam."

She looked at the floor and bit her lip.

"I'm sorry," she said.

"No."

"I seem to want to talk."

He sat back, to allow her to.

"No. Let's go outside."

They walked to the door. He was hesitant, allowing her to go first. On the front stoop she sat, and he stood above her for a moment, studying the shape of her head. He knew a renewal of desire, and thought what he had felt inside was cleaner, purer. He tried to return to it.

Above them, the sky was abnormally clear. He could see not only the outlines of stars but something of the depth of their network, layer after layer. He remembered how once the universe had been described to him as an enormous cone, and it was as though he could see just beyond the rim of it.

"It was. Please sit down."

He did.

"I love this story, and I may never tell it again. It was in New York, Mr. Henna. My father had owned a factory upstate, I think I told you, and when it collapsed, he went to work as a salesman for one of his competitors."

Her head moved forward a moment, as though she were seeing some new figure on the lawn, but when he looked, he saw that her gaze had in fact turned inward. He looked at the lawn, and the street before it, and thought of his family in this early darkness, finishing dinner.

"They moved him to New York, we lived in a large apartment on Riverside Drive. I was frightened to death of the city. I was used to lawns and I was used to houses, and now I huddled by the window of my bedroom, looking down on the lights below. I thought it was lovely, but I couldn't imagine a place for myself in it. Women were so brazen, it seemed. They had such large breasts and they wore their hair as if they were so proud of themselves, with big red gashes on their mouths, this bright red lipstick. I thought men would like that, to be kissed by lips like that, and I would look at my own lips in the mirror, and wonder what they could possibly do."

She scratched her ankle and drew her legs up, so that her head was fairly resting on her knee.

"I went to City College, the only place my father could afford to send me. I did not want a Jewish lover, I thought I would be consumed by one, they all had so much energy, were so hungry. The war was about to happen, I remember. I saw Sam walking on Riverside Drive. He wore a muffler and a long tweed coat. How wonderful he looked. I took my book and sat down on the bench and prayed that he would talk to me. He never did. He, well, he already had someone."

She paused and closed her eyes.

"It is so easy to see him as he was then. Easier than remembering how he was in the last days. Sam. The way his mouth would open. I could still be there on the bench, watching him pass by, ignoring me. I could be there in a second. What's changed? What has changed?"

She breathed hard.

"I stopped going to the bench. I gave up. Until once, in a bookstore on upper Broadway, he came up to me and said, 'You stopped sitting there.' And I said, 'Where?' as if I didn't know. 'On the bench,' he said."

Something was pulling at her mouth. Her hand fluttered.

"I didn't know what to say. It's so impossibly a fairy tale, Mr. Henna. Tell me, is every courtship? Does everything begin wonderfully? Is it all a long falling off? Do you know what I said? Of all the things. 'I will be there tomorrow, at two o'clock.' And I ran out, and I bought red lipstick, but I couldn't put it on, couldn't bring myself to. I wore my best coat, I said he'll either have me or he won't, but it must be the way I am. And at two o'clock he came with corned beef sandwiches and we sat on my bench, we talked about our schools, and where we'd come from—dull talk, I knew it was dull—I could feel the losing of him, the sense of him saying, 'She is not what I'd hoped,' and I wanted, Mr. Henna, I don't expect you to understand this, I wanted the feel of him inside me. I didn't care if I never saw him again. I'm sorry."

She shook her head.

"I keep saying I'm sorry, but I'm not. I wanted the feel of him inside me. When virgins think of men's penises, they always think of them as being huge. But his, I did not think—I was not afraid of him. He was so fair, I thought he would go in me like a long soft finger made of something like velvet. That is how I saw him."

She was breathing hard. Henna thought an enormous flow had been unleashed.

"And I could feel the possibility of his going. I could feel his boredom. When he looked away and a long silence came, this is what I said—God! how brazen!—'I cannot wear red lipstick in a gash on my face. I am not proud of my body like other women. I cannot wear it like a badge. But I want you to have it.' Then I started crying. Impossible! To say those words, and then fall apart. And he knew, of course he knew, and he didn't take me away and have me. Not Sam. He said, 'That is the most interesting thing any girl has ever said to me.' And he laughed, he was delighted. At long last I had become interesting."

Her breathing shortened. He could feel the crest of the story.

"And the fact was that as soon as I'd said it, my desire went away, and was replaced by an enormous fear. I did *not* want him to have my body, but rather to *say* that, to be brazen for once in my life, to give these romantic rages a voice. Once having done that, I was frightened, and prayed he wouldn't. And he didn't. He knew. He was not *all* literature, not then. He had his intuition."

She looked ahead, he followed her gaze. Nothing was between them and the sky, the layers of stars, the enormous rim of the universe's cone.

"I had to ask him, finally, when it was time. And afterwards, I think he expected me to say something interesting. But what was there to say? My virgin's imaginings had gone away, and there was blood. How it humiliated me. There on his bed. I knew a thing now the way it was, and something in me, something hard and awful and something, I'm afraid, Sam never quite forgave me for, could not forgive him for making my life less interesting than I'd imagined it from the window on Riverside Drive, where the feel of a man in a muffler and a tweed coat might be like velvet if you can only catch his attention, only sit on that bench and wait for him to notice you. He is a thing of wonders."

Long, heavy tears fell down her cheeks, but she did not sob.

He put his hand on her back, very gently. She let it rest there for a few moments, then shifted her back just slightly, to let him know he should remove it now.

When it was gone, when his hand was back in his own lap, she shuddered.

"How good of you to listen. It is unfair that that story has to be told now, to a stranger."

"I'm not a stranger."

"No. I keep calling you one, though, don't I?"

He could see, now, seven, eight layers beyond the initial layer of stars. He pointed this out to her.

"Oh, yes."

She hardly looked. She was not interested in stars. He hoped that she would begin another story. Instead, she was silent. She looked down at the walk in front of her. He was afraid that her silence meant it was time for him to leave.

"I feel humiliated just now. I'm sorry."

"No . . ."

"To be saying those things. What virgins think of."

"It's all right."

"To be able to sit with a woman now, to see our lives as a long . . . whatever. A long dream, from the first sight of a man on Riverside Drive to the bills his death left behind. You can only see that with a woman, I suppose, someone with whom you share the initial . . . suspense."

One finger went up and ran along the line of her cheek. She moved away what hair had fallen there. She stared out at some point between herself and the walk. In the blankness of this moment, Henna could find no place for himself. He had no idea what would happen next. Then, as if to answer him, her head moved as though it were a body in some grand circular orbit and came to rest on his shoulder.

He could feel his body stiffen. It was so unexpected. He looked down at her head and wondered what he should feel. The perfect roundness of it now filled him with pity.

Her hand was on his sleeve. Nothing in her pose, in her movements or in her touch held anything of the sexual. Henna felt like a statue with an enormous broad lap, something a body could fit itself into without in any way expecting a response.

Then, after only a few moments, she lifted her head slightly off his shoulder. It seemed to hover a moment in air. He waited, then reached for it, to draw her back.

"No. No, Mr. Henna. I am quite aware of the significance of that gesture. I needed a shoulder to rest against for that amount of time, and no more."

"Are you sure?"

She said nothing.

"Tell me more about him, then."

"Sam? Why, so you can gloat, feel superior?"

"No."

"He could not do what you do. He couldn't live in the world. He farmed and he wrote his father for money and he tried hard to think of himself as a man whose life had substance. But the farm only fed us, and he was saddened to learn there were necessities other than eating. That a woman might like to have clothes, and heat, that boys, when they break their arms, go to hospitals. Even his father, in the end, gave up on him, thought of him as wasteful issue. The only thing that remained of Sam was his beauty. His face never really changed, though there were lines in it, but not the way other men's faces changed, not the fat-necked, swollen way men's faces change when they are out there, day after day."

Henna feared she was about to turn to him and consider him in some judging way. Instead, she turned away, looked off to the side, as if this comment could touch him in no vital part. The omission unsettled him; he wondered where, in her view, he fit in.

"I found myself silently betraying Sam, by becoming attracted to faces like those, like your friend Valenti's, repulsed at first, but then thinking how I'd like them to take me out in a fast car—the most superficial things, Mr. Henna—take me out to one of those cheap, flashy restaurants and order me a steak, and I would drink booze and be someone's wife, and talk to other women and have something in common with them. Sam had such beauty, but being alone with him, in a room, I nearly always felt an impulse to open a door, be interrupted by a phone, a knock, it was like going back to childhood with Sam, being two children in a room to whom nothing, really, had happened."

Henna had to breathe hard to cover the sickness he had begun to feel. That she had admitted to being attracted to Valenti was more than he could accept.

"What's the matter?" she asked.

"Valenti is a pig."

"I know that. I didn't mean it."

"But you said . . ."

"I know what I said."

He could say nothing. There was a blankness at the heart of things: in his center was a space waiting to be filled. With lust, with anger, with decision, with sadness, anything at all would do. It was as though she'd gone inside him and cleared out a room and not decided yet what to put there. He only knew it was all up to her. He could not manufacture anything. His desire for specific things from this woman seemed long ago, a working out of a problem based on insufficient information.

"What is the matter?"

"Nothing. Where did his, his father go? Was he here for the funeral?"

"Yes. He came. I hated him. I hated him for the last letters. He asked me if I needed anything. I wanted some pride in the end. I said no."

"And he left it at that."

"Yes. He left it at that."

Henna stood up. He wanted to know, immediately, what her plans were for him.

"Where are you going?"

"I don't know."

"Mr. Henna, have you left your wife?"

"I think so."

"Did you come here thinking you could have me?"

She was not looking at him. These were not easy words for her, clearly.

"I thought so, but now, now I don't think that anymore."

She nodded, still not looking at his face; looking at the lower half of his pant leg, somewhere in that vicinity.

He nodded his head, too: being where they were, he could not think what to desire from her. His thoughts of the night before, when he was back in his own yard, seemed aberrant imaginings, not thoughts of this woman, but of some other, some imagined woman. He thought now of desire as a thing that could only happen in the dark, when faces and features can only be made out by the touch of fingers on them. Then he remembered how he'd felt in her room before, she in her Chinese robe; circumstances had done it then. His life up until that moment had worked to make him swollen. Now a clear division had been reached, he was on the other side of a cleft in his life. She had put history and memory in front of him, and he thought things now were as complicated as they'd ever been with Nancy.

"I am glad," she said.

He started to move down the walk toward the road. He was not sure why. He thought it was perhaps that he wanted to know less what she would say next, or direct him to do, than what the slant of his own feelings would be if he put distance between himself and her.

"Mr. Henna," he heard her say. Inside himself he was pleased at his momentary freedom of response. She could say, "Don't go," now, and he would still continue on this passage. He wanted to know how it would feel to look at her from a distance.

When he reached the road, he turned around. He saw her sitting on the front stoop, the shift draping her legs so that only her ankles and feet were visible. Beyond her he saw the house he had come to love, full of darkness now. Just above the house, suggesting itself like an interloper, he saw the barn. Everything was affected by history now, by how much more he knew now than when he'd first approached it. He looked at the car and felt an urge to laugh at the man who had driven in it all day, full of plans, the man who thought he could come here and take over. He could feel history like a new structure to put beside the house and barn. But there was still a unity in what he saw: history was no crazy architectural eyesore, it was done in the same style. He could see this woman on a bench in New York, waiting for a boy to pass by. Even her thoughts about the boy, that she had wanted to "feel him inside" her, really changed nothing. She had imagined it would feel like velvet. Even Samuel Adams, whatever else he possessed, lacked that singular gift. Henna could connect to him at least there.

What had troubled him most, her professed attraction to Valenti, though still able to cause a pang in his heart, had to be seen as she'd wanted him to see it: not as a desire for Valenti's corporeal being, but for a life she saw as attractive; steak in restaurants, cocktail lounge booze, the company of other women, wives. Adams had stranded her here. Any boat happening to go by would attract her. Though he could never have known it before, Valenti's philosophy wasn't totally wrong, only incomplete; it wasn't that anything could happen to anybody anytime. There were too many strikes against that, and the odds were too low. It was that we carried around with us unconscious gifts. Valenti would better have said: assume nothing. He remembered when they had first talked about New York, the Taft Hotel, O Sole Mio. He had known these weren't her hangouts. What he could never have known, until now, was that she might have thirsted for their cheap glamour, from her room on Riverside Drive.

It was her tiny space in the physical picture he was looking at that made him hunger for her again, not in the lusting way he had in her room before, but in subtle, delicate ways. A woman like this, one who could talk so eloquently, go so far beyond him in the realm of language, you'd have to watch out or you'd actually start seeing yourself as a tiny, diminished thing next to her. He'd have to pick her up to know her true weight. He wanted to do that, to establish a simple balance. She was drawing him down to the place where he was no more than a woman to her. He thought other men might laugh at him for not just going for the obvious. She had rested her head on his shoulder! Valenti would have made quick work of such a gesture. But imagining what would inevitably follow from such an assault, he was glad it was he who had stopped by, his boat she had flagged.

He started up the walk. He had found the place where desire rested, felt comfortable with it. His hands at his sides felt like new tools.

When he reached her, she was looking down at his shoes. She seemed to study them.

"You don't have to go, you know."

The words coming out seemed to pull skin from her throat, so aching and startled were they.

He put his hands on her head, lifted it to him. Under his hands, he could feel a slight tension.

"I have only asked you to stay the night."

"I know that."

He kissed her lightly on the lips. His own strength was a

wonderful surprise to him. He was only frightened that it might go at any minute. He sat down next to her.

Things felt as though they were ending now. She rubbed her knee.

"May I tell you one more thing, Mr. Henna? I don't know what you'll think of it. Do you know the line from Yeats—no, of course you don't, no reason why you should." She looked embarrassed for a moment. "It is from a poem by William Butler Yeats. The line goes: 'I'm looking for the face I had before the world was made.' That line haunts me, Mr. Henna." She turned eagerly to him. "Because, look at me: I sometimes think the world has ignored this face, like Sam's, done nothing to it. When you kissed me, I remembered looking in the mirror and wondering what these lips could be to a man."

He touched them with one of his fingers. "They're beautiful. They're good."

"Do you suppose most women—Yeats's woman—are looking for exactly what I have: a face to which nothing has happened?"

"You've lost your husband. That's not nothing."

"No. But I lost the sense, years ago, that this was a life."

He took her hand. They sat on the front stoop with their joined hands dangling beside them.

"I'll sleep on the couch," he said.

She nodded. There was no hesitation, but the nodding was slow and careful.

He remembered their first meeting, his taking the ball from Valenti, her refusal to talk sense until he created sense for her, how she had looked at him then, the way in which their understandings had always been made in silence, made by nodding heads and eyes adjusting to an enlarged presence as if to the suddenness of light.

"On the couch," he repeated, so that she should know exactly what his intentions were. Then he asked, "And Johnny?"

She bit her lip. "That will not be easy." When she stood, he watched her shift fall from the places where her body had caught and bunched it, until it hung and clouded her.

"Wait here," she said. "I'm sorry. Wait here until it's time and then, then I'll call you."

She looked up at the house, not at him. When she passed and he heard the door click shut, he knew a brief moment of panic. His greatest fear since coming here had been hearing that door shut and having no reason to come back. But there had always been one. There was one now.

Across the dark landscape that lay in front of him, he imagined his wife and sons keeping a vigil for him. He was certain now, for the first time, that he would not be home tonight. He imagined Nancy tucking the boys in, the color of the light in the kitchen as she stepped into it. He tried to return to the feel of Mrs. Adams' body beside him on this stoop, the feel of her head against him. There was a kind of comfort in the recollection. The landscape before him was suddenly not so dark and suggestive; his sense of loss became like a pinpoint of light in the far distance. He realized he could hear the sounds of the woman inside, making a place for him.

Above him, he could hear her changing.

That is, the creak of her feet on the wooden floor suggested—he was charting her movements with the keen attention with which he'd applied himself, outside, to the pattern of the stars—she was moving from the vicinity of the bed to the vicinity of the closet. He sat on the couch below, the light turned out, himself in darkness, and guessed at the sound of a coat hangar jangling, emptied. He imagined the shift falling from her, leaving her briefly naked, imagined her covering herself quickly with her nightgown. She would still be frightened to be naked with him in the house. They had passed that part, where he was a danger to her, but the memory of it would, he knew, still be in the room with her. He thought she could come downstairs now, naked, and he could watch her make up his bed for him and treat it like the greatest gift anyone had ever given him, but still not touch her, not grab her. The thought of a sordid thing happening, the quick and the unlikely and the quickly over, was as repulsive to him as, he was sure, it was to her. He waited, fully dressed, in the dark.

Outside, he had sat for more than an hour before she'd called him in. He'd seen the light in Johnny's room go on, been momentarily frightened that Johnny might stick his head out and discover him still there, then saw the light go off and relaxed from his crouching position, felt things empty from him. He'd had no thoughts about time, no particular eagerness for this to progress: he was satisfied to be waiting, watching stars. He was, after all, where he thought he wanted to be: the front stoop, the couch, what difference did it make? He had no desire for sleep, not then, not now. When she'd opened the door finally, she told him simply to come inside and wait while she made up the couch for him. His waiting felt like a thing composed of chambers, first one division, then the next, first the stoop, then the couch, then he would wait for the night to pass. That the object at the end of his waiting was unclear presented no problem to him. The waiting was exquisite and pleasurable. Above him, the sound of her feet on the wooden floor was as comfortable as the sound of a child breathing in its sleep.

When she appeared on the steps leading down to the living room, he saw her framed by the only light in the house: the light spilling out of her room into the hallway. The wisps of fine hair seemed to spray out of her head. The nightgown she wore was as shapeless as her dress had been: a long white box. There seemed to be layers to it.

She did not see him at first.

"Mr. Henna?"

"Here."

She drew a hand up in front of her eyes. He groped for the lamp switch.

When it was on, he saw that what he thought were layers was instead a stack of folded sheets she carried and, on the bottom, a small pillow.

He peered at her. They both got used to the light.

"You don't have to sit in the dark. He is asleep, I think. There will be hell to pay in the morning."

She moved to the couch. He stood up, and she began draping it in sheets.

"Are you sure . . ." he started to ask.

"Yes, I am sure, and please don't ask. Let's not bother with asking whether this is really what we ought to be doing."

She tucked in the sheets so efficiently. He watched her body tense as it bent. She seemed smaller than he'd ever seen her. In action, she seemed to diminish in size.

"There are no neighbors to peer out the window and notice the widow woman has taken in a man for the night, so let's not invent any."

When she was finished, he nodded and put his hands on the sheets.

"You didn't have to do this."

"But I did. Would you like a cup of tea before we turn in? I think I have some."

"Camomile?" he asked, he knew, absurdly, to show her a little of his education, newly arrived at. He stifled it instantly.

"No. I don't think I have any. Orange pekoe is about as exotic as we get around here."

"I'll have some."

He waited again, while she made it; that is, he entered the next chamber. The sitting position he seemed to have been in for hours was strangely comfortable, but he had liked having her above him more than having her in the next room, preparing something for him. He thought of his wife again. He wondered, should he call her? It was too easy to imagine that conversation, how little of the truth he could get at with Mrs. Adams beside him, or in the next room. He wasn't even sure how he could explain this to anyone, much less his wife. He thought that he and this woman were digging, slowly, toward something. He wouldn't be unhappy if she entered the room now and said, "In ten years, if you are faithful to me, I will show you my breasts." He thought that might give him ten years' worth of energy, his life on the farm would be slow and worth enduring. When finally the moment happened, he would be a man approaching old age. His muscles, his face would have changed. He would be worthy of it. Their love would be a thing so aged and entirely felt he couldn't even begin to guess at the details. She would be in her late forties, but it didn't seem beyond imagining that he could make a child on her.

When Mrs. Adams came in, though, he had to adjust his thinking as if to a change in atmosphere: here was a woman with whom he could contemplate making a child, sitting before him in a thin white shift, inciting him not with lust but with a prayer for time to pass, for dangerous terrain to have been crossed. The tea was hot, unsweetened. He could have been anywhere. When he looked at her, he had to remind himself this was the same woman he'd been dreaming, imagining, charting the movements of with an attention he'd not been able to summon in business since the first time she'd lifted her head and said: I will listen to you.

What had he said that had gotten him this far? He couldn't remember. The tea scalded the top of his mouth.

"Will you go to work tomorrow, Mr. Henna?"

She sipped her tea, seemingly oblivious to the difficulty of her question. It was as if she'd said, "Do you mind taking it without sugar?"

He cleared his throat and looked at the floor between them, not sure what kind of question it even was. Were they supposed to allude to normalcy now, as if what had happened outside, on the stoop, left normalcy intact?

"I don't know," he said, and startled her. Her eyes went wide for a second. "My car," he remembered. "My car's going to be ready tomorrow." How insignificant the Fairlane had become, where yesterday he'd thought everything depended on it. He sipped his own tea harshly, as if to move bluffly past the heat, to get it down, settled in his stomach. He felt impatient with ritual.

"Are you," she said, then smiled to herself, "are you a good salesman, Mr. Henna?"

They were sipping tea in a room lit by a single lamp. He thought it was like being on the shore of a new country, just having arrived, and sitting around a campfire, telling stories of the old. It was this part of ritual, the statedness of it, that annoyed him. He wanted to move on without having to make statements about the past. It reminded him of D'Alio in the woods on Saturday. The reminder was not pleasant.

"I guess I am." The tense seemed to be what she required. He was answering her in kind. If she asked him to sell something now, called a neighbor over, he supposed he could do it. Despite the evidence of the day, he didn't think you lost basic skills that quickly.

"Tell me how you do it."

She was nearly hiding behind her cup. He wanted to pull it down, make her face him: we are somewhere else now.

"Why?"

"I am . . ." She looked at his chin, the shoulder of his shirt. "I am fascinated by this thing you do."

But I am here now. I have no other life but this. He wanted to tell her, but couldn't imagine saying those words. It would be the way it was with Johnny before, begging for an understanding that never should be asked for.

"Well." He cleared his throat. She had given him her history, after all. Perhaps all she was asking for was some return.

"You start, that is, before you start you knock on the door and step a foot or two backwards. It's a trick. That way you don't look like you're leaning in, begging for anything. You look like you could be refused, it wouldn't matter so much to you."

"Psychology," she said. "And then?"

"Then, well, the secret is not to sound like you're selling anything."

She waited. He didn't know how to go on. The words sounded depressed coming out of his mouth. They had no urge to be spoken.

"What's the matter?"

"Nothing."

"I want to know what it's like, to be in a car out there, what the assumption is, what the world looks and feels like, when you look at a house and say, 'I'm going to go in there and make a sale.' "

The way she said the last part depressed him, too. It was not something a woman should say, "make a sale." He was not sure why, but the idea of women and sales, or at least this woman and sales, was difficult for him.

"You don't, you don't really think about it. You know what you're selling is something people need. You, for instance . . ."

He wouldn't finish. He wished that she would allow that part of his life to be over. He could see himself going into a pitch, and how absurd he would feel.

"You don't like talking to me about it, Mr. Henna?"

"No."

"Are you ashamed of your work?"

"It's not . . ." He had, finally, to say it. "It's not my work."

"No. It is. Don't be like Sam, Mr. Henna. Don't be ashamed of that part of life."

He looked at her, astonished. It had been his effort, all day long, to try to accommodate insurance to his new vision of what his life would be. When he thought he'd succeeded, at the end of the day in the professor's house, he'd been jubilant. But as soon as he'd come here, he'd wanted to abandon it. Now it seemed to be the thing she was asking for, that he stay the same.

She took his cup and her own, settled them on the table beside her.

"Are you tired?"

"No," he said.

They sat in still light. He thought, sadly, that their plans were different now. He wanted to turn out the light and lie there, with her upstairs. What she was asking for was too much, just now. Perhaps in the morning it would make more sense.

"There is a Woolworth's in town. I'm going to go in, Mr. Henna, and I'm going to see if there's an opening. I am no better than those women. I have no more resources than they do, and it's time—I admitted that. The greatest stumbling block I know is the one Sam gave me—that we are different from those people. That we deserve more."

She was creating an imaginary world in the space between them. He could see her as she imagined herself, and in his mind he embraced this woman, told her she did, in fact, deserve more, asked her to be patient, to let him sit with her at each dinner, support her as best he could, nurture his love over time and finally . . . he thought of the imagined child and felt his own imagination pull back, no longer able to go that far. He resented her for the bleakness of her vision, how strong a pull it exerted on his own. But he said nothing.

"It's late," she said finally.

He reached over and shut out the light. They sat together in the darkness. She didn't move. He went to her and embraced her. The clumsiness of his movement found his hands glancing across her buttocks, a gesture he wanted to pull back.

She said, "Stop," and he did, instantly, breathing hard, regretting having done it. It was a gesture he should have waited years for, yet his vision was so waffling, so affected by hers, that he had given in to the first impulse.

"No," he said, "I didn't mean that."

"Mr. Henna, is it all right for you to stay here?"

He thought he would cry, but when he looked up at her he saw she didn't hate him, was, instead, concerned.

"Do you know what I mean, Mr. Henna?"

"Yes. Yes, it's all right."

She stood up. He sat with his hands clasped in front of him.

She took the cups and went into the kitchen with them. At the top of the stairs, she looked down at him. Then she came down the stairs and sat again across from him.

"I want you to know this. I know what I am doing. But this is the truth, too: I want you to be here. I want you to stay the night."

She sat a few moments longer, then got up and left him. He sat a while, cursing his hands for their ill-timed sweeping of her body. Then he lay back, breathing hard, and wishing for her presence again. The house in darkness seemed a blunt finger pressing at his heart. He saw the sham in all his dreams of waiting ten years before being given a chance at her body. He remembered his children, as babies, lunging for things before they'd acquired the skills for grasping. He was no farther along than they were.

He thought then of work, of arranging an excuse for tomorrow. The ability to move was beyond him, his body felt amorphous, a maze of unfocused longings. Again, his boys appeared to him, his absence like a chill hovering over their dreams. He should call, he should make connection. But beyond the sound of their voices, he could think of nothing to say to them.

He dreamt that night that his son lay beside a tractor, mangled by it, his severed hand lying beside him in the grass. In the dream, Henna lifted the hand and attached it to Thomas' body. Then he carried the boy to the river that bordered Adams' property and washed him there. Nancy was there, Nancy and Mrs. Adams, Leo, his mother, Mr. Vanaria, Valenti. Valenti was dressed, ready to take him to work. They left the others swimming, and Valenti's car brushed past cornstalks. Mrs. Adams, in the back seat, said, "The new baby will be fine." This caused bright, conflicting eruptions, low in him. He was still carrying Thomas' hand, it had somehow been separated from Thomas. He tried to get Valenti to turn back, but the car would not go in that direction.

Then Thomas was looking up at him, bright, eager, beaming, from a desk at the front of a classroom. The boy motioned for him to sit down. The boy had both hands, but Henna still carried the severed one. Mrs. Adams stood beside him. She carried no child. He wanted to ask her about it, but she wouldn't respond. Nancy came in and took Thomas away. Nothing had been said, but somehow it had become known: Thomas was not his, had never been his. He had no child. He watched them walking out onto a long, blank playground in which his car waited, Valenti inside it. Valenti said, "Come on."

He woke with a surge of desire for Thomas that was like a huge, gnawing hunger, one without hope of satisfaction. He saw a ceiling above him and thought, at first, it was his own. He could go, check on the boys. Then, slowly, the details of the past twenty-four hours were returned to him.

He did not know why he was here. He felt the sheets resting on his still-clothed body, and the pillow under his head, and knew exactly how they had gotten there. He could remember the incidents of the night before, his touching of Mrs. Adams and then his chastisement of himself, the talk they'd had on the stoop—all of these were clear, but they were like incidents from a story whose point has been forgotten. Of the moment, if there had been one, when a decision or an act, purely motivated, had set these scenes in motion, he remembered nothing. He was in a strange house, far from his own, far from knowledge of his children's welfare, on nothing more substantial than a whim.

Rising, he heard the floorboards creak beneath him; he thought the house contained a tension that forced upon his every movement annoying considerations: he couldn't even move without making a racket. He tried to remember the last thing he had said to his wife. The dream in which she had denied him fatherhood seemed to contain as much of his claimable life as the memory of her that morning at the breakfast table. Why had he wanted so badly to leave her?

He thought of getting into Adams' car, driving to his house, checking on his own boys, but then what? Stay there or drive back here? His life seemed hinged between the two; he couldn't locate its center. He'd thought his family would be safe, but that was foolish. Nancy could not take care of them, not alone. He remembered that Thomas had gone into the Round-Up to buy him something. The thought of that present—where? under Thomas' bed? On the shelf? how had she explained his absence to them?—was unbearable.

He stood, and cursed the floor for creaking under him. He made his way up to the bathroom in the dark. At the top of the stairs, he opened the bathroom door, switched on the light.

Johnny's door was open. He turned down the hall, and found the woman's door open as well. Nor was she in her bed. They had deserted him. He was alone in the house.

He walked downstairs, into the kitchen. They weren't there either. He glanced outside, saw nothing. The moonlight made the first rows of corn look eerie, as if they each held mirrors up to the sky. They had to be outside. He opened the back door, to listen.

And heard nothing. He stepped out. The night was chilly. Good that he'd slept in his clothes. It was strange how, outside, the place began to feel more familiar. He looked at the barn, the top of the house, and the onset of sexual feeling became his first understanding of why he was here. He had to balance his feeling for his son with it, and it made him feel as weirdly uncomfortable as when, in his dream, he'd carried Thomas' bloody hand into the knowledge of his new son. He had to go back into memory to determine just how close he and the woman had come together: he remembered brushing her buttocks, kissing her dry lips, the extent of his contact. He had berated himself even for that. Now he wondered why.

He followed the path of the moon in the direction of the irrigation ditch. The ground was hard and surprising: by day you tramped across such ground, thoughtless and sure of yourself; by night it became sinister, full of unseen bumps. Twice he tripped, expecting to elicit laughter. Where were they?

When he arrived at the irrigation ditch, he slid down on his ass, certain that any other approach would land him there anyway, and less gently. It turned out to be a wise approach. Several yards ahead of him, he caught sight of the woman's white shift, and crouched immediately backward. He could not find the boy, but heard his voice, a mumble of indistinguishable words. He would have to move closer to hear.

He hid back among the cornstalks, where everything was abysmally dark, and tried to move closer. When he again peered out, he appeared not to have moved at all. The woman was as far from him as she'd been previously, the boy's voice still a muffled, ghostly sound. His eyes could absorb more now. He could see that the boy was not there.

He headed up along the furthest row of stalks, risking getting caught in her sight. She seemed not to be moving, though, was turned, instead, facing in the direction from which the boy's voice came. He saw the outline of her arm, craning upward, then reaching back to touch her forehead. Finally, she turned, and he could hear her words exactly, seeming to address the tomato plants.

"Come here," she said, just above a whisper.

He thought she was addressing him, and made ready to reveal himself. But then the boy appeared. He looked as though he were coming out of the fields, though he must have been standing just beyond Henna's vision. When he was within her grasp, she reached out, clasped him, cradled his head. The boy clutched her buttocks in a way that was infinitely sad, yet which filled Henna with a longing for transference: he wanted to *be* the boy, be Johnny.

They stayed that way so long Henna began to tire from the stillness required to watch them. He thought of the way she held him, and saw his own dreams ridiculed in the passion with which her fingers curled around the boy's head. To think that his body could elicit a yearning like that.

From the beginning, hadn't he been made aware of their exclusiveness? Their beauty in the moonlight, clasping each other with a passion burned and finished on their mutual caring for Samuel Adams, seemed a mocking of him. The boy would not have to say another word, Henna could do all the talking for him: just exactly what do you think you can do here? His initial offer, to be a hired hand, to work for fifty cents an hour, seemed the most sensible of any he'd made.

He imagined that just being allowed to watch this would be the furthest intimacy he'd be allowed here. Why not go now, leave them in this state? Where had he ever gotten the idea he could be a figure between them? Whatever they had said or done to him, it had been to get to each other, to this embrace.

He knew now that the logical step would be for him to return to a place where he might find an embrace of his own, but he couldn't help it, he wanted still to be between them, to warm himself at this particular fire, to announce himself in such a way that all tension was dissipated, unity achieved, he would be welcomed with open arms.

The sound of the boy's voice blunted his hopes, though.

". . . to go" was all he heard, but the tone was unmistakable. He referred to Henna.

The boy was seated now under the tent of his mother, facing her breasts, so that when each of them spoke, Henna had to work to hear what they were saying. This strange business of listening in on nocturnal intimacies! It was as if, at night, human sounds were devalued, had to fight for elbow room with crickets, wind, rustling cornstalks, sounds that went unnoticed during the day.

"He has nowhere to go."

Hearing the woman's voice soothed him. He was surprised when he realized she was actually defending him.

"You said he has a family. You said he has boys."

"He's left them."

"You could tell him to go back."

The boy dug at the earth.

"I can't tell him that."

"Why not?"

"It's his choice, isn't it? He could go somewhere else, but I can't tell him to go back to them."

Henna could not see the expressions on their faces, but could easily guess at them. Her head dipped above the boy's; Johnny's pointed at the earth. He knew now why movies had never truly needed sound.

"Besides, he is my friend. I deserve a friend, don't I?"

"I don't have one."

"Well, you should. Don't be like me. There are boys around here."

"I don't like any of them."

"Johnny."

"I don't like anyone."

She touched his head.

"Johnny, we can't live this way. We can't live the way your father lived, feeling superior to everyone, feeling we don't *need* anyone. It never works, you know that."

The boy shook his head.

"You never cry for Dad anymore."

"I have cried for him, Johnny. I have to stop. I have to see things, don't I?"

"What things? See what?"

His mother was crying now. The boy's voice went softer.

"It's me who's responsible now. No one else. Do you see that?"

"What was wrong with Dad?"

She touched the earth. She seemed to be making a circle with her fingers.

After a silence, she said, "He didn't know how to live."

She looked at Johnny, to see what was registering. Henna watched their silhouettes. Behind them, in a house across the river, a light went on.

"Do you know that your father could have been anything he wanted to? Truly. He could just as well have been a . . . a cowboy, Johnny. And you think that's glorious, don't you? You think that's wonderful. But it is a blankness, Johnny, an absolute nothingness that needs to be filled. He was a flawed man, Johnny. He missed some hardness that kept him from functioning like the rest of the world."

The boy moved slightly back, reached up with one arm to scratch the other's elbow. The woman's chin went forward, her head bent toward him. She reached outward, as if to extend the explanation. Then she aborted the movement, touched her own forehead. They leaned toward one another in silence.

"You want to leave this place," Johnny said finally.

"Yes."

"Dad was happy here."

"Happy in the way an idiot is happy."

Johnny's hand swung out and caught her on the shoulder. She rubbed the sides of his head and shook it.

"Don't call him an idiot," Johnny cried.

They both seemed shocked by the suddenness of violence. "I wasn't calling him an idiot. Your father was not an idiot."

"Why don't you *cry?*"

"I can't cry all the time!"

"You invite men in instead."

"Johnny."

The boy stood up.

"He is not here in the way your father was here."

"Use words," Johnny said angrily.

"What words?"

"I know what sex is."

"Then not for sex. If you are such a man, so capable of handling complexity, I will say that: not for sex."

Johnny started to move away from her, back into the fields. As she got up and moved toward her son, Henna watched the moonlight catch her dress in such a way that it seemed to flare up for a moment, then die. He had been watching them with such a loss of self-consciousness it was only when they were out of his field of vision that Henna fully realized they had been talking about him. About his body, its darkest dream! He felt as separate from this man, the possibilities for whom they discussed, as if he had physically separated from him, left him sleeping, dangerous, on their couch.

He looked now into the ditch and wondered if they had truly been there, or if he had only imagined them, acting out a scene calmly, then lashing out at one another and disappearing. He moved through the stalks and found himself among the tomato plants when he caught up with them. They had moved to where the rows of lettuce flattened out the farmland for a space. It was the woman's shimmering gown that caught his eye again. He hoped the tomato plants were sufficient cover, and crouched down.

"What for? What for?" the boy was saying.

Then: "We don't need him," when she failed to respond.

He watched the expansion and contraction of the boy's chest—Johnny wore only pajama bottoms—and wondered, dumbfounded, how he had managed to incite such passion in what was, after all, a stranger. What was so life-or-death about his being here? Johnny now reminded him of one of those actors in the movies for whom every incident required teeth gnashing, hair pulling, eyes raised to heaven. He had always assumed, watching them, that there was something he was missing, some force in life he hadn't a clue about. He felt that way now.

But something odd happened then, forcing his attention closer. He thought he must have missed some small action on the woman's part, something the boy had reacted to, and flinched from. The space between them suddenly seemed filled: it was as though an electrical current passing between them had announced itself, become visible. When her voice finally exploded—he'd never heard it so loud, so guttural—it was as though a new presence had entered the field, a third voice.

"You're going to condemn me to this, aren't you? This. This. This was a failure, but because he's dead we have to treat it now like a shrine."

Johnny reached for her nightgown, twisted it in his hands. Henna thought he might tear it away from her body.

"Is that man going to sleep with you?"

"No."

"In your bed?"

The boy's voice was caught, tripped over something. He started to cry.

"No one is going to . . . Johnny, come here. We will not even discuss . . ."

The boy took a step back.

"Listen to me, please. Why should we make this go? Why? It was an idea, nothing more. Your father could have had any idea. Suppose he'd started a—oh, I don't know—a brewery, a grocery store, a gas station—would we be required to enslave ourselves to that, too?"

"Just no men. No men."

He was casting about with his hands.

"But I need help. There are things I need to learn to do."

Her hands reached out as though to catch something. She began to move toward the boy, but when she reached him he only swung out at her. She tried to catch his blows, and when she failed, started to fight back. Henna watched them, in the eerie white band of light the moon provided, striking at each other. He wondered how long he could watch it before interrupting.

Finally, though, and just as quickly as they had started, the two of them stopped. They were both on the ground in a moment, then the boy seemed to disappear. Henna could only see the woman, the spread of her shift sprayed out against the ground. Her sobs were long and deep. When she looked up, she seemed to be staring right at Henna, addressing him.

"Imagine this man you worship so tenderly," she began, her voice low, "for a moment, would you, imagine that long body, those full shoulders, that head. And think about the morning he got up before us. It had to be three or four in the morning. Early enough to be safe. Johnny, we thought he loved us."

The boy was again visible. His hands went up, but he seemed to have trouble finding a use for them. It reminded Henna of an infant's first fumblings, his sons' early pawing at their eyes.

"We thought—well, no matter what we thought. He had to plan it, Johnny, you can't just do it. There is a hose involved, it has to be cut, and fitted. Do you suppose when he cut that hose that he was thinking of us? Was there some plan for us there?"

The boy's hand reached out, tried to cover her mouth. Her head ducked backward, found safety.

"Was there even regret? No. Imagine, Johnny, what happened that morning, what had to be going through his head, and find, please, the love for us there, which you would return with sacrifice . . ."

The boy struck out at her.

"Don't hit me. Christ. Goddamnit. You will know the truth, whatever there is of it to know. It was your father's way, when he was out of ideas, to end his life, no regard for you and me."

The woman seemed to hover over her son, rocking gently, like a gauge wavering between two points on a compass.

A separate part of his dreams returned then to Henna, unannounced. He had made love to her against a garden wall, in a field like this. He thought, as he watched her reach out for her son, of the way her body had somehow melded with his in the dream, the pattern of her shift as it slipped over her thighs. It had been a long painful broaching of her body, more pain than pleasure; no wonder he had had to go over the actual events, on waking, to determine just how intimate they'd become. Her words now, and the strange authority the dream had seemed to invest in him, made him want to reveal himself, to stop being such a careful keyhole peeper at their most intimate confessions. He thought he'd somehow gone beyond that now.

He stood up among the tomato plants and watched her freeze in motion, and the night was again still. He was surprised that he could affect this.

"Is that you?" he heard her say.

He waited a moment, until he was certain she'd intended *him* and not some fourth participant, then stepped forward and revealed himself. Neither of them moved; the boy was just behind his mother, in the shade of her body. Henna could not tell if any part of them touched.

The way they looked now, each of them staring up at him from the ground, made him want to reach out his hand, pull them upward; their need had the power to affect him that way, as if they were falling into a huge hole and only his hand could save them.

He wanted to approach them now with a surety in the very way he walked that whatever they needed, whatever the desire, he could fill it. He wished that things were as simple as geography, that they had no ghosts to rid themselves of, no mysterious, mute needs, but were simply what they looked: two children lost. He wished he could do something as unambiguously helpful as pointing the way out of the woods, the direction home.

But as he moved forward, he was struck by a self-consciousness as strong as any he'd felt on this farm. Adams was dead, Adams had been erased, emotionally, by what she'd just said; yet, in looking at them, and moving his leg among the neatly planted tomatoes, he had never felt so strongly the sense of himself as interloper, with no true place here. What could he say to them? Move toward them, yes, hope that the moonlight was as kind to his figure as to theirs, and say what? He felt the beginnings of a huge thirst. He would have to say something. It would have to be the right thing. They would only wait so long, then they would turn away from him.

Their eyes looked enormous when he was close enough to see them. He looked at the darkness in the boy's features, had to remind himself: he is ten, not forty.

"Go away," the boy said.

"I don't like to see you fight," he answered.

The boy started to turn to go. Henna caught his arm. He may have pulled too hard; he wasn't sure, but he thought he heard the arm snap. At that instant, he pulled the boy to him, letting go of the arm. The boy uttered a cry. He felt the small body next to him then and received the vivid shock of its lightness, its youth, as if he'd been expecting something altogether more formidable. Henna reached for his arm again, to check for breakage, and received a series of blows, short, expert, as though he were a bag the boy had practiced punching for weeks. He gasped and hugged the boy to him, remembering his dark look, his lightness, and reaching blindly for some synthesis, felt the boy's skin bunch in his hands; soft, a child's skin. The boy cried again.

Henna grabbed him in one final hug. As the skin gave under his fingers, the boy uttered a different kind of cry, one that sounded strangely close to laughter. Henna didn't want to let go of the boy, but the sudden image that under his grasp was a laughing face was too wild a hope to resist. He remembered his sons, their laughter on the floor at home, his bearish body hugging them. There seemed to rise then, in the field, a glowing sense that they had finally come together, his gifts with this child. But when he let go, the boy started to run. His face betrayed nothing, no laughter, only a concentration on escape. Henna watched him run into the wild, comforting embrace of the orchard. The boy's hair flashed for a moment, then disappeared.

Henna dropped down then, to rest. He was afraid to look at the woman, afraid that he'd held Johnny too long, endangered him too much by nearly breaking his arm, afraid that she might have turned against him. He could look no higher than the lap of her shift, reflecting briefly on how inviting it had looked just moments ago. The presence of the just-finished event with the boy made him think how ridiculous it was to have ever seen invitation in that lap, or on the farm. He felt as foolish as when, once as a young man, he'd been walking home past the river to McKenn Street, and a car containing two women in their twenties stopped ahead of him, and one of them glanced out her window, to get a better look at him. He had already started off toward them when they took off, laughing. He felt an anger now, too, for finding himself here, on her husband's earth, having been defeated by her son. Had she been leading him to this, treating his assumptions as serious propositions only to prove to him finally how foolish it was to assume he could ever *be* anything here?

She said nothing. She looked down at her lap. He stared at her, waiting for her to say something. Whatever it was, he would listen, patiently, and then he would go. He wondered, as he stared at her, what had become of his desire.

"Mr. Henna," she began.

"I don't like this fighting. I don't want to see you two fighting on account of me. I thought . . ." He wondered, again, why he had begun answering her before giving her a chance to accuse. He opened his hands.

"I warned you this would not be easy."

He looked at her, astonished.

"What? What would not be easy?" He tried to hold back his anger, couldn't. Neither could he help injecting into his tone a tinge of hope. "You tell me what this is. You're holding the cards."

"Am I?"

"Yes."

"My son does not want you here. Isn't that clear? Don't persist in trying to win him."

"I was trying . . . This is stupid. I was thinking of my sons."

She looked at the ground a moment. "Where do they think you are tonight, your family?"

He shook his head. "They don't know."

She looked at him, and lifted one arm so that it grasped the forearm of the other. It seemed an exact duplicate of something her son had done, before, as he had watched them from among the tomato plants.

"Would you like to go back to them?"

Her chin hardened. He thought hard how to answer. If by saying yes he could force her into a more open declaration of her feelings, he would do it. But how did he know it wouldn't hurt more than he wished it to, forcing her instead into a deeper silence, one the two of them might never come out of?

"I don't know."

He had dreamt of living here, had seen it in waking dreams as a thing so desirable he would risk his life for it. Now he had seen her naked, held her hand, had her make up a bed for him, slept under the same roof, and he wanted more. In entering a dream, he wanted proof of his whereabouts, something like a name on a dotted line.

How could he make this clear to her without making of himself some coldhearted bureaucrat of lust? Wasn't it the long, slow awakening he desired, the hushed promise, "In ten years I will show you this, then that"? He would have to make her see the simplicity of what he needed, the promise stated, in clear language, of what he could expect.

"Tell me," he said, as though she had been following him.

"Tell you what?"

When she looked up, her cheeks were puffy, her face drawn out as though she had, in fact, heard everything he'd thought and was not afraid now to register the pain.

"I thought this was what you wanted!"

"It was," he said weakly.

"Did you not come here, begging to stay, to make us dinner, to take care of us, to be our friend? Wasn't that your promise, Mr. Henna? Or did I make that up? Was it I who begged? Go back to them."

He reached out for her as she said it, as surprised as she to hear himself calling out, "Ann!"

They both took a moment, as though to register some change in the atmosphere. The direct way they had begun to stare at each other was a little frightening for both of them, as if they were on the edge of a declaration each of them shied instinctively away from. He took her hand, kneaded it gently, then released it and said, "Let's go in. It's no good out here."

He stood above her now, allowed his hand to gesture that she should take it.

"Come on."

She studied his hand, then went back to looking at the ground.

"Are we going to stay here?" he asked. "I'm tired."

"I'd like to stay and wait for him. I don't know where he's gone."

He could see she was shaking now. He wasn't sure why. She looked down at the ground, away from him, perhaps ashamed.

"No matter how he acts, the need remains . . ."

She stopped, stammered, seemed to paw at the earth, reminding him briefly, startlingly, of a colt.

He touched her arm. She still would not look at him.

"Go on," he coaxed.

"No." Her head seemed to wrench away. "I have said it."

He reached for her chin and drew it to him. The kiss she allowed him was brusque: it told him nothing. She had said it, though. He felt the rest, all the difficulty, washed away. He tried to reach for her shoulder, but she moved past him, started walking toward the irrigation ditch.

He started to run toward her. "Ann!" He said the name freely now. He actually had to run: how had she gotten so far from him?

When he reached her, he felt she'd moved into another realm altogether. She would not look at him.

"What's the matter?"

"Nothing."

"No."

"I am ashamed of myself."

"What for? All we did was touch. This is innocent."

She looked up at him.

"Johnny might have seen."

"He suspects worse."

"Exactly."

"Hey."

He took her head in his hands. There was no hesitancy now. He did not have to apologize. He could stroke it smooth, explore it to his heart's content. He was amazed by the wonder of her small, perfect head, astonished that it had somehow become his to hold.

He kissed each of her eyes gently, aware now and considerate of her fears. He vowed to kiss this woman carefully, and he touched each part of her face: forehead, cheeks, chin, neck, and saw the way her face absorbed it like gentle rain, like beads of it standing out on the places where he'd kissed. Her hands reached out like a little girl's might, looking for support. He reached out and carried her to him, lifting her just an inch above the ground. Her eyes were closed when she kissed him, and she immediately hunched back, frightened of the act. Careful, Henna, he thought.

He stood inches away from her, and didn't move, conscious, though, of the shaking of her body, its attempt to reach control. He would wait until it did so. See, he wanted to say, how little you had to worry about me! Then her hand reached for his face, touched the stubble on his chin, then his neck, finally she lay against him, a tiny sob falling from her as she did. She stood like that a moment. He was entirely still. He thought it might be raining. The atmosphere was one of extreme wetness: her tears, the bubble of semen between his erection and the shorts he wore, distances and distances between them, safe layers. I will protect you. He let his arms, his stiff body say that, and it was as if he went away, or flew above them, surveying the farm, the land that was now his, while a vacant body stood at attention, allowing this needful woman to rest against it.

Finally, she pulled away. She stood, not looking at him, looking, again, at about chest level, and wiped her tears. She took a hard look over the farm, and he wondered if she hadn't had his thought: this was his now. He waited for her palm to make a gesture, a silent gesture, giving it to him.

She began to walk away from him. He followed her, quietly. Halfway back to the house, he tried to take her hand. She pulled it from him.

"What's the matter?"

"Nothing."

"You're tired. You want to go back to the house."

"Yes. That is it."

But there was more. She wasn't telling him. Pulling her hand away had been like a pulling of things from him. Was it so easy to lose things, one slip of the grasp, were they lost forever?

He stopped her, laid his hand on her shoulder, lifted her face up to him. This, too, she resisted.

"What? Tell me what I should know?"

She looked up at him. Her eyes gave nothing away. She kept secrets as though she were drawing tighter the chest she kept them in. Her body itself had become tight, a drawing down of lines.

He ran his finger along the line of her scalp, drew a half circle on her face. She moved away from it, leaving his hand in the air, drawing a circle.

"We don't have to go inside," he called to her. "We could sleep outside. Under the moon."

She said nothing, continued walking.

"Ann. Mrs. Adams."

She smiled a cold, darting smile, a miser of a smile.

He approached her and tried to hold her face again.

"What's that supposed to mean?"

"What?"

"That smile."

"I'm not aware of controlling my facial movements."

"Don't talk like that."

"Like what?"

"Like we're back at the beginning again."

She continued walking toward the house. He followed her, walking just behind, studying the slope of her head, the movement of her body under the shift, for some sign of where the change had occurred. She made a fine, sober figure walking toward the house. He had to remind himself she had, only recently, touched the stubble on his chin with something he had interpreted as love.

Inside the house, she made no motion for him to follow her; she seemed, instead, to behave as though he wasn't there. He watched her go sadly up the stairs and into her room, a girl returning from a disappointing evening at a school function, one in which romance hadn't happened. Her gown seemed to hang more loosely on her disappointed body than when he'd first seen her on the stairs. Her neck, disappearing through her bedroom door, seemed the most fragile thing he had ever seen.

He sat down on the couch. The darkness was horrible. He tried to return to the smell of her, the closeness, the presence of her face inches from his own. His erection struggled painfully upward, he worked hard against the creeping knowledge that she had, in the field, wanted from him the one thing he'd been afraid to give her. He imagined Valenti saying it: "She was askin' for it, Jack." He closed his eyes, winced. It was horrible to suspect it, and to be sitting here, the event past. But what could he do? Go up now? It seemed crazy. He'd opted for carefulness, he would follow his option.

When had the night become so dark? His body, under the

sheet, would not rest, could never be coaxed into sleep. It wanted to *lift*. It knew a pure straining, the entirety of him, like a being entirely ready for change, a cat in summer dying to lose its fur. She was still in the house. She was above him, maybe sleeping, but perhaps not, perhaps wishing to prolong the moment, too, to not count him defeated but allow him another chance. It was worth a try. There would be no sleeping otherwise. Carefulness had been the wrong choice.

Quietly then, he ascended the stairs, pushed open the door. She lay in bed, under a single sheet, staring up at him. The nightgown she'd worn outside hung from one of the bedposts. In her silent staring was neither invitation nor denial. Her eyes seemed to have lost color, they offered him a perfect blankness. He felt a stabbing sadness like the one he'd known below, when he'd thought it was over. Her head turned on the pillow, to look away from him. Her eyes closed.

He felt an impulse to remove his clothes. The moonlight in the room made things look so starkly beautiful he wanted to be a part of it. He moved to the side of the bed and knelt there. Then he pulled back the sheet and discovered her body.

The course of movement became astonishingly clear. He touched the skin at the base of her neck with his lips, felt it rise toward him. Then he began the long descent of her body, feeling with marvelously tactile lips—how suddenly expert they'd become!—the texture of her skin under him, giving and receding. It was delicious, more than his mouth could handle. He became afraid his lips, tongue, gentle teeth, might be causing her pain.

When he reached her thighs, the smell of her made him reckless. He nosed into her center and felt her tense against him, then her hand forced him backward. She said, "No."

He sat beside her on the bed and touched her face. This was beyond logic. The idea that there might have been a moment when she'd accept him, that he'd missed it, seemed a fragment from remote time, a system they'd moved beyond. She buried her face in his hand, then one hand reached out for him, one moment in a kind of clasp, then forcing him back. He stood up.

She studied him coldly now, soberly through a wet mask of hot tears.

"Go away," she said. Her body shook. She pulled the covers up and turned away.

"No."

"Go away. Please."

"I think you are the most beautiful . . ."

She covered her tears.

He moved on top of her. A sheet lay between them and he was still clothed. He threw his shirt off and felt their skin touch. He moved to where his head was between her thighs and clasped her to him.

"The most beautiful. I love you. I love you."

He was moving so far beyond himself he'd lost track even of amazement. He knew a desire to taste her again, and began to pull the sheet down. There seemed any number of ways to make love to this woman: it did not have to be any way he had learned before.

He held to her thighs then and pressed his face down between her legs. Gently, he stroked the insides of her thighs and then a sound came and a movement upward of her body told him that something was finished. He stayed where he was until she pushed him away.

They lay in silence now. They heard the boy enter the house. Henna could feel the woman's legs stiffen. Johnny clumped quietly up to his room, pushed at the door, hesitated. Then he approached his mother's room.

Her hands dug into Henna's scalp, she was pushing him away. He saw red, but hung on. The boy did not enter. He poised on the edge a second, just outside the room, then turned and went into his own room, closing the door behind him.

Henna crept up, then, until he was beside her face.

"Go now," she said.

She would not look at him. Pleasure, if there had been any, had drained from her, too.

"Please. I want to sleep."

He stood above her. She seemed entirely serious. There were no tears now, not even the invitation of emotional complexity.

Quickly, he grabbed his shirt, then bent down to kiss her. He could feel the hardening of her features under him. She offered not her cheek but the bone of her cheek. Kissing it, he was amazed at what he had done, the degree of intimacy to which he'd aspired. What had been accomplished? He wanted to know. He sat on the bed.

"What . . ." he started to say.

But there were no words. The woman stared at him, her gaze returned to that vacuum in which this incident had begun. His hand moved to touch her eyes. She pushed it away. Soon, he could tell, she would begin to cry again. Strangely, this heartened him. In uncertainty and lust, he was trying to move all other events away from this event, to let this stand alone, to force her to consider him for what he'd been on this bed, what comfort and what beauty, if any, he had created here.

He moved the back of his hand in an orbit against her face, touching chin, cheek, forehead, cheek, chin.

Then he stood up and left her to sleep.

9

IN THE MORNING, he awoke in the panic of a body in flight, held down by a large weight, unable to move with the swiftness its will described. He thought of the night before, of his attempt to make love to her on the bed, the sweetness of it rising in his belly, but he felt the dull sense, too, that it hadn't been enough, hadn't cemented things, had been more an end than a beginning. The knowledge was painful, but he knew it to be only waking knowledge, rife with self-doubt. They had slept apart, she had had her separate thoughts. Perhaps, this morning, she would welcome him.

He clung to that possibility, and made a plan. He would be ready for them. He would have breakfast on when they awoke. He would be dressed, freshened up. They would not have to find him in this state, on a rumpled makeshift bed, probably needing a shave.

He heard a car outside the door and wondered whose it could be. It clattered noisily, gears grinding, the driver obviously a new one. Probably here to ask directions. Or water for an overheated engine. When he thought how he'd been missing from his house an entire night now, he became frightened: Nancy could have the police out after him. But police cars didn't drive like that. They approached noisily, but it was a matter of announcing themselves, not grinding gears. She might then have called Valenti, but would Valenti, the only person on earth who could guess his present whereabouts, disturb him here? Henna didn't think so, and, that being the case, felt safe.

He lifted the covers off his still fully dressed self and heard the car clatter to a stop. He would go to the door, answer to the request as master of the house. First he shoved the bedclothes aside, hid them in a ball beside the couch. Whoever it was, he would not want to have to answer to any unexplained messiness, the wavering eye that said, "Are things really on the up and up here?" Look at me, he would want to say, I am dressed, I am ready to begin my day, a day like any, like a million others.

He looked out the window first, to check, and saw Mrs. Adams at the door of the car. His first thought was: How did she get out before me? Because he thought she was only helping, as he'd intended to help, he didn't notice at first glance that the car was Adams' own.

She looked up at the window. Could she see him? Impossible to tell, but he didn't want to risk it. He closed the blinds; who had lowered them? He remembered last night, before going to sleep, being able to look at the stars through the windows. One more peep revealed Johnny, with her. And she carried in her arms, hefted, really, because it was enormous, a brown bag. He closed the blinds again and waited for them, trying to re-create, and find hope in, the look in her face as she'd glanced up at the window and, he was certain now, seen him. There was little hope to be found, though; her face had looked pinched and determined, a way he hadn't seen it in a while. Even her arms, the way she carried the bag, the muscles bunched against flesh, had the power to cause in him now a kind of sickness in the loss of hope.

When they opened the door, they found him sitting on the couch, his hands folded in front of him. Henna thought that, inadvertently, he had fallen into a pose that spoke penitence. He knew his head was lowered; in this position, it was hard to hold it high, and anyway, how was he supposed to look in this position, the last in the house to wake, with their already having carried out a plan regardless of him? Her face, confronting him, betrayed her own lack of resolution: she looked as though she'd planned to use a certain face, a face like a strategy, and then, seeing him, dropped it. She simply looked at him, bag in hand. The boy's face, though, looked flushed and excited, as though he'd been for a long, invigorating run.

"Where have you been?" he asked finally, when it seemed she wasn't going to say anything.

"To the store." She managed a hesitant, slightly embarrassed smile, then looked down, away.

"How'd you get there?"

"We drove."

"I thought you didn't know how."

She was looking at the doorway. It angered him, that she wouldn't look his way.

"Sam once tried to teach me." She shook her head, then smiled to herself. "I don't know quite how we did it. Johnny helped."

She touched Johnny's head. The boy looked at Henna with an astonishing expression: he thought the boy was asking him to approve of this.

"But you were all right? You did it all right?"

"I think so. We stopped and started. We stalled quite a bit."

She looked out the window, perhaps wondering if he had noticed her final failure with the car. Then she spoke into the bag.

"Here, we have things now: bacon and eggs, some ham, milk, juice."

She started the slow move into the kitchen, as though it were difficult to get past him, he was one of those wary, malicious cats mice were always having to tiptoe past in cartoons.

Then she was gone. The boy had followed her, not looking past her or even considering Henna once the statement of his triumph had been made. How did the boy know enough to help her with the driving? That was simple: by watching his father. It would have been easy, of course, for Henna to have said yesterday, "Tomorrow we'll go for a lesson." She might have waited for that. Then, too, if he'd been smart, he might have removed the need for this trip yesterday when he'd gone over the contents of her kitchen. He'd been afraid to guess at the need for milk, cautious as to too fine a broaching of the farm's mystèries. Here, their morning gesture suggested, you've been paying too much attention to mystery, not enough to what's in front of your nose. He thought back over the series of questions he'd asked since they'd come back into the house—where've you been? where are you going?—the dull, oafish questions of the spectator. He thought he'd affected something last night. Now he could only remember groping for her, never really touching. It was as though he had done nothing but add thickness to the layer that existed between them.

From the kitchen he could smell bacon now. He thought: I should be cooking that.

Inside the kitchen, he watched her, over the stove, the smoke from the cooking bacon rising. She brushed it away, as though it were a part of her, her hair.

"Let me," he said.

She looked up, first noticing him.

"I can do it."

The boy sat at the table, focused on his mother, eager to be served.

"You could get into an accident, you know, doing that. Driving."

"Town is not far."

She turned the strips of bacon.

"Do you like your eggs sunny side up, or scrambled, or however?"

She talked like a waitress in a diner. He remembered her vision of herself behind a counter at Woolworth's. Perhaps she was practicing.

He seemed to be invited to eat with them. It was something, at least. It was not holding her thighs, or kissing her breasts, but neither was it a complete denial of him. He would just have to wait until things became clear to him.

"Scrambled," he said.

"Good. That's how Johnny likes them."

He looked down at the boy. They seemed finally to agree on something. The boy was still having trouble looking at him, though.

She made them breakfast. Surprisingly, she was capable of soft, yellow, fluffy eggs, eggs that tasted of butter. He didn't know why he was surprised: she had taken care of a husband and son for more than ten years. But in the time he had known her, she'd seemed to have lost this ability.

"Delicious," he told her.

The boy ate as if he'd been starved. Indeed, he had. Henna remembered he'd eaten none of the food prepared for him last night.

The woman's attitude toward him through all of this seemed a careful balancing of him against a plan she seemed to have arrived at, oblivious to him, while he slept. She asked him no questions, only looked up now and then to meet his gaze with one of her own in which he was asked, quite clearly, not to ask questions, not to upset the balance. The achieving of breakfast seemed an act she was proud of. Her look appeared to ask some acknowledgment of this.

When they were finished and the dishes had been cleared, he sat with Johnny and the two of them watched her, at the sink, washing them. She wore the same brown shift she'd worn yesterday. Only that, it seemed, hadn't changed.

"Johnny, you'll go out now."

"I don't want to."

"But you will."

The boy felt the edge of the table, ran his fingernail along a groove in the wood.

"You need another driving lesson."

"Not right away. Go on out now. I'll call you for lunch."

The boy rose and went to her. Her head was dipped over, staring into the sink, at work on the cast-iron skillet she'd used to cook the eggs.

He held to her dress with one bunched fist, paused, hesitating over some internal detail, then shot Henna a quick look, dark and warning. Henna wanted to gesture: What? What can I do now? But the boy turned away and slipped out the door. His mother looked up, out the window, and when he was far enough away, lifted the cast-iron skillet and set it to dry.

She dried her hands on a towel, went to the side drawer, the one in which she'd kept her husband's death certificate, and extracted a pack of cigarettes.

At the table, opposite him, she lit one.

"Since when do you smoke?"

She nodded her head, coughed. The smoke bothered her eyes. She stubbed it out onto a plate.

"I'm sorry. I don't. It seemed a good idea."

A film of smoke hung over the table. Through it, he watched her eyes darting across the wood. The illusion of competence had been just that. She seemed frightened now.

"So tell me. What are your plans?"

Plans? He had none. He had been sitting, waiting for her to tell him what the rest of his life was to be. What did she expect him to say? She had undone his plans, and now, it seemed, the worst was about to happen. She would ignore every good thing that had happened, she would strip him down to his worst, then send him out. She would even take memory with her, it seemed; where was the recollection in her face that they had made a kind of love last night? On the morning after the night when they'd first made love, he could remember Nancy singing.

"I'm not sure."

There was some hardness in the look she gave him, as though he'd admitted, in company, to a secret she'd prefer he kept hidden.

"It is nearly nine o'clock. If you're not going to work, you should at least call. I assume that's when you report to work."

"Earlier, usually."

He considered the phone: dial seven digits and he would be catapulted back into the world of Cutler and Lavolli, Valenti and Freddie D'Alio. He assumed by now they knew. Nancy would have called Valenti, the office would be buzzing with talk of him. He couldn't enter that room, not now, not even through the medium of the telephone.

"Then . . ."

His fist pounded the table. The gesture had not been planned.

"Tell me."

"Tell you what?"

"What any of this meant. You can't go back to the beginning. You can't pretend like nothing ever happened between us. Like I'm just returning the car now and I should get the hell out of your life . . ."

She paused, and looked at the table, appearing again impossibly young. He had stripped years from this woman.

"No, I am not saying that, Mr. Henna."

He held back. He took out one of his cigarettes and inhaled deeply. The sun must have just passed from behind a cloud. He watched now a swath of light cut across the room, forming a bar of which her head was the very center. Light was always collaborating with her; she seemed to have a corner on it. A moment after noticing her head grabbed by this new entry, he felt the lifting of it into separation, as if the head itself, her wonderful head, was becoming lost to him.

"Where'd you get the money? For all this?"

"There is cash in the house. I used most of a ten. I have ten left. You said the check will be here in a week. I can, I assume, draw money immediately."

"No. You'll have to wait."

She closed her eyes a moment.

"I can't think. I suppose we'll live."

"Look, is it because of what I did?"

"Is what because of what you did? Mr. Henna, please make yourself clear. Do you expect that everything is changed now because of what you did?"

As quickly as that, she could make him feel that nothing had happened. He thought of his actions the night before, how overwhelming he'd expected them to be. In her head, as he left, had she been thinking of milk and juice, the things they needed?

"No." He shook his head.

"Would you like some coffee? I think you should make that call."

She rose to put the pot on the stove.

"I don't want coffee."

"Are you sure? I could make it."

"I know damn well you could make it, and make breakfast and drive a car and do a million other things if you wanted to. Since I've come into this house, all I've been telling you is how I love you, and you, you're more interested in learning how to drive a car."

She looked down at the coffeepot.

"Yes. That is true."

He stood and lifted his wallet, pulled out forty dollars, all he had, and slapped it down on the table.

"Here. Now you can get by without anybody."

He was not sure why he was doing it; it was as though he

wanted to force something, whatever it was that lingered at the edge of their conversation, into the open.

She looked down at the money.

"No. Please."

"You don't need anybody now."

"That would be true without the money, Mr. Henna. It is not a matter of money."

"I give up, then. I can't go around guessing all the time. I just want you to tell me, do I stay or do I go?"

She looked at him as though she were saddened by what he'd just said.

"Shall we go out?" she asked.

"Why? Are you afraid to stay in the house with me?"

He meant it as a kind of joke: see where all my carefulness with you has gotten me? She stared seriously at the table, seeming to want to convince him of something.

"No. I am not afraid."

He tried to get her to look at him again, failed.

"Let's go out," he said.

Outside, he followed a step behind her, feeling hot in his clothes. Their movements were slow; he felt the lack of a direction keenly. The walk seemed ceremonial. He remembered how last night in the field their bodies had responded to one another. Now, under his clothes, under her shift, their bodies moved as if under a burden. His own felt slack, disinterested. He knew a desire to sleep, to rest.

"Shall we sit down?" she asked.

They sat in the same lawn chairs where they'd first sat, when she'd first opened up to him. This registered, but not emotionally. He felt the aching dullness of one whose emotions have ground down, become blunted. He knew that somewhere inside him a vast disappointment was waiting to be awakened, but he didn't know where it was.

She sat in the light, with her hands folded. The light on her hair, on her dress, ought to have moved him, but didn't.

"You said last night, that there was a need."

"I said that."

She looked out at the farm. She pinched her eyes and lifted her head, as if she were an old woman with failing sight.

"Well?"

"When you left my bed last night, Mr. Henna, I was aware—it was very clear."

She stopped.

"What?"

"Do you think this is easy?"

She was again, for the thousandth time, about to cry. He looked away from her, wondering why he was putting her through this. He felt he already knew.

"No," he said.

"A need. I said there was a need."

When he looked up, the woman's face seemed to have recovered somewhat. She looked as though she were working her way, with difficulty, through some treacherous inner passage.

"Did you suppose we could fall into something," she began, "like teen-agers, based on lust? That a night of love would lead to . . ." Instantly, she seemed to reject the detached, austere tone of reflection, and her face again sharpened. "I have had that. God, I have had that."

She put her hand to her face.

"I am going to learn to drive, Mr. Henna. Would you have taught me that, or insisted I stay here, while *you* go out, preferably stay here wearing white, and waiting soulfully by the fence of the farm, for your return, cradling my belly . . ."

She held off. Her hand at her forehead began to shake, but she did not cry.

"I am sorry. I was not talking to you."

She closed her eyes, then looked directly at him.

"But can you see, how important it is, that I continue life in a fashion not patterned on the past? I lay there last night, after you'd gone, and I thought that, and it seemed to me that there was, finally, a choice: I could have a life, with Johnny, in which I was able to do simple, magical things—drive a car, have a bank account, determine what supper would be. So we will keep this farm, until Johnny's ready, and then we will sell it, and I will do whatever I have to to make that happen, including selling baubles at Woolworth's, which I am not above—in order to have a vision, Mr. Henna, which is my own."

She paused, and breathed.

"Which is a son, and that is all. And if you want to be my friend, that is fine, but I will not take your money. When the time comes, when Johnny goes away to college, I will sell this place, and I'll move back to New York."

She had been talking quickly. He allowed the air to settle now, her breathing to slow down to normal, before asking, "And do what?"

She lifted her hands, palms upward, staring in front of her.

"Oh, there must have been something on my mind, mustn't there, before I looked out the window and saw that handsome boy."

She shook her head.

"Oh, that sounds sentimental, I know. But I must have been thinking of something, I could not simply have been a vacancy. But I'll never find out here, will I? There's nothing here."

She looked around, and he looked at the farm with her. He imagined it with other people living on it. He was not sure how it had happened, but he could look at the barn now, and see it held up, repainted. For the first time, he saw how tentative had been their hold on it.

When they looked at each other again, they each seemed to be embarrassed. Henna thought to himself: There is nothing to say. He was not sure he wanted to be here now.

"Tell me about your sons, Mr. Henna."

"Why?"

"You haven't spoken of them. You have never said . . ."

She let the words drop off. Said what? Where now were his sons? Who lived in their bodies?

"My first boy, my first boy is called Thomas."

He looked down at the ground.

"He's ten, he's Johnny's age. What do you want to know?"

"Anything."

"He . . . he's a good boy, I suppose."

He tried to re-create Thomas. An unexpected surge of feeling came upon him. He knew that nothing about Thomas was extraordinary, that the boy would probably never make him proud, but as he began to re-create him, in his body and in the way he held his head and spoke, in his separation from Henna and in the very fact that, at this moment, he was conducting a life independent of his father's, eating or looking at a book or sitting in a chair, he thought he saw something of the world itself, and he knew he'd been wrong about Adams, knew that Adams' detached reflection on the beautiful thing he'd created would never be a thing to keep him on earth. What Thomas was, an imperfect and difficult creation, could exert a much stronger pull than a child like Johnny ever could. Dying men, he'd heard, didn't think of mountains and beautiful sights, but of the smell of coffee, and things left undone.

He must have not been talking for a long time.

"All we can finally claim, Mr. Henna," the woman started to say, but he rushed his hand at her, to stave her off. The gesture was large and almost brutal, cutting the air, but he wanted none of her generalizations. He did not want to know what he could claim. He wanted to consider Thomas from this distance, sitting in a chair, looking at pictures in a book, pictures of movie stars in their strange and glamorous poses, their poses that shunted life aside and went for an essence that wasn't an essence at all—the essence was, rather, in the way his son would look at them.

When he was finished considering this, he looked up at her.

"I'm sorry," he said. "You wanted to say something."

"Finish talking about your sons."

Why had he ever wanted her? She seemed cold and distant now, a woman who spoke in a foreign language. It was not that he wanted anyone else, but she, now, began to seem like the farm around her, a thing that had been made, could be inhabited by anyone. No, that was not true. She was inhabited, that was where the difficulty came. She had no real need for him, and now he felt foolish for having been attracted, for having made such a large and messy display of himself. He saw now that what she had been to him was a new country. The insight flashed and then disappeared, leaving him only with the sense that there was another country, an older one, to which he already, and immutably, belonged. He saw that, even given a chance now, even were she to say, "I will have you, Mr. Henna," in the way he might once have dreamt, he would hold back.

"No. I'll go," he said.

Her face registered no surprise, no resistance. He remembered her body last night, his desire for it. But it was as if that body and its promise would have to blaze constantly—the farm, the boy, every accoutrement of life here would have to blaze as her body had in order to keep him. He would not be comfortable otherwise.

He stood up. She followed him into the house. He found his briefcase beside the couch. He asked her, because he knew he would not come back, and because he would want hard facts, not imaginings, to remember this by, if there was a picture of her husband he could see.

She told him to wait, and went upstairs. He stood in the empty room feeling uncomfortable. He could feel his clothes hanging heavily on him. He wondered how clean they were now.

In the inner pocket of his jacket, he still carried Adams' bills. He took them out, held them, weighing whether he should take them or not. He tried to imagine himself writing out checks for Adams, at his desk at home, among his things. Gently, he laid them down on a table.

When he looked up, he felt ashamed, as though she might have caught him at something. The light at the top of the stairs caused memory to awaken in him. He felt a falling off of resolution. How bright, how wondrous life had seemed in that room yesterday! When he had seen her breast fall like a swan's wing—how innocent he had been on that bed, looking away! he would kiss it before the night was through—when he had placed the earring in the hole in her ear and touched her need, the way it had come when least expected. He thought that he might never again know life more fully, and that he might be giving up something now. When she appeared at the door, he saw her body embraced by the light, and he knew again the need to hold her, what it had been to hold her. She seemed to know, too, what he was returning to, and shut the door behind her.

She came down the steps holding a black-and-white photograph. She handed it to him.

The picture had been taken on board a ship. Adams, tall, blond and possessed of an enormous jaw, a head shaped like a large block with tiny ears on either side and longish tufts of curly hair on top, stared at the camera with a wide, square smile, his eyes black slits in which it was impossible to see anything, no inner man, no sense of what he thought beyond the smile. If he looked at it long enough, he would begin to see the aptness of her description of him: he had the lines of a man in a children's drawing. You were invited to fill them in. Beside him, approaching the camera and showing off in a way that made him think of the word "saucy," was a younger Ann Alther Adams, her hair cut shorter, so that it stopped at her neck, and an unruly curl at the front. Her face was screwed up into a smile that was like pointing out her tongue without exposing the tongue at all. She looked like someone ready to begin life, she looked to have the requisite energy. He turned the photograph. April '49, it said.

He tried to imagine himself on that boat, in steerage with his mother, returning from Europe, looking up at this girl in first class. And he could know, could sense, the desire he would have felt then, to talk to her, feel her skin, be embraced by her. And he would see the man beside her and say, "How tall! How strong! To be him!"

But it had not happened, and, finally, he was not that boy anymore; it was nothing but a negation of all the things that had happened to place himself in that position, to put her and Adams so far above him that only by their blessing did his life have meaning. Another life had been waiting for him. When he knew this, his desire did not go away, but lost some of its power.

He looked around the room then. He could recognize nothing, not the couch he'd slept in last night, or the chairs, or the light filling the room, as belonging in any way to him. It had begun as a room he'd had to intrude into, and it ended there, as though it were turning away from him, having used him, now finished.

When he turned, she couldn't look at him. One temple throbbed. He remembered the first sight of her in the overstuffed chair, the way she had looked up, the specificity of what he had presented her with then. They had gone through it.

He gestured down at the bills he had laid on the table.

"The insurance check will be here soon," he said.

She nodded. He handed her the photograph then, and touched her once on the shoulder. The gesture was comradely. He took time only to savor the texture of her plain dress between his fingers. Then he was out the door.

On the road in front of her house, he looked back once into the windows, into the rooms, expecting to catch some sight of her. The sun made bright shields of each pane of glass. He started to walk.

10

AT A DINER in Lexington Center, he stopped and ordered a cup of coffee, then, spying the rows of sugar-coated doughnuts in a glass tray behind the counter, asked for one of those. He was hungry. The walk had made him hungry.

The diner was empty except for two cops sitting down the counter from him. They sat and sipped coffee as if the effort pained them, as if it were a difficult thing, the drinking of coffee. Their hats were pushed back on their heads. He looked at the creases in their high foreheads, their blue uniforms. It was going to be a hot day.

Behind the counter, through an opening just to the right of the racks of doughnuts, he could see the cook, a gray-haired man wearing a white cloth cap and smoking. He peered out through the opening while he smoked. There were no customers, there was nothing yet for him to do.

Henna drank the hot coffee and put the doughnut into his mouth. He tasted the jelly inside. He hadn't expected it, had not known what to expect.

"Jelly," he said to the waitress.

She nodded, not sure whether he was about to register a complaint. He smiled, to let her know he was delighted. She did not return the smile. She wiped the counter. Down the counter from him, one of the cops looked at him curiously: who was this guy? Henna licked at the sides of his mouth, where the sugar from the doughnut had collected. He smiled at the cop, then took away the smile and just nodded. The cop turned back to his partner and said something, but the partner did not turn and stare at Henna. They both looked forward and drank their coffee seriously.

The cook was looking at him now, too, staring out as if he were thinking deep thoughts about Henna. Henna knew he needed a shave, and must look pretty ridiculous in a rumpled shirt, with sugar deposited at the sides of his mouth. He also knew he was a free man. He had nowhere to go. If he wanted, he could continue walking, no particular direction in mind. The cops would eventually have to get back to work, the cook had to stay behind that opening and if someone came in, if Henna himself were to say, "I want a hamburger," that cook was obligated to make him a hamburger. He was not free, and neither was the waitress. If he said, "More coffee," she would have to get it. He marveled at this, that he was the only one in the diner who did not have to obey anyone else's beckoning. He could stay as long as he liked, drink as much coffee as he wanted, no one could say anything.

His thoughts were on his family, had been since he'd left Adams' house. He wasn't sure they'd welcome him, or if they'd even be there. He'd have to cut through an agony of resistance before things could ever be normal again, if indeed they ever could be. He had left them. He had untied his life and let it drift. Now he wondered if a man had the power to reconnect to such a thing, if the tarp was wide and strong enough to withstand such a rip. He thought of his first son, and he still did not love him as he should. Then his second son, who, the morning before, had thrown a cake of soap at his head. Then of Nancy, and he saw with clarity how she must see him now, how far and how dangerously he had ranged from the ambitious young man she had married.

The direction he'd taken, consciously or unconsciously, was leading him toward Waltham, toward Warren Street. But he had not known, until he'd entered this diner, sat down with his coffee and confronted the world here, that he was a free man, that no irrefutable law of the universe demanded that his steps take him to Warren Street. He remembered an extraordinary moment in his life, a snowstorm that had come by surprise, his third or fourth year of selling insurance. He'd gone farther out that day than he'd expected, and it had been a fruitless day. When the storm came, he'd had to pull over to a roadside café. It was so sudden, and so torrential, that he thought he wouldn't make it home that night, and this, combined with the bad day he'd had trying to sell insurance, had made him consider, from behind snow-pummeled windows, with a cup of coffee before him, how a life was such a fragile thing, how easily it could fall apart, how dependent on things like weather it was. He'd sat there and looked across at another man, similarly stranded. The two of them had gotten to talking. Within an hour, he'd sold the man an insurance policy. Outside, the blizzard continued, but he'd had a wonderful sense then that his life was protected.

Now that sense, though he recognized how young he had been at the time, was still with him. All these years, he had been protected: nothing had happened. Weather, and illness, had never been serious adversaries. He had been allowed to do

his work. A woman had allowed him to give her children.
Everything he had ever wanted he'd gotten. And yet he'd
worked so hard to keep his life small. The cook, the cops, they
were doing the same thing: looking him over, wondering who
he was, trying to fit him into the rigid scheme they carried inside their heads. Who was this guy who looked so unhurried?
What's he up to? That he had no job to go to would, he knew,
make him look like a failure to them. But he was not a failure.
He was a man in the middle of his life, sipping coffee in a diner,
weighing his options. He was a free man, and he was protected,
because if insurance was no longer there for him, there were
other things he could do. He had a body, he had strength. He
knew how to drive a car. He could talk, he knew the language.
Whatever else a man needed seemed beside the point. A mowed
lawn, a house, wife, children, none of these were strictly necessary. You had to work hard to make them so.

The cops were getting up. They took their time, stretched,
hitched up their pants. The one who hadn't stared at Henna
was young, dark, probably no more than twenty-five. He
seemed to be imitating the older one beside him, taking his
time, hitching up his pants only because the older one did. He
was a young cop, and he looked very serious, like he wanted to
do right. He was sure there was a right way to be, a thing
agreed upon, and that was what he wanted, not to go against
that. His face was tense with the effort, but the tension made
his face more handsome than Henna thought, otherwise, it
might be. Like his, it was an Italian face, and, also like his, when
such a face is given over to sloth, to lethargy, it goes to a kind of
swimming fat that had frightened Henna in some of the men of
his youth, the Lotharios, the ne'er-do-wells. He watched this
cop now as he followed his partner to the cash register. They
each had separate bills. They paid the waitress, and she smiled
at each of them. The older cop took a toothpick.

Henna thought he'd follow them out. He had not decided on
anything, but he didn't particularly wish to stay and be stared
at by the cook. He picked up his check, then reached into his
pocket for his wallet, opened it and saw there was nothing in-

side. The forty dollars he'd had with him had been left on Mrs. Adams' table. In his pocket, he found eleven cents. He thought he had more change, but he'd slept in his pants last night, had crouched in a field, tripped and fallen, somewhere his change had been lost. The bill, coffee and doughnuts, came to twenty cents.

The waitress was looking at him. She looked over at the cops, who were about to leave.

"I have eleven cents," Henna said, before anyone could ask him. He made it simply as a statement, not as an apology.

He looked over at the cops. The older one, holding the door, looked down at him, and Henna could recognize the signs of disgust beginning to affect his features in the way his eyebrows went up and his eyes opened out. The younger one, readjusting his cap, said, "What? What's the bill come to?"

Henna looked at it, though he was sure.

"Twenty cents."

The older one said, "You've got a problem."

The younger one looked at his partner, then at Henna.

Henna said, "I thought I had more. I thought I had forty dollars."

He opened his wallet.

The younger cop approached the counter. "I think I can help him out."

He reached into his pocket and counted out nine cents for Henna.

"And you wanted," the cop said, "you wanted to leave Jenny a tip?"

"Oh, yes. Oh, sure," Henna said. The cop gave him another dime.

Henna looked up. The young cop was saving his pity. This was a business transaction.

"You'll be all right? You need more?"

"No. I'll be fine."

The young cop looked at him, nodded his head, then started to leave.

"I want your name," Henna said. "I want to pay you back."

The man said, "You don't have to pay me back."

Henna took down his name and address.

He watched the two cops cross the street, get into their patrol car. He looked at the money before him, then watched as the waitress scooped it up.

"That's mine, right?" she said.

He nodded, then he left the diner.

He wondered, as he did so, if he wasn't becoming small again, as if all he could do with his sudden and astonishing freedom was to set himself in the same direction he'd been taking for years. He was hot, though, and suddenly thirsty, and nostalgic for the clink of change in his pocket, the sense that he was someone in the world who could take care of his own affairs. Questions of small or largeness seemed beside the point. He took off his coat and, silently counting up the miles ahead of him, started off on the path homeward.

A NOTE ON THE TYPE

This book was set via computer-driven cathode-ray tube in Janson, a film version of type cast from matrices long thought to have been made by the Dutchman Anton Janson, who was a practicing type founder in Leipzig during the years 1668–1687. However, it has been conclusively demonstrated that these types are actually the work of Nicholas Kis (1650–1702), a Hungarian, who most probably learned his trade from the master Dutch type founder Dirk Voskens. The type is an excellent example of the influential and sturdy Dutch types that prevailed in England up to the time William Caslon (1692–1766) developed his own incomparable designs from them.

Composed by American–Stratford Graphic Services, Inc., Brattleboro, Vermont
Printed and bound by R. R. Donnelley & Sons Co., Harrisonburg, Virginia

Designed by Judith Henry